I0645328

PRAISE FOR S.D. TOOLEY / LEE DRIVER

"Author S. D. Tooley delivers the exciting Sam Casey series with suavity and grace in a writing style which will rivet the reader to the roller-coaster plotting."
— *EuroReviews*

"Tooley entices through nuanced characterizations, intricate plotting, and detail-laden prose."
— *ForeWord Reviews*

"An exciting mix of police procedure, spiritual 'intuition,' creeping suspense, and page-turning narrative."
— *Library Journal*

"For those readers with an interest in the religion of Native Americans and specifically the Sioux, they will find tantalizing hints of these practices within the pages."
— Leslie Doran, *Mystery News*

"Sam Casey is amazing—a beautifully described and magically interesting character…the plot, characters and pacing are all excellent."
— 4 Star Review, *Romantic Times*

"The fusion of mystery and urban fantasy makes Chasing Ghosts a wonderful thriller. Lee Driver writes fabulous paranormal whodunits that star interesting characters struggling with a world that makes no sense."
—www.alternative-worlds.com

"Lee Driver's Chase Dagger/Sara Morningsky series is one of the few truly dependable mystery series being published today. You always know what to expect with Driver: the unexpected."
—Craig Clarke, Top 1000 Reviewer

Awards won by some of the below titles: IPPY, Readers Choice, ForeWord Magazine, Ida Chittum Award (The Skull-YA), and a finalist for a Derringer Award (Sara Morningsky, short story).

WRITTEN AS S.D. TOOLEY

Sam Casey Series

Buried Secrets
The Tunnel
Destiny Kills
What Lies Within
Echoes from the Grave
Restless Spirit
Nothing Else Matters
When the Dead Speak

WRITTEN AS LEE DRIVER

Chase Dagger Series

Nightfall
Vaporizer
Fatal Storm
Chasing Ghosts
The Unseen
Full Moon-Bloody Moon
The Good Die Twice

For Middle School/Young Adult Readers

The Skull

SHORT STORIES

Mysteries to Die For

Includes:
    The Thirteenth Hole
    Sara Morningsky (a prelude to the Chase Dagger series)
    A Diamond in the Ruff
    Solving Life's Riddle

Killer Double

A Sam Casey / Chase Dagger Mystery

S.D. Tooley

Full Moon Publishing

Library of Congress Catalog Number: 2023935359

ISBN   9780997670738

Published May 2023

Printed in the United States of America

Full Moon Publishing LLC
433 Mystic Point Drive
Bluffton, SC 29909
www.fullmoonpub.com

Logo Design by Lesley Staples

From the Author

Having created two separate series back in 1998, I have decided to combine the characters in both my Sam Casey Series and Chase Dagger Series (written as Lee Driver). Both are cross genre mysteries so it wouldn't be a stretch for Sam's Native American mysticism to work well with Sara's shapeshifting talents and Dagger's lab-enhanced abilities.

PROLOGUE

Vancouver, British Columbia

The figure slowly stood, removing his Cartier glasses and setting them on the desk. The view of Coal Harbour behind him was postcard perfect, as was the man. Tall and trim, salt and pepper hair, which gave him a hint of distinction, and deep-set eyes most would say were piercingly cold. The hotel suite in Vancouver, British Columbia, was just one of his residences.

He no longer had an assistant. The last one had been with him for years, totally trusted, until he turned. Since then, Jonathan Keyes, the Director of BettaTec, only trusted himself. If someone could get to Fredrik Hensen, he could get to anyone. Keyes wouldn't take that chance again. Interrogating Fredrik had proved fruitless. Either he was very loyal to his new allegiance or he had not been the traitor. Either way, there was an adversary out there, and until he could figure out who it was, he would handle everything himself.

He watched the man approach. Even in a suit Levitt Crane looked like a research physician. A mild hint of antiseptics seemed to trail the doctor. Working in a lab all these years had added weight to his frame. And when had he developed a balding pate? But the doctor's smile was disarming, his round face as pink as a baby's bottom. He stepped forward and reached out a hand to Keyes. "So glad you could see me on such short notice."

"Has he been wanded?" Keyes' question was directed at the two dark-suited security guards standing by the door.

"Yes, sir," they replied in unison.

"Please, sit." Keyes directed Crane to the conference table as a butler entered and placed a tray on the table. The butler filled two coffee cups as the two men chose chairs across from each other, sparring positions. All that was missing was a chess set between them.

"I wasn't expecting you." With a wave of his hand, Keyes dismissed the butler. The two guards opened the doors and the butler stepped into the hallway. The heavy doors closed with a sucking sound. The entire suite was soundproof. The guards remained in front of the doors, barring anyone from entering, or perhaps from leaving.

"Which is why I appreciate your understanding. I didn't plan to be in town long."

"Keyes sat back, crossing one leg over the other, and taking a languid pose, a panther waiting for the right moment to attack. His gaze dropped to the Jaeger-Lecoultre watch, and he smiled when it caught the attention of the meek doctor. After all, only Keyes could afford a seven hundred-thousand-dollar gift to himself. Director Jonathan Keyes headed up a shadow network which operated below the radar of every alphabet government agency. He had the best scientists, the best mercenaries, and cutting-edge technology at his fingertips. He didn't fear the government or outside saboteurs. It was those in his own network he had to guard himself against. Keyes was born suspicious. Anyone as rich and powerful as he was had enemies. He had every reason to distrust the person sitting across from him.

Levitt Crane gave the watch a passing glance, more interested in the furnishings, the artwork on the walls, Persian area rugs, and remote-control blinds. A smile played across his lips.

"Cream?" Keyes raised the cut glass creamer. When Crane declined, Keyes poured some into his own cup. "You are a long way from your lab, Doctor."

"Come now, Jonathan." Crane noticed the Director bristle. No one called him by his first name. Actually, no one was certain if Keyes was the Director's actual name. "We both know the research ship was destroyed. What I can't understand is why you would destroy your own ship, not to mention all those employees on board. The fact that your handlers allowed me to contact you tells me that you are also curious about my survival."

"Hate to disappoint you, but I didn't destroy it. I had important research planned on that vessel, so I was just as shocked as anyone.

Unfortunately, I have no proof as to who was responsible."

"No one knew the location. The ship was camouflaged, wasn't even detected by radar. The entire Navy fleet could pass by and not see it."

Keyes eyed the doctor over his coffee cup. Was it his imagination or did Crane still think he was responsible? "Which is why I think it was someone in the Agency, someone with knowledge of the location."

"And what? Placed a bomb on board, killing himself, too?"

"Whoever it was used one of our own satellites which is why I know it was an inside job. He didn't have to be on the ship."

Crane thought about that while he watched Keyes take a longer sip of coffee. "First, you thought Mother was the traitor."

"Yes, but she's dead along with those loyal to her."

"Obviously there were others who weren't able to escape."

"Obviously."

"Guess it makes sense that you wouldn't blow up your own ship. I saw what they were making on the fourth floor. Really Jonathan, your lab is responsible for killing over one hundred thousand people a year."

That steely glare locked onto Crane, but his guest didn't appear affected. Keyes stole a quick glance at the guards, then leaned across the table. "What we did on that floor brought in millions of dollars a day, Crane. What did yours bring in? I know about your selling of organs. You didn't think I was aware of the side business you had going for years?"

"I was doing a great service for those needing organs. But the drug business? Really? Carfentanil is one hundred times more potent than fentanyl. Have you no shame?" Crane didn't hide his disgust. He watched Keyes shove a finger behind the knot of his tie and pull, then loosen the top button of his shirt. "You may look at your product as only profits, but do you have any idea what that drug does to people? First you feel hot and dizzy, then your chest feels like an elephant is sitting on it." He lowered his voice and smiled. "Finding it hard to catch your breath, Jonathan?"

The Director's eyes widened as he looked at his coffee cup, then at

Crane.

"It's in the cream, Jonathan."

"Guard," Keyes yelled, but it sounded more like a gasp.

"Don't bother. They work for me now."

Even with the muscles stiffening from the drug, Keyes was still able to contort his face into a mask of fury. "How dare you?" He struggled to raise an arm. "Antidote, in my top drawer."

Crane didn't move from the table.

"Money?" Keyes tried to remain calm so he could reason with this lunatic, but he was aware of what the drug did. "Ten percent?"

Crane laughed. "And do you think I'd live long enough to see the ink dry on the contract? Besides, I detest drugs as well as the stupid, weak people who use them. I'd give a medal to the traitor who blew up that ship." Crane finally rose and walked around the table. He lifted the Director's left arm and removed the watch.

The Director's eyes widened. "I'm… I'm not…"

"Always loved this watch."

"You…you were on that ship." Keyes struggled with each breath. "You should be…"

"Yes, I should be dead."

Leaning close, Crane whispered, "What makes you think I'm not?"

1

Hilton Head, South Carolina

Small footprints dotting the shoreline were quickly devoured by an ocean wave. Two boys searching for the best seashells to take home were scouring the beach at sunrise. Their family had been vacationing on Hilton Head Island in South Carolina for as long as they could remember. It certainly beat the Chicago beaches which were closed too many times to count because of unsanitary conditions.

Connor and Caleb were six-year-old twins and not looking forward to leaving, nor the start of the school year. They wished they could have spent all summer on Hilton Head, but their parents had the timeshare for only two weeks. The school year didn't start until after Labor Day.

Water clutched at their bare feet as they walked, head down, stopping every now and then to dig out a half-buried shell. The water was holding on to the warmth from the summer's heat while the humidity made the air feel as thick as gauze. The boys didn't care. Heat and humidity didn't faze them after the arctic winter which had blasted through the Windy City.

"Ugh, what's that?" Connor winced as he pointed. Freckles dotted his bronzed skin. He was shorter than Caleb who took great pleasure in reminding his twin that he was five minutes older and one inch taller. It was easy to tell the two apart. While Connor had red hair and freckles, Caleb was blond and blue-eyed.

Caleb leaned down, hands on his knees. Lying on the sand was a helmet-sized creature that resembled something dropped from a UFO. "That's a horseshoe crab, dummy. You would have known that if you had paid attention when we toured the museum. It's part of the tick and scorpion family rather than a crab." Caleb also prided himself at being the smarter of the two.

The crab was a muddy brown color and resembled a huge tick with a long spiny tail. "They use the tail for digging," Caleb added.

"It's still ugly. Does it sting?"

"No."

"It looks like a skull. What do you think killed it?" Connor straightened, bored with this latest find and eager to find better and bigger seashells.

"Sun probably. It can't live on land for long. They wash up with the tide, and if they land on their backs or can't get back to the water, they die." Caleb saw a new crop of shells deposited further up shore by the tide.

They each carried bags containing several dozen shells. Their parents had told them not to get their hopes up. This was not the best beach to find large shells, but it didn't stop the boys from searching.

Connor looked over his shoulder. "We're pretty far from the condo. I can't see mom and dad anymore." In the distance was a row of houses lining the shore and tucked behind tall grass and marsh, a safe distance from large waves hurled by the seasonal hurricanes. While their parents preferred to sit on beach chairs and enjoy their coffee, the boys had taken off with a warning from their dad not to go too far.

They had wandered onto a strip of beach lined with marsh grass and small dunes. Clusters of other seashell hunters had ventured in the opposite direction. The boys had this section of the beach to themselves. It was void of any houses much less swimmers or beachgoers.

"This is weird shaped," Connor said as he bent down to pick up the cylinder-shaped shell. "Is that a…?" He screamed and dropped the object.

Caleb poked at it with a stick. "Is that a finger?"

"It can't be, can it?" Connor leaned closer, now intrigued.

While Connor studied the finger, Caleb poked at another object tangled in seaweed. "Looks like another horseshoe crab." But when he dug it out of the seaweed and flipped it over, both boys screamed. It wasn't a crab at all but part of a human skull.

Two men emerged from behind a sand dune and watched the retreating figures. Using gloved hands, they added the body parts to others in the cooler, then quickly picked through the remaining seaweed. Moving farther down the shore they used a monitor, its beam lighting up human parts in a green glow. Finally satisfied they had located all they were going to find this time, they snapped the lid shut. With a quick glance to make sure their movements were unseen, they disappeared behind the dunes, crossed a foot bridge, and returned to a black SUV.

One team, posing as a couple, had infiltrated the curiosity seekers as a throng gathered where the boys had found the skull only to find the two bags of seashells, dead horseshoe crabs, and seaweed, but not one body part. The boys had insisted, the crowd was disappointed, and the parents were embarrassed. The family returned to Chicago with a warning to their sons not to mention the issue again. A team scoured newspapers for two days after the discovery. There had been no mention of what the boys had seen.

2

Cedar Point, Indiana

"Do you really need that much firepower?" Sara scanned the abandoned warehouse. Dusk had settled quickly, given that the skies had been overcast all day. This unincorporated area was near an abandoned quarry. The warehouse had been used years ago to house trucks and digging equipment. Two additional buildings hunched nearby, listing slightly from the shifting earth. The warehouse most intact proved to be the perfect place for nefarious activities.

Several semis had been unloaded an hour ago, leaving two tattooed thugs standing guard over the cargo stored in the warehouse. Dagger had taken shifts with Skizzy for a month to time the deliveries and pickups. Tonight was the best time. Tomorrow more unmarked semis would be backed into the warehouse, pallets of drugs and cash would be loaded, then driven off to parts unknown. Semis dropped off pallets, another trail of semis would pick up the pallets the next day.

"Isn't it overkill?" Sara added, noticing that Dagger was ignoring her. Other than promising no innocents would be harmed, he hadn't explained to Sara exactly what he, Skizzy and Simon had planned. Skizzy had already used drones in the shape of birds to blot out the cameras on the buildings with black paint. Last thing they needed was to be on the cartel's hit list.

They were tucked behind a ridge dressed in black clothing and ski masks. Skizzy and Simon were hidden somewhere planning all kinds of mayhem.

"How does it look, Skizzy?"

"Good to go," they heard in their ear buds.

"Simon?"

"Oh, yeah. Let's light it up."

From three directions, what looked like miniature missiles shot toward the warehouse. Dagger's shoulder bucked from the rocket launcher. The two thugs were resting on the back of a pickup, headphones on, listening to some profane music, eyes closed, feet tapping. They didn't hear the glass breaking. Skizzy had also sent drones to the roof to drop containers of napalm down the shaft. He wanted to make sure everything in the building was incinerated.

The explosion lifted the pickup truck several feet off the ground. The young thugs ripped their headphones off and leaped from the truck. Their legs were like dancers, two steps forward, two steps back. They weren't sure whether to grab a bucket of water or run for their lives. With a thunderous roar the roof caved in, and a rolling inferno engulfed the warehouse. The thugs clawed their way into the truck and hightailed it for parts unknown. Even the angels couldn't help them once the cartel discovered the loss of billions of dollars and drugs.

"Oh my god," Sara gasped. "I've never seen anything so white hot." Flames licked at the sky, but the warehouse was too far off the beaten path for anyone to notify the fire department. Sara was glad to see the drugs and money destroyed, but these three guys were getting way too sophisticated with their destructive methods. She wasn't sure whether to be amazed or worried. She watched Dagger load the launcher into the back of the van. "Won't those guards get into trouble when the cartel realizes how much product and money they lost on their watch?"

"Yep. They'll probably kill them."

"You promised no innocents would be hurt."

Dagger turned to Sara as he nodded for her to get into the van. And dammit if he didn't have that smug grin plastered on his face.

"I said I wouldn't hurt them. I have no control over what the cartel might do to them."

Sara slammed through the front door, practically closing the door on Dagger. She ripped the cap from her head, sending a yard of streaked hair tumbling down her back. Dagger calmly closed the door and locked it. He unzipped his black boots and left them by the door, tossed the ski mask on his desk, then walked to the bar and grabbed a beer from the refrigerator.

"I think you need a drink." He shook the tangles from his collar length hair and waited for her response.

She stood, arms folded and glared, her turquoise eyes penetrating. "I don't need a drink."

He poured her one anyway, a Tia Maria on the rocks. He carried both drinks into the bedroom and set them on the dresser. "Our clothes smell like smoke." He stripped off his shirt. Next came the black cargo pants revealing black briefs.

"Don't you have a conscience?" Sara demanded. "What a stupid question. Of course, you don't."

Dagger took a long pull from the beer. "Sure, for all the victims hurt by the drugs these cartels pedal." He carried the beer into the bathroom and turned on the shower. The tiled shower could hold at least eight people comfortably, no shower door or curtain needed.

Sara trailed after him, drink in hand. "I'm sure you barely made a dent in their operation." She took a sip of her drink, then set it on the counter.

"I don't know about that. Tonight the same thing was executed at factories outside of Miami, New Jersey, and Los Angeles. It won't end their business, but it will cripple them. "He stripped out of his underwear and disappeared behind the wall.

"Don't tell me Mother sanctioned these operations." Sara let out a heavy sigh. "Of course, she did."

Dagger peered around the corner, his body soaped up. He eyed her hair and sniffed. "You smell like smoke, too." He wrapped a muscular arm around her waist and hauled her into the shower. Sara screamed but didn't stop him from removing her clothes and soaping every inch of her body.

* * * *

Ten miles away, just off the coast of Lake Michigan, the Watcher ambled through debris under an unused overpass, avoiding what looked like human waste. The derelict he was trailing was twenty yards ahead, shuffling past makeshift homes of cardboard and bedsheet tents. Newspapers moved as bodies underneath shifted in their sleep. Not all alcoholics or addicts slept at night. Some used the nighttime hours to steal for their next score or bottle of liquor.

It was hard to tell his target's age. The alcohol and drugs had darkened his teeth and lined his face to the point where even a mother couldn't identify her son. He knew his target liked isolation which is why his refrigerator cardboard box he called home was at the farthest end of the underpass. Vehicles rumbled on the nearby expressway as the odor of diesel filled the air. With a heavy sigh, the drunk crumbled to the ground, his hands empty, unable to have scored enough tonight to purchase his next bottle.

Sitting on the ground was not an option. Always known to plan ahead, the Watcher had stashed a bucket under a nearby bush. He retrieved it, turned it upside down, and sat with his back to any of the other homeless who might awaken. He reached into his pocket and pulled out a pint bottle of whiskey.

The sound of the cap unscrewing brought the drunk's suspicious eyes to his benefactor. He quickly relaxed and tried out a smile. Only one corner of his mouth upturned.

"You do realize that you are one of eighty-eight thousand people who will die this year due to alcohol." When the Watcher held up the bottle, a shaking hand quickly snatched it. The statistic just shared with him didn't appear to register as the disheveled man took a long gulp of the whiskey. He leaned back against the graffiti-filled concrete wall with a satisfying sigh. "Some say you are only harming yourself." He grabbed the drunk's left arm, pulled up the stained sleeve, then turned it over to check the inside wrist. "There's spousal abuse, kids going hungry because food money is spent on alcohol or drugs. And then there are the number of victims of DUI accidents." He pulled a permanent marker from his pocket and removed the cap. "Over two hundred people die every week due to drunk driving." The drunk took another swig and closed his eyes as though listening to a bedtime story.

The thin tip of the marker outlined an image on the wrist. With quick strokes the horns were outlined first, then the chin and face. The drunk's eyes fluttered, the lids now heavy. Even his right arm felt too heavy to lift the bottle. He was fascinated at what his benefactor was doing.

"Now, they label you as having a disability. How long does it take you to run through your government checks every month?" The eyes were next, vacant and almond shaped. He used confident strokes, details engrained in his memory. Then the teeth, long and pointed. A ratty beard under the chin looked like a ruffled collar. The nose was pointed, bone ridges on the top of the skull resembled the surface of a planet. "Excellent job, as always." He raised the drunk's arm so he could see the finished work. But the drunk wasn't listening, the unfinished bottle lying in his lap. "You can take my word for it. Now you can go to your maker knowing I have released your demon."

3

"How are you doing, Jake?" Captain Lamon Robinson reached a mitt-sized paw across the desk and gave his former detective a vice grip.

"Good."

Jake's wife, Sam, planted a kiss on Robinson's cheek. "We miss you. I don't see Jackie that much anymore, other than a text or phone call every now and then." The couple each claimed a chair in front of Robinson's desk.

"Yeah. Besides the store, she's busy nagging the builders every second, making sure every brick in the house is just right." He lowered his linebacker-sized body into the special order, high-backed chair. It protested with a groan. "I heard from Frank."

Frank Travis was Jake Mitchell's former partner. He was currently awaiting his assignment after finishing training at Quantico.

"They didn't assign him yet?"

"He's pretty sure it will be either Dallas or Atlanta."

"Better than Chicago," Sam said. "That's only thirty minutes from here and we know Frank hates cold weather. I'm sure Claudia wouldn't want to raise a child in Chicago. Great restaurants and a nice place to visit but get out of town before nightfall."

"Did you want coffee? I can have Becky get you some."

Jake pushed his chair back and stood. "I can get it, as long as you haven't moved the break room."

"Nope. Still there." Lamon watched Jake head past the sea of desks, then turned to Sam. "How is he really doing?"

"Much better." Sam had seen the signs of PTSD even though Jake denied it. He had been drugged and held prisoner for three months by a disgruntled ex-cop. Everyone thought Jake had died in an explosion. The make-shift hell hole where he had been kept was dark, his movements restricted by a studded dog collar. The ring of scarred welts around his neck always drew stares, even today when he walked into his old precinct. Once back at work, he had trouble walking into dark places, hearing a car backfire. One search for a suspect had led Jake and Frank into a dark basement. Jake made it forty feet into the dark abyss until he had to retreat, leaving his partner in possible danger. That's when he knew he had to quit, couldn't put Frank's life in danger. He was glad Frank had been admitted into the FBI. That made Jake's decision to quit the CHPD easier.

"He told you about the case we worked in South Carolina, right?" Sam raked a hand through her unruly hair, a Methuselah tangle of curls which Jake found sexy as hell.

"Oh, yeah. Civil War history, ghosts. Right up your alley."

Sam slid a business card across his desk. "Jake joined my one-woman PI firm…CM Investigations.

"Casey/Mitchell? Couldn't come up with a clever name like Ghost Busters?" A shadow of a smile crept across his dark face.

Jake returned and set a cup of tea in front of Sam and a coffee for himself. "Sam has five hundred of those cards. We can probably wallpaper one bathroom with them."

"You should have brought more," Lamon said. "Never know who I might run into."

"So glad you said that." Sam reached into her purse and pulled out a stack of cards wrapped with a rubber band.

"Jake, your wife is a marketing genius. No pressure. She just flashes those baby blues or shows a shapely leg." Lamon set the cards to one side next to the cardholder containing his own cards.

"So, what have you got for us?" Sam asked.

Lamon pulled a folder from the bottom drawer as he explained. "Thirty years ago I was a rookie in Jersey. My partner and I were on patrol when we got a call about a body near a frontage road. Two teens looking for a place to park off of I-80 found her. She was a suspected street walker, as they were called back then. Strangled with her own scarf. Over the following five years ten more men and women had been killed, all with the same M.O."

"Serial killer." Jake grabbed sheets of notes from the Captain. "Pretty thin file."

"I wasn't in Homicide at the time so the first case was the only one I copied. Besides, the bodies stretched along I-80 from New York to Ohio. Press gave the killer the name of the Keystone Killer cause I-80 was called the Keystone Shortway in New Jersey. Another nickname was the I-80 killer."

"Did they catch him?"

"Oh yeah, Sam. John Wallace Baker was his name. Discovered he was a truck driver who used I-80 every day. By the time he was caught, the body count totaled twenty-four. After his arrest he confessed to eight more murders along that stretch of highway, but the bodies were never found. His lawyer had said Baker might offer to give the location of the bodies in exchange for being moved to a different prison."

Jake studied the photo of Baker. He was thirty-four at the time of his arrest, but a youthful, arrogant smile gave him a James Dean appearance. A bad boy look that women would find attractive and older women might trust. Jake rippled the sheets of paper in his hand. "So why are we here? Seems like the case was closed."

"Actually, he was killed in prison five years later. Rumor was he paid someone to kill him. Left a handwritten will with a request that his brain be donated to science for research. Felt scientists could study his compulsion in hopes they might identify a genetic flaw."

Sam caught a photo of an image in the file in front of Lamon. "What's that picture?"

Lamon held it up. "It's a demon. The killer drew it on the inside of each victim's wrist. That was one clue never released to the press. Baker drew it in permanent black marker and never facing the victim, always so we would see it. According to the killer, he felt prostitutes were the bane of society and had to be eliminated, a cleansing of the earth."

Jake handed the pages back to Captain Robinson. "I take it something happened. Another body?"

Lamon pulled out another folder. "Homeless man was killed last night in the southern part of Chicago off Lake Michigan." He handed the folder to Jake.

Sam leaned close. They spent several minutes studying the report. "I don't see a correlation. Victim obviously wasn't a prostitute, body wasn't near I-80. And he was homeless," Jake pointed out.

"Thing is," Robinson said, "he had a drawing of a demon on the inside of his wrist." He handed Jake a color photo of the image on the wrist of the deceased.

"Copycat?" Sam suggested.

"You tell me." Lamon rocked back in his chair, much to the protest of the leather.

"You know cops can't keep their mouths shut. Someone years ago must have shared the photo. Maybe someone in the medical examiner's office," Jake offered.

Sam cradled her cup of tea. "Did Baker have any kids, male relations who might be picking up where he left off?"

"Divorced, wife died a couple years after Baker. No kids. What few relations still alive had changed their names and are living stellar lives." Lamon studied Sam. She had that look he was all too familiar with. "What are you thinking, Sam?"

"Where's his brain?"

Robinson snorted. "I knew I shouldn't have asked."

"Really, Sam?" Jake said with a smile. He had been known to humor his wife's strange theories in the past.

"I'm only curious if they did examine his brain and if they found any neurological explanations for his compulsions. Maybe they were able to identify them in other suspects, maybe someone who idolized Baker."

The two men appeared to breathe a sigh of relief. Robinson half expected Sam to accuse zombies or Baker's ghost. "Guess I could make a courtesy call. And while I'm at it, I'll make a call to the lead detective. I have some pull in Chicago. If successful, I'd like you to take a look at the crime scene. See if anything turns on your spidey senses."

4

"Good job, six-one-seven." The image floating over Dagger's desk revealed a feminine face, more robotic than human. Connie was the name of the computer, but the face belonged to Mother, the head of AlphaTec.

Dagger, Skizzy, Simon and Sara were huddled around the desk, although Skizzy had skooched his chair back several inches as he searched for unseen wires.

"I thought Mother said your rag-tag group was small in numbers." Sara sat with her arms crossed, still fuming over the unknown repercussions on the two warehouse guards.

"Well, depends on your description of small. Smaller than BettaTec's? Yes. Smaller than the members of the United Nations? Yes." The robotic eyes blinked, and dammit if the hint of a smile didn't play on its lips.

"You just ain't gonna tell us, are you?" Skizzy skooched back further, wondering why he had opened his mouth. As if on cue, the robot image swiveled to face Skizzy. He hunched his shoulders, unable to move back any farther because his chair had already hit the bookcase.

"What's important is the job got done. Put a dent in the LaPalma Cartel. They lost over ten billion in cash and products with a street value of eighty billion dollars. The fact that over one hundred pounds of fentanyl has the capability of killing twenty million people, that's a lot of lives. That's how much they seized in Nebraska in 2018."

The image swiveled back to Dagger who was sipping from a steaming cup of coffee. On the desk were two envelopes, one for Simon and one for Skizzy. Simon's eyes scoured the walls, then rested on the floating head. At first it had only been Dagger and Sara who knew about Mother, AlphaTec and BettaTec. But Dagger had needed Skizzy's and Simon's assistance on several important jobs. Skizzy took it all at face value. After all, it only confirmed his suspicions of secret societies, covert governments, Big Brother, aliens, and spies around every corner. He even looked the part of a paranoid schizophrenic with his wild hair, eyes that appeared to wobble in opposite directions, and disheveled appearance, as if he had just crawled out of a bomb shelter.

Simon didn't need the full details at first. Having been a sniper turned mailman, he loved the action and asked few questions. But too many strange and unexplained things Dagger dragged him into had made him cautious as well as curious. Simon had mentioned recently that he was getting too old for all this excitement and thinking of retiring. The money Dagger, actually Mother, had paid him was all he needed to turn in his papers.

Simon finally found his voice. "What about the tunnels?" He waited for the image to swivel in his direction, but it was Dagger who replied.

"Explosions closed them. I'm sure it was a buildup of gas. Guess those guys had eaten too many refried beans." Did he just see the robot frown like a disappointed parent?

"More people killed?" Sara's accusatory tone was directed at Dagger.

"I'm sure Mother's people dropped leaflets from a helicopter warning the cartel to stay out of the tunnels." His dry tone wasn't appreciated by Sara. Skizzy and Simon, though, barked out a laugh. Dagger handed an envelope to Simon and one to Skizzy. "We thank you for your service." Skizzy was the only one to open the envelope and count each bill.

"The missus and I are headed to Florida in a couple days. This should come in handy. May even look for a retirement home down there." He shoved the envelope into his shirt pocket. "Happy to oblige. Anything I can do to get this shit off the streets." Simon stood on wobbly legs. It was a wonder his spindly legs could hold up the barrel chest hanging over his belt. It was the twinkling eyes and quick smile that made Eunie, his wife, laughingly refer to him as a black Santa.

A sigh was emitted from the robotic face. "Things should be quiet for a while until the cartel regroups. In the meantime, follow Mister Simon's lead and take a vacation." The monitor clicked off, causing

Skizzy to sweep the ceiling with his gaze, expecting the robot head to have been sucked into the mother ship.

5

"Juice, Padre?" Sara set a glass in front of Sergeant Martinez as the cop eyed the plate of homemade cinnamon rolls.

"Don't tell me you made these from scratch." He dragged one onto a plate and tried calculating the calories. No matter how many miles he pedaled his bike or struggled at the gym, one visit to Sara's and he gained it all back, plus some.

"Sara makes everything from scratch," Dagger said from the opposite side of the table where he was eating his second cinnamon roll. "She detests chemical additives."

"But you never gain weight. Neither does Sara."

"Metabolism," Dagger replied with a grin. They were seated in a kitchen of chrome and white marble. Vases of fresh flowers, floral dishes and curtains helped to liven up the clinical feel of the room.

Although Jerry Martinez had been part of several strange cases that always followed Dagger, he was kept at arm's length because of his buy-the-book personal rules. He wasn't fat, but he also wasn't thin. Martinez cared only about closing cases. Most detectives dressed the part, as though they watched too many cop shows…shoes spit-shined, expensive suits and ties, crisply starched shirts. Martinez's appearance was more Columbo, a cop's cop who looked as though he spent one too many days on surveillance without a change of clothes.

"So, what's up?" Dagger knew Padre never showed up without an ulterior motive. The former seminary student turned cop also kept Dagger at arm's length. He valued his street sense but suspected this mystery man worked under everyone's radar. There may be a dark web, but Dagger worked in a dark world.

"Huge fire a couple nights ago near the quarry. No one hurt, thankfully, at least that we know of. The fire was so intense we doubt we'd find anything other than teeth."

Sara's laser stare at Dagger drew the cop's curiosity. She ate her cinnamon roll with a knife and fork, but the knife appeared to be aimed at Dagger. How like a woman.

"And you want me to collect the teeth?"

Padre chuckled. "Such a comic." The laugh was cut short. "Thing is, the same stuff you and that squirrely friend of yours used to kill that creature a few years ago appears to have been used at this warehouse. We suspect that building contained something nefarious, maybe drugs. Now, you and that friend, who isn't quite of this planet, wouldn't know anything about that, would you?"

"Nope." Dagger licked his fingers but there was a twinkle in his dark eyes.

And was that a heavy sigh Sara was trying to stifle? Padre turned on her. "What about you, Sara? Where were these guys two nights ago?"

"Out with Simon."

"Simon, huh?' Now it was Padre's turn to sigh. "And where did the three go?"

"To the Hideaway to play pool," Dagger quickly replied. "Don't badger the lady."

"Badger?" Padre looked shocked. "Am I badgering you, Sara?"

"Never. But do tell me, who owned the warehouse? Maybe it was arson."

Padre wiped his mouth with a napkin, taking his time to decipher any clues the two might drop. "Thing is, it was a fake company name, fake address, fake owner." He turned his Cheshire grin toward Dagger. "Like someone else who appears to have fake everything."

"Now, Padre. When have I not been straight with you?"

"Oh, gee. Maybe from the first day we met?"

"Did you want us to take a look through the rubble?"

How like Sara to divert his attention, Padre thought. "No need, little lady. Our boys are going through it now." He stabbed another glare toward Dagger. "Now that it is finally cool enough to enter." Padre stressed the word cool. "Course, you know, I could always verify things with your secretary." Padre rose.

"I wouldn't disturb him. He gets ornery if you wake him," Dagger said. He and Sara followed the cop into the living room. The house used to be an automobile dealership. But since it was built unknowingly on reservation land owned by Sara's grandparents, they had to vacate it. She had lived there with her grandmother until her death. Dagger offered to move in to defray costs since he and his rowdy macaw had been kicked out of the office he used as his P.I. business.

Padre slid open the glass door to the twelve-hundred square foot aviary revealing a second, grated door. The scarlet red and blue macaw swooped down from a fifteen-foot-high faux tree and landed on the perch near the door. The bird eyed the cop cautiously. "Hey, Einstein, where was Dagger two nights ago? Was he with Skizzy and Simon?"

Behind Padre, Dagger ran a finger across his own neck as a warning to the macaw. Einstein had a photographic memory and was known to answer the phone and act like a live rolodex whenever Dagger needed a name or number.

"AWK, UP AGAINST THE WALL AND SPREAD 'UM. AWKKKK."

Padre chuckled again. "You know, I can confiscate your bird as a witness."

"You could try, although I think he would peck out your eyes and eat your fingers before you reached your car."

Padre shrugged. It was worth a try.

"Besides," Dagger continued, "he would need a lawyer, and I've played a lawyer before."

Padre chuckled at that. "Yes, among other things."

"Wasn't it just in the paper," Sara said, "about some tunnels the cartel uses which the DEA destroyed? It seemed to occur the same time as this fire. Do you think they are connected?"

"Already checked with the DEA. They denied they had anything to do in our town much less with what went down in those tunnels out west."

Dagger huffed. "Right, and the government is always honest."

6

"That was the Captain," Jake said as he hung up the phone. "His contact is allowing us to take a look at the crime scene." He took a seat next to Sam who was trying to corral Dillon, their fifteen-month-old, onto her lap.

"Exactly where are we going?" Sam grabbed Dillon's chubby hand before he knocked over her cup of tea.

"The body was found under a closed off exit ramp that used to be used by employees of a nearby shuttered brewing company. The crime scene is cordoned off with a couple officers guarding the place."

"That's strange, especially since they should be through with the investigation."

"Bodies, victims. I do wish you wouldn't talk in front of my grandson." Abby lifted Dillon from Sam's lap and carried him to the patio door. "Do you want to help Uncle Alex rake leaves?"

"Alex doesn't rake. He sucks them up in that Kubota thing he drives, then puts them in the mulcher," Sam said. "And please, don't let Dillon ride that thing."

"Alex will drive slowly with Dillon on his lap." Abby walked out and set Dillon down. The toddler ran off at a fast pace.

"He'll be fine, Sam." Jake had to constantly reassure Sam's protective instincts.

"Well, hearing words like victim and body isn't as bad as my son's foot being cut off."

"Alex won't let anything happen to him."

Sam turned back to Jake. "Any other details?"

"He was homeless, reeked of alcohol. They are having the contents of the liquor bottle analyzed. Place is full of prints and human waste so I'm certainly happy it's not in our town. No identification on the victim, age between thirty and sixty. Hard to tell after years of abuse."

"Do you think we'll be able to get close?" Sam folded the morning newspaper and set it aside.

"Maybe if you wear something low-cut," he replied with a grin.

Five miles east in Cedar Point, Indiana, a green light pulsed in Dagger's vision. He took a seat at his computer in the office above The Hideaway bar. The apartment had been Dagger's home for several years after setting down roots in Cedar Point. One of Mother's operatives, was the owner of the bar.

"You called?" Dagger asked when the robot head appeared above the desk. Sara sat across from him, sipping a cup of hot tea. They had been headed to breakfast when Mother contacted him. Sara wanted to try a new restaurant over the border in Illinois.

"There is a report of a homicide in Chicago."

"Really? Only one? There's about one a minute in Chicago, if not every second." Dagger didn't know why Mother didn't just show her face. After all, he knew what she looked like, well, only when she appeared as a hologram one day. But why continue with the mechanical voice? "Good. He's cleaning up the scourges of society."

"Nice."

Dagger didn't have to hear Sara's response. He could feel her glare from across the desk.

"Why is this the concern of AlphaTec?"

"Naturally, there were numerous sets of prints at the crime scenes, considering where the bodies were found. We are concerned with one partial print which did not show up in the police database, nor Interpol's. However, we may have a match in ours."

"Because he's a BettaTec operative?"

"Since it's only a partial, we can't be sure at this point."

How like Mother not to give him the full details. "And you need us to do what?"

"What I need you two to do is check out the crime scene, see if you can find anything the police couldn't find. If police are still at the scene..." Now the robot head turned in Sara's direction. "...perhaps you can overhear details about the crime scene." The robot head swiveled back.

Questions started forming in Dagger's head. Something didn't add up. "What aren't you telling us?"

"Please report back when you return."

"Wait."

The brows of the robot image raised, as though questioning the interruption.

"I haven't seen any activity on the Director's computer in days."

There was silence, as though the robot were conversing with a panel. "Interesting. Even if he were traveling, he would be using his laptop. We will check it out."

With that the image disappeared.

"Well, it looks like your breakfast is a drive-thru."

"Someplace with bagels, please." Sara would rather cut off her arm than eat a fast food meal of mystery meat.

7

When the expressway had been redesigned, an exit ramp to the lakeshore had been closed off, leaving boaters to take a frontage road. A nearby brewing company had closed decades ago so the state saw no reason to offer an exit ramp for such little traffic.

The viaduct was isolated from residential areas, which made for a lengthy walk when the homeless had to lug tents and mattresses. Jake used a frontage road to access the area, then another turn which brought them in through the south side of the crime scene. He parked the Ford Explorer on a gravel road which led to an overgrown berm overlooking Lake Michigan. Not far north was a poor man's yacht club, the building listing as much as the docked boats. It was a fisherman who had found the body when he had climbed the berm to eat his lunch.

A salvage and scrap metal yard claimed an acre of land a block away. The crunching of metal could be heard above the cooing of pigeons overhead. Jake checked to make sure he hadn't parked the Explorer directly under the pigeons.

Sam's attention was drawn to a larger bird resting on a guardrail overhead. It was a hawk. With any luck it would feast on several of the filthy pigeons.

Two officers pushed off the front of the squad car. Both young and eager, they hitched up their gun belts as they approached. Although anxious, they also looked bored. Babysitting a crime scene was obviously not their idea of action. "This is a restricted area," the beefy one said.

Jake showed his business card. "We're working with the Chasen Heights Police Department. Captain Robinson has been in touch with your lead detective. He shared some information with your department but wanted us to examine the crime scene."

Sam didn't wear anything low cut as Jake had jokingly suggested, but she didn't have to. Her hair was wild but controlled, thanks to her late father's genes. Her eyes were even bluer than her father's and could be icy but mesmerizing at the same time. The two beat cops had a hard time dragging their attention away from her.

"Has your forensics crew already been through here?" Sam asked, stepping closer to get a view of the area where the homeless and belongings had been removed, except for the makeshift cardboard home at the far end.

"Yes, and were already forced to turn things over," the rail thin officer replied. He obviously didn't attend the gym as much as his partner. He was more a Barney Fife.

Sam edged closer. "So it isn't restricted anymore, right?"

"What do you mean by 'forced to turn things over'?" Jake knew Forensics submits evidence, logs it in, so why use the term forced?

"Gotta ask the boss," Bruiser said. Although his words were directed at Jake, his eyes were still on Sam.

Sam studied the taped off area, hoping there was a road or walking path on the opposite side from where they stood, somewhere closer to the crime scene. If only she could touch something, the concrete wall where the deceased rested his head, the cardboard box he used for shelter. All Sam had to do was touch something the victim or killer touched to pick up clues about a case.

"Any of the other homeless see or hear anything?" Jake asked.

Barney Fife hitched his gun belt again. "Gonna have to ask you to leave now." A sudden twang drifted into his voice, as though channeling Barney.

Jake tugged on Sam's arm. "Thanks for your time."

"We can go around to the other side," Sam whispered as Jake led her away.

"I have other plans." They climbed into the vehicle and went back the way they came. Jake pushed a button on the dashboard to dial Captain Robinson.

Robinson's voice blared from the speaker. "What did you find out?"

"Zip. Two patrolmen wouldn't allow us near the scene and made a strange comment. They said their Forensics team was forced to turn over evidence. Know anything about this?"

"Shit. No, I don't." Robinson sighed.

"This isn't a national security threat," Sam countered.

"No, it isn't. Where are you headed now?"

"A salvage yard nearby. See if they have a security camera pointed toward the area."

"Good. In the meantime, I'll call my contact."

The gray hawk followed the vehicle as it pulled into the salvage yard. It landed on a nearby telephone pole and watched with unusual intellect. The couple exited the vehicle, but before entering the building, the woman stopped and turned, her gaze searching until it rested on the hawk.

What's happening, Sara?

Whenever Sara shifted into her hawk or wolf form, she and Dagger could communicate telepathically. Sara Morningsky was a shapeshifter. Believed to be folklore, she had discovered the ability when she was six years old. Her grandparents had been the only people who knew. But with both grandparents deceased, it was Dagger whom Sara trusted with her secret.

There were two patrolmen guarding the crime scene. This couple showed up asking questions about the investigation but were told the case was turned over to another agency. Now the couple is headed over to a salvage yard.

How close is it to the crime scene?

Maybe a block away.

They are looking for surveillance tapes. If they are able to get one, follow them and see where they live.

8

Dagger entered first, having located a side door several yards from the main entrance. He hadn't expected the massive property, wrought iron fencing, or mini-estate sized house where the couple lived.

The hallway and beyond were dark, but neither Dagger nor Sara needed lights to see. He signaled for Sara to check out the room to their right. He could see gym equipment and what looked like an office sectioned off in a corner. What they were looking for might be there. Sara disappeared while Dagger crept toward a doorway on the left. He saw a family room with a widescreen TV, sectional, chairs, and an elaborate bar. His attention was drawn to what looked like a safe on the wall behind the bar. It appeared to have a keypad which he knew wouldn't be a problem breaking into.

He had checked the address Sara had given him and discovered that the couple were Jake Mitchell and his wife, Sam Casey. Further digging told him they owned CM Investigations, a private detective firm.

When Dagger turned back to the gym to see if Sara found anything, he felt a presence. No sooner did the presence start to say, "hands up where I can see them," Dagger had already spun around, gun raised. Facing him was a brute of a man at least two inches taller and twenty-five pounds heavier than himself. The eyes were cold, face ruddy. Hit man crossed Dagger's mind, especially with the repulsive scars circling the brute's neck. But this was different. His brain clicked through several scenarios—gun for hire, Special Forces. No. The sense of law enforcement rolled off of him. Dagger could smell a cop a mile away. If he had to guess, he'd say FBI.

Cold eyes glanced at the weapon Dagger held. "Nice piece. Kimber .45 caliber. You have excellent taste." Just as quickly, Jake's gaze snapped back to Dagger' face. "Looks like it's just you and me."

Sara emerged beside Dagger, her gun raised. Jake knew there was someone else somewhere but thought he or she was standing guard outside. He and Sam had watched the intruders on the surveillance monitor disengaging the alarm at the gate and then jumping the fence. Almond-shaped, azure-colored eyes appeared to glow in the dim hallway. Long hair glistened, full lips, the entire package was mesmerizing. Maybe that was how this thug distracted his opponents.

"Yes, you definitely have excellent taste."

The light in the family room came on just as Sam appeared at Jake's side, her gun raised. It was a wonder there was enough space in the doorway for four people and four guns. Now it was Dagger's turn to be distracted by shapely legs, electrifying blue eyes and a sexy mass of blonde hair a guy could easily imagine spreading across a pillow.

"It appears we both selected way above our stations in life," Dagger said.

The silence in the house was evident to everyone but Sara. She could hear the humming of the refrigerator, the ticking of a large clock somewhere, like a grandfather clock, the hissing of water filling ice trays in the freezer. Guns remained pointed, gazes unwavering.

Sara broke the silence. "Well, this is awkward."

Sam smiled. Besides, her arm was getting tired. "Mom made chocolate cake with cream cheese frosting."

"I'm in." Sara lowered her arm. Her gun disappeared into a jacket pocket.

Sam placed her gun on the desk to her right. "Put the coffee on, sweetheart."

The two men watched the women leave, their eyes on the shapely figures, sexy walks, and flowing hair.

Dagger clicked his tongue. "Yep. We are two lucky sons-of-bitches."

With formal introductions made, the men settled in the kitchen watching the coffee perk while the women disappeared into the dining room. Sara set the tray of cups and saucers on the dining room table. Sam set the cake next to the tray along with plates and forks. A small leather pouch on a leather cord escaped from under her blouse which caught Sara's attention.

"Is that a medicine bundle?"

Sam held it up. "Yes."

As though noticing the décor for the first time, Sara studied the inlaid tile running down the center of the table, the Navaho rug under her feet, the furnishing and wall hangings in the sitting area to her right. Her eyes settled on Sam's blonde hair and blue eyes.

"But you're…"

"Sioux, half of me, on my mom's side." Sam was puzzled at the young woman's features. She looked more island than Native. "And you?"

"Assiniboine."

"Montana?"

Sara nodded, then smiled. She felt a sudden kinship, regardless of their adversarial positions.

Jake carried in a carafe of coffee, Dagger trailing after, his eyes surveilling his surroundings. Jake wondered if he was figuring out what to steal first. There had to be something in the house he wanted, and he had a hunch what it was. The man was a cop's nightmare. He had untrusting eyes, dark hair pulled back in a ponytail, wore a diamond earring, for crissake, and exuded danger from every pore. Jake doubted the guy would get past a checkpoint at an airport.

A sliding glass door opened somewhere, and voices could be heard in the direction of the kitchen.

Sam handed Sara the knife. "I don't know how big of a piece you want so help yourself."

A woman in a traditional Native dress and wearing a squash necklace of turquoise and coral stones entered followed by a man with bronzed skin, hair in pigtails, and carrying a sleeping toddler. The knife Sara held clattered to the table.

The woman looked at Sara curiously, then smiled a warm smile that put Sara at ease.

"Mom, this is Sara and Dagger. My mom, Abby Two Eagles, and our family friend, Alex Red Cloud."

Alex's distrust of strangers was evident in his glare. "I will put Dillon is his bed." Alex retreated from the room.

"Don't mind Alex. He's really a teddy bear when you get to know him," Sam said. "He lives out back in the gate house. Even has a tipi and sweat lodge back there."

"Really?" It had been years since Sara had seen a tipi much less a sweat lodge.

Abby walked around the table and clasped Sara's hand. "*Wíyuškiŋyaŋ waŋčhíŋyaŋke.*"

Sara looked puzzled, then smiled. "*Philámayaye.*"

Abby laughed and cradled Sara's face in her hands. "See. You remembered."

"What did she say?" Dagger demanded.

"Mom said welcome to our home to which Sara replied 'thank you.' See, you can take the girl out of the reservation but not the reservation out of the girl."

Abby stepped closer to Dagger. "Welcome." She sandwiched his hand between hers. Her clasp was firm.

He could feel her penetrating eyes studying him, but her face didn't give anything away. There was something about the way she stared, not so much at him but through him.

She finally released his hand. "Please, everyone. Sit. I am curious how you all met." Abby walked around to the head of the table and sat down.

"No cake for me." Dagger's words were sharp, but he didn't care. He didn't like the hold Sam and her mother appeared to have on Sara. She knew better than to involve anyone from the outside with their lives. They needed to find the surveillance video and get out.

"Trust me," Jake said as he poured coffee into cups. "Never say no to my mother-in-law. And once you taste her desserts, you will never say no again."

Alex returned and took a seat across from Dagger. A smile played at the corners of Jake's lips. Dagger may have thought he was clever and would find what he wanted in the house, but now he was nothing more than a rare specimen being studied and dissected by Alex and Abby. Dagger must have realized this as his death stare leveled at Jake, an acknowledgement that he was in deep shit.

"How old is your son?" Sara took a bite of the cake and almost swooned. She had never tasted anything so good, not since her grandmother's baking.

"Year-and-a-half. His name is Dillon."

"He looks just like your husband."

"Like a mini-me," Sam said with a laugh. She glanced at the baby monitor sitting on the buffet against the wall and could hear Dillon's steady breathing.

Dagger stared at the cake and reluctantly took a bite, aware of the laser stares from across the table. One bite led to another.

"I knew your *unci*." Abby dropped the bombshell in a tone that could have said "it's supposed to rain tomorrow."

Dagger noticed Sara's eyes start to tear.

"Grandmother? How?"

"Ada Kills Bull, right?" Abby took several bites of cake as she watched the young woman. "Fort Peck Reservation?"

Sara nodded slowly. She could sense Dagger ready to stand and storm out of the house, so she placed a firm grip on his arm.

"I met her years ago at an annual pow wow held at Eagle Ridge Reservation."

"But how…" Sara had so many questions, she didn't know where to start.

"In good time," Abby said.

"Abby is *wicasa waken*," Alex said, his eyes daring Dagger to utter a word.

"Medicine woman?" Sara asked. Her grip on Dagger's arm appeared to tighten which Alex and Jake found amusing.

Abby refilled her coffee cup, took a sip, then placed her clasped hands under her chin. "So now, who will be the first to speak."

Dagger felt as though he were sitting at the table of a mafia family with the Native woman head of the family. He wasn't so sure he could escape the house without guns blazing.

Sam was too busy licking her fork which left Jake to reply.

"Captain Robinson asked us to look into a homicide. He thought it might be a copycat killing from a case he worked more than twenty-five years ago when he was a rookie in New Jersey. Sam and I went to the site but the officers guarding the crime scene said another agency had taken over the investigation. So we left."

"You forgot the part where you retrieved a surveillance tape from a salvage yard." Dagger pushed his plate away with a smile. He hadn't been the one to follow Jake and Sam. It had been Sara in her hawk form.

"We were pretty sure we weren't followed." Jake knew Sam's spidey senses would have alerted them to a tail. But the only thing that caught Sam's attention was a hawk on a utility pole outside the yard.

"We have high-tech binoculars, or a rifle scope. Take your pick."

The two men appeared to be engaged in a high-stakes game of one-upmanship. Abby swung her attention to Sam.

"Of course," Sam started as she cut herself another piece of cake, then handed the knife across the table to Sara. "It is known that killers like to return to the scene of the crime so either we are entertaining the killer in our home, or he has a very good reason for being there and for his interest in what we learned." Sam purposely left Sara out of the equation. She didn't appear dangerous and wondered how she ever got mixed up with Dagger. Sara seemed too smart to fall for a bad boy.

"A man of mystery," Alex deadpanned, his suspicious nature never wavering. "You definitely don't look like a choirboy."

Dagger either liked the cake or just needed to keep himself from reaching across the table and wrapping his hands around Alex's neck. He helped himself to another piece.

"We have a client who was also curious about the homicide," Sara replied, feeling the anger circling Dagger like a fog. "Our company is Dagger Investigations. Naturally, we have to honor client privilege."

"And obviously," Dagger said between bites, "our client doesn't have the connections yours does." Dagger knew that was a lie. Mother knew everything.

Abby turned to Jake. "And you can't or won't share the information?"

Jake was sure Abby knew better than to ask, so why was she trying to help them? Words Abby had spoken in the past crept into his head. *Keep your friends close and your enemies closer.* She obviously sensed something about their guests.

"Maybe if they had called ahead or buzzed the intercom at the gate rather than breaking into our house, I might trust them."

This surprised Abby but incensed Alex. She tamped him down with a slight flick of her wrist, then turned to Dagger. "How did you get past the alarm system?"

"We are good at what we do. Your security system is Level One at best. A five-year-old could break into it."

Jake knew they had one of the best systems. There obviously was technology out there even the FBI hadn't discovered yet. "It appears we have the upper hand here. We know why the body is important and how it relates to crimes from twenty-five-years ago."

Dagger pushed his plate away and appeared to stare at something over Jake's shoulder. What he was seeing was a monitor on the side of Jake's face. His internal computer scanned Jake's face and now stats appeared over Jake's right shoulder. Next, he looked at Sam's face and her stats appeared, but Dagger didn't have time for a deep dive into all the stats.

Dagger slid a card across the table. "When you are unable to identify the killer, let me share the video with my client. Although I am surprised you don't already know about the killer seeing that the FBI probably took over the case and you are former FBI. You must still have contacts there. Former Marine, a degree in criminal investigation, five years with the Bureau, then a detective with the Chase Heights Police Department." He turned to Sam. "You've had an interesting career. Your godfather was the police chief, your father an investigative reporter for the Post Tribune." He paused as something flashed on the screen. "Spent time at a mental retreat. Wonder what that was for."

"That's enough." Jake wondered when Dagger had time to research their backgrounds. Did he take their pictures and then looked them up after spotting them at the salvage yard? Maybe checked their license plate and obtained their address? Or did he have a contact at the CHPD? "So, you have your own intel. If it's that good, you should be able to research a case from twenty-five years ago in New Jersey and get your own details on the case we are investigating."

"And maybe you should talk to your contacts at the Bureau and find out what they know."

"Really, gentlemen. Perhaps you should all talk to your respective clients." Abby stood. "We will reconvene tomorrow morning for breakfast. Alex and I have work to do." Alex cast an unspoken question of "we do?" Abby smiled at Sara. "We will try to get in touch with Ada tonight."

"You can do that?"

Dagger stood to leave. He had to get Sara away from these people. "Thank you for your offer of breakfast, but we can't make it."

"Nine o'clock sharp."

Dagger whispered to Sara, "Did she just order us to come back?"

"When *wicasa waken* makes a request, you honor it." Alex started stacking up dirty plates.

Fat chance, Dagger thought.

"What do you think?" Jake was standing on the balcony outside the master bedroom talking to Captain Robinson on the phone. He had already sent him a copy of the video which had showed an unclear view of the face of whom they thought could be the killer. Unfortunately, it didn't show him actually committing the crime.

"Drawing looks eerily the same as the others from twenty-five years ago. I'm going to show this to a handwriting expert just to ease my mind that the killer hasn't risen from the dead. Let him compare this drawing to the ones from earlier cases. Now, about the FBI. They claim it wasn't their people who took over the case."

"What? Then who was it?"

"Good question. Why don't you contact your former boss and see if he can shed some light on this mystery group who claimed the body and swept through the crime scene."

Jake found this puzzling. It's a crime to pass yourself off as a police officer much less a member of the Bureau. Why is this case of interest to so many people? "Can you do me a favor, Captain? See if you can find anything on Chase Dagger and Dagger Investigations. His partner is Sara Morningsky. She mentioned to Sam that she used to live on a reservation in Montana. I don't know of a Dagger Investigations in Chasen Heights, but maybe it's in Indiana. Do you have any contacts with the police departments there?"

"I take it this Dagger guy ruffled your feathers."

"He's got a shitload of bad rolling off of him. I wouldn't be surprised if he had a record. And he has pretty good intel because he knew some things about me and Sam, especially that Sam spent time at the Binyons Retreat."

"What about her? Think you were entertaining a present-day Bonnie and Clyde?"

Jake thought about that innocent face, those eyes. "No. She didn't strike me as anyone who would do harm. I'd bet she takes in every stray cat and animal she sees on the road."

"Right. And he uses them for target practice."

"I know it's late, but if you can get me any info first thing tomorrow morning, I'd appreciate it. Abby invited them for breakfast."

"Said the spider to the fly."

9

"Stockholm Syndrome," Alex said as he rubbed sticks to start the fire. "That's the hold he has on her. Probably kidnapped her walking home from high school." Alex blew on the wood chips, then kept rubbing the sticks. "What is he, maybe thirty, thirty-five? And she looks eighteen."

"She's older than that, maybe early twenties," Abby said. She watched Alex labor over starting the fire. He always had to do things the traditional way when in his tipi. "She is vulnerable, afraid. I believe her grandmother sheltered her because of what she is. I sensed her timidity. Probably afraid of crowds. Dagger is very protective of her."

"He certainly doesn't want her hanging around with us." The rubbing grew more intense. "He looks like a terrorist. And that hair. What modern man wears a ponytail?"

"Says the man whose hair is in pigtails."

Alex stopped rubbing and glared across the pile of wood chips. "I'm allowed. It's tradition."

"Hmmm." Abby stifled a laugh.

"I didn't see wedding rings. What are his plans with her?"

"Alex, you are talking as though she is your daughter."

"She is family, part of our Native family, as is Sam. I feel an obligation to make sure she is safe."

"They have matching earrings, or didn't you notice."

"So? You think they exchanged them in view of the spirits so now they are committed?"

Abby already knew how they met, what their feelings were for each other, and she caught a glimpse of Dagger's past life. All she had to do was touch them for several seconds, but she needed more time with Dagger, or perhaps the spirits will fill in the blanks.

"Do you think she is safe with him?"

Abby considered that for a few seconds. "I think Sara can be almost as dangerous as Dagger." As she watched Alex struggle with the sticks, she reached under the blanket, pulled out an electronic lighter, and held it against the wood chips.

The grey hawk folded its forty-inch wingspan and settled on a branch of a maple tree outside the wrought iron fence surrounding the property. Nightlife scattered but animals had nothing to fear from this hawk. The only animals in danger both day and night were two-legged.

Sara had waited until she was sure Dagger was asleep before leaving the house. He was adamant about not returning for breakfast as requested and would find another way to obtain a copy of the tape, perhaps wait until everyone left the house. She knew he would be angry if he knew where she was going.

The one-hundred-acre property was surrounded by woods. In the distance the tall buildings on the Chicago skyline lit up the shore. There were only a few lights on in the house, mostly nightlights. The hawk lifted from the branch and headed for the back acres where the gatehouse revealed a light on in what looked like the kitchen. A glow in the distance appeared past the house. A hawk's visual acuity was eight times stronger than a human's. The glow was coming from a thirty-foot tall tipi. The scent of smoke filled the air.

Strong wingbeats propelled it closer. The hawk landed on the peak of a rotary type clothes pole. Hanging from a clothesline was a traditional dress. Drumbeats and rattles could be heard from the direction of the tipi. The hawk dropped down to the dress and quickly shifted. Sara found the dress to be slightly too large, but it would do. If Abby were as powerful as Sara felt she might be, could she really communicate with her grandmother? It wasn't enough to hear her grandmother's voice, she wanted to see her.

Cautiously she approached, the cold ground chilling her bare feet. The structure was large, at least seven hundred square feet. With a tipi this size, she should have no problem entering without being seen. She could feel the silky hide skin of the entrance flap. Sara gently pulled back the flap then quickly slipped inside. The odor of burning sage brought back memories. Even in human form she could use the hawk's vision to see in the dim light. There were cooking bowls and pots nailed to the lodge poles, blankets covering every square inch of the floor. She suddenly realized that the sounds of rattles and drumbeats had stopped.

"Come closer, my child," Abby said.

So much for being stealth, Sara thought.

"Sit by me." Abby patted a pillow next to her. "We were expecting you."

Huh? Even though the tipi was warm from the fire, Sara felt a chill. Had the dress been left on the clothesline on purpose? If so, did Abby and Alex know of her shifting abilities? How could they?

The impulse to flee was strong, but her curiosity was stronger. She wanted, needed to talk to her grandmother. All fears set aside, Sara quickly took a seat next to Abby. She flashed a nervous smile first at Abby, then Alex. The anger in his eyes when they first met was gone. Maybe the anger had only been toward Dagger. He was sitting across from her smoking a pipe.

"I have only spoken to grandmother at her grave. Sometimes she answers, or at least I think she does. Do you think we can talk to my parents, too?"

"We can try. Let us start, Alex."

"I've had a few too many in my day. Who hasn't?" The room was dimly lit with candles. It was a wonder it hadn't caught fire. That would be an excellent way to eliminate the world of another worthless piece of shit. But then the authorities wouldn't be able to see his work of art.

"See, it isn't so much that you are a pothead. I don't care if someone relaxes with a glass of wine or a joint after a busy day. But you don't have a typical job, do you? You make your money selling this shit to kids. That is unacceptable. Hanging around high schools is one thing. Teens should know better. But grade schools?" The Watcher paused in his drawing to stare at the face of a twenty-something millennial, or whatever they called them these days.

He had followed the man for weeks, witnessed his stomping grounds. The dealer never changed his attire, always dressed in jeans, dark hoodie and sunglasses. Probably so his followers could recognize him more easily. Not only did he hook young people on pot, but he also got them to push it.

The single-wide trailer was the pot dealer's lair. A place to eat and sleep and store his goods in storage bins under the bench seats. After a hard day's work of pushing pot on unsuspecting youth, he obviously kicked back and sampled his own goods. Would have been better if he had spent time cleaning this rat trap. Empty pizza boxes were stacked on the counter. Overflowing ashtrays were on a coffee table. The entire trailer reeked of pot, garbage, and dirty laundry.

"How are you doing, Kenny?" The black strokes of the fine tip marker were precise, as though stamped by a machine.

The young man stared, not really focusing. His head was swimming in a fog of retribution.

"Did you know that today's marijuana contains a much higher level of THC than in your grandparents' day? Those brownies you make and hand out to friends are potent. With today's pot you can easily become addicted and go through withdrawal. What do you think that does to a young body like the ten and twelve-year-old customers you have? Hallucinations, paranoia." He was disgusted by the drool trailing down the man's chin. "I juiced yours a bit. Can you feel it, Kenny?" He slapped the young man's face. "Don't fade just yet. I want you to feel your pounding heart rate and spiking blood pressure. A taste of your own medicine is a good thing." He finished the drawing and was tempted to sign his artwork. He raised Kenny's hand to show the inside wrist. "What do you think?" But Kenny was no longer focusing.

10

Dagger set his cup of coffee down on the desk and gazed at the catwalk leading up to Sara's bedroom door, closed tight since she slammed it shut last night. His bed had been too damn empty and cold. All because of last night. According to Sara, he had been rude, obstinate, a bully and dozens of other adjectives he couldn't remember. But he was being himself. She should have remembered that he was distrustful, suspicious as well as protective of her and their privacy. Sara was drawn to Abby and her daughter. Even the house with its Native American décor. It brought back fond memories for Sara. But it should have also brought back horrible memories of when her parents had died in a fire, when an angry crowd of neighbors and friends descended on their home believing Sara's father was a mythical Manitou, a shapeshifter, something evil that should be destroyed. That was when Sara, then six, had first shifted and escaped the fire through an attic window. Unaware of what was happening to her, she didn't know how to shift back. When she located her grandmother, she suddenly was aware her grandmother could hear her in thought only. Ada had taken her to an elder on the reservation who could help. Ada suspected that Micha was also a shapeshifter and would be the one to train Sara on how to control her abilities.

Dagger turned his attention back to the computer screen, to the newspaper articles he had pored over since six in the morning, when he could no longer sleep without her body next to his. Water over the dam. Sara forgives quickly so he expected her to come down any minute.

The articles he had read about Jake Mitchell were interesting, especially how he received the welted scars circling his neck. His death had been faked by a fired police officer who kept Jake chained in the dark basement of a shuttered sanitarium. Since he felt the newspaper had been weak on facts, Dagger had accessed police reports and found horrifying details. The scars were from a studded dog collar Jake had been forced to wear. The ex-cop had used a cattle prod on Jake when he grew aggressive and drugged the water bottles to keep him complacent. It had been a six-year-old boy, curious about an unused tunnel in his apartment building, which led authorities to the sanitarium and the basement where Jake was being held.

Sam's history was fascinating if not slightly unbelievable to the average person. Dagger was anything but average. At the age of five Sam had watched her father and his wife die after someone rigged their car with a bomb. She had been catatonic for two years. As a cop, she watched the police chief die in her vehicle when a bomb meant for her blew up her Jeep. This placed her in another catatonic state resulting in her stay at the Sara Binyon Retreat.

But the most interesting thing about Sam Casey was how she solved crimes. In one case she claimed animals and grass bent in a way that led her to mass graves in Indiana. In another she touched an unearthed button owned by a killer and saw the murder taking place, heard the name of the killer. It aided in the release of a prisoner wrongly convicted and due to be executed. More recently the ghost of a boy led her to the grave where he and his father had been buried during the Civil War, unearthing a priceless Confederate coin. This had been in a town in South Carolina.

There were other instances of Sam's talents. Her childhood at five was somewhat similar to Sara's when she was six. Both had watched a traumatic ending to family members. Dagger set the coffee cup down and walked over to the aviary. A splash of blue and red flew from the faux tree. The twelve-hundred square foot aviary was humidity controlled and had a tiled floor for easy cleaning as well as Astro Turf under the tree. The scarlet macaw landed on a perch near the grated door and rubbed its beak against Dagger's fingers.

"What's new, Einstein?"

The bird trained one eye on the stairs leading to the catwalk. "AWWWK, MEN ARE IDIOTS."

Dagger shook his head. Einstein had a habit of repeating things he hears, and he was now repeating what Sara obviously said last night.

"You don't think she's still mad, do you?"

The macaw dipped its head as though responding in the affirmative.

"Well, it's time we woke her up, right?"

"UH OH." Einstein shook his head hard enough to release several feathers.

Dagger shrugged off Einstein's negative reaction and took the stairs two at a time. He knocked first. When he didn't receive a response, he opened the door to a room filled with sunlight and a bed that hadn't been slept in. You could roll a quarter on the floral bedspread, and the accent pillows had been placed with precision. Where could she have gone? The backyard? The store? Then he saw the open patio door.

Dagger pulled up to the gate and laid on the buzzer. He saw the camera on the post. In daylight the house was impressive, all flagstone and stucco. The detective business must be doing well. By accessing the monitor on the Lincoln Navigator, he had discovered where Sara was by the tracker earring she wore. A red blip on the dashboard screen gave him the exact location, although he also had a tracker on his watch.

Someone inside obviously recognized him since the gate slowly opened. He raced the Lincoln Navigator down a brick drive that had to be at least one hundred yards long. The Navigator came to a screeching halt. Jake was standing just off the patio cradling a cup. Where was everyone else? Even if Sara had decided to attend the nine o'clock breakfast, it wasn't even eight o'clock yet. Had she been here all night?

Dagger stormed out of the vehicle, fists balled. "Where is she?" he shouted. He picked up speed and charged at Jake. The cup went flying as both men hit the ground with a thud. They were up on their feet in a second, ready for round two.

"Who are you talking about?" Jake demanded.

"Sara. Where is she?" Dagger shoved. "What have you done with her?" He took a swing at Jake who was surprisingly quick. But Dagger was ready and swung with his left fist, connecting under Jake's right eye.

Jake responded with an upper cut to Dagger's left cheek, then a double punch to the gut. The twenty-five extra pounds Jake had on Dagger made it feel as if he had been hit by a sledgehammer. Now he was pissed. Dagger started with the feet. Jake wasn't surprised this guy knew kick boxing or was a black belt holder. He pulled Dagger into a headlock to keep him from using his feet.

"Stop it, NOW!" Sam's scream broke Jake's hold long enough for Dagger to spin and apply a kick to the solar plexus as Jake shoved against the offending leg. The two men dropped to the ground like fallen trees.

"Really?" Sam stood over the men, hands on her hips. "Are you still in grade school?"

They lay on their backs trying to catch their breaths. If they were embarrassed by their schoolyard brawl, it didn't show. Dagger measured his breathing, not wanting to give Jake the satisfaction of knowing his punches harmed him. Slowly Dagger propped himself up on one elbow, feeling something trailing down the side of his face. Jake took a slow, deep breath, reached into his shirt pocket, and pulled out a cigarette and lighter. He took a long drag, turned his head and blew the smoke in Dagger's direction. "You hit like a girl."

Dagger snorted. "A snail moves faster than your lard ass."

"Two-hundred ten pounds of solid muscle. You'll realize that when you look at your face in the morning." He studied the blood trailing down Dagger's face. "Then again, you should probably have that cut looked after."

"If you're looking for Sara, I'll take you to her. She stayed in the tipi last night with mom and Alex," Sam said.

"Shit," Dagger whispered.

"Jake, will you keep an eye on Dillon. He's in the kitchen playing with knives."

Jake jerked his head up.

"Only kidding. I'll go get the golf cart from the garage."

Dagger struggled to his feet. "She's a riot. You obviously don't keep her on a leash."

* * * *

"You've got blood on your face," Sam said as she drove the golf cart down the asphalt path to the back acreage. "Someone might think you've been in a fight." She checked out the grass clinging to his black shirt and cargo pants. "Then again." She nodded at the bottle of water in the cup holder. "That might help."

Dagger poured the water on a hankie and wiped his face and lip, wincing when he got near the cut. "Sara wasn't home this morning. I figured she left early but had no idea she left last night."

"And you thought she might be here because…" she prompted.

Dagger didn't reply.

Sam studied him. He appeared younger than Jake by a few years. He either didn't have time to shave or had one of those faces that had a perpetual five o'clock shadow. She bet that if she searched through his closet he only owned black shirts and cargo pants. Either that or he was wearing the same clothes he wore last night. She noticed his earring, identical to the one Sara wore. Hair pulled back in a ponytail was dark, as was his skin. More Italian or Greek, Sam thought.

"How long have you known Sara?"

Dagger slid his eyes to her, then turned his head to study the vines growing over the fence surrounding the property. He felt something trickling down his face and pressed the hankie against it.

"Okay then. Not a talker, only a fighter. It isn't smart to be possessive."

"Sara and I don't socialize. We value our privacy."

"Maybe you shouldn't decide that for Sara. She hungers for friendship."

"You know nothing about her."

"True, but I can certainly tell when someone is being stifled. It will eventually come back to bite you in the ass."

Dagger ignored her comment. All he knew was that Sara wasn't safe here. She wasn't safe anywhere but on her three hundred acres of secluded property.

There was a slight turn in the path which led to a small ranch size home. A vegetable garden near the house was surrounded by chicken wire. Beyond the gatehouse was a thirty-foot structure, a tipi, where Abby, Alex and Sara were standing. Dagger climbed out of the golf cart, but the site of Sara in Native attire stopped him cold. She hadn't driven here. Her PT Cruiser was still at home. She had shifted in probably her hawk form which meant she didn't have clothes. Did Abby and Alex now know Sara was a shapeshifter? All kinds of emotions raced through him. If they had witnessed her shifting, the wolf would have killed. Yet Abby and Alex were still breathing. His anger and concern dissipated when he saw the joy in her eyes.

Sara rushed into his arms. "I spoke to my parents and my grandmother last night. Dagger, it was wonderful. They are happy. They found each other and grandfather, too."

Ignoring her question, Dagger glared at the two Natives. What shit have they been feeding her? Had they given Sara peyote and she hallucinated?

Sara pulled back from him. "What happened to your face?"

Dagger touched his cheek and drew back blood.

"You should see Jake's. They're matching bookends." Sam left the golf cart on the path, and they all walked back to the house. It wasn't that far, and it was a colorful walk past flower beds in full fall colors. She heard Sara's voice, excited from her night in the tipi. But Dagger was quiet. Sam saw his tenseness, the set of his jaw, the dark of his eyes. Was Sara safe from his anger when they returned home?

"You have a beautiful garden. I bet it's beautiful in the spring."

"All year, Sara," Abby said. "Alex does a wonderful job."

"I have some flowers and a vegetable garden." Sara hadn't noticed Dagger's growing anger, but she could feel he was distant, closed off. "We have three hundred acres of open prairie, a stream. My grandparents are buried near the stream. It was a shock when an auto dealer purchased the property and built the building only to discover it was reservation land owned by my grandparents."

"Sara." Dagger's voice seeped caution and anger. They reached the driveway where the Navigator sat, its car door still open. Dagger turned to Abby. "Thanks for your hospitality, but we have to leave." To Sara he said, "Get in the car. We're going home."

As if not hearing a word he said, Sara snaked her arm around Abby's. "Abby and I are making fry bread. Bring my bag from the backseat, please." With that the women headed to the house with Alex trailing, stopping briefly to give Dagger the snake eye.

Jake watched as Dagger pulled a gym bag from the back seat and slammed both doors shut. He couldn't resist a parting shot. "I believe PetSmart has a sale on leashes."

11

While Sara showered and Abby placed a jelly roll pan of bacon in the over, Sam cracked eggs, her mind conjuring up a list of questions. Why did Sara have extra clothes in Dagger's vehicle? Where are the clothes she arrived in last night? Where were her shoes? If Dagger wasn't sure Sara was here, why was he prepared with the gym bag?

"Sam, those eggs aren't going to crack themselves."

"Oh, sorry." She glanced at Dillon who was shoving mandarin oranges in his mouth. He was always quiet when there was food in front of him. Dillon was a perfect likeness to Jake, from the soft brown eyes to the husky build. Like Jake, Dillon would never have to lift weights to have a toned, muscular body.

The kitchen was bright, a window box highlighting a variety of plants, a testament to Abby's green thumb. Plants seemed to die just by Sam breathing near them. Bowls containing measured ingredients needed for the fry bread sat on a large island counter.

"Can I do something?" Jake had cleaned up and changed out of his grass-stained clothes.

"Thanks, Jacob. You can set the table. Also, place the pitcher of orange juice and glasses on the table."

"I'm ready," Sara said as she entered the kitchen, her damp hair tied back in a neat braid. "Where do we start?"

Dagger was sitting on a cushioned chair on the flagstone patio, studying the various stair-step gardens with brick borders and a number of bird feeders and birdbaths. He had to admit, he needed to do more work on Sara's yard. She did have vegetable and flower gardens but most of the acreage was wild grasses and wildflowers. Sara had placed a hummingbird feeder on a shepherd's hook. However, after seeing this manicured yard and magazine cover quality landscaping, it left a lot to be desired for their own property.

He swung his attention to the five-car garage and wondered why a portion of the roof was a bubble window. Then he spotted a telescope on the second-floor. Just as he was about to get nosy and check it out, Alex took a seat next to him.

"Jake likes to study the stars."

"Either that or he peers into neighbors' bedrooms."

Alex ignored the comment. "Is the young woman with you of her own free will? You are obviously much older."

"What? Like she's been kidnapped or something? Why didn't you ask Sara last night? You spent enough time with her."

"Which obviously bothers you. You are too possessive for your own good."

"Why the hell does everyone think that? Did she say something?"

"Alex." Abby stood at the screen door. "Come make your special seasoned potatoes and leave the young man alone. Dagger, would you like a Bloody Mary?"

"Thanks, but it's a little too early for me."

He heard Alex mumble, "I doubt that," as he entered the house.

"On second thought, yes, I'd love something stiff about now." What he also needed to do was lecture Sara about choosing friends and not reporting back, but even he knew this wasn't the time or place. If he had to be honest, though, he was more than suspicious. He was jealous. Was Sara's life so boring now that she needed to find something or someone new and exciting? Even her grandmother warned her not to get close to people. It was dangerous for Sara to make friends, even though Dagger knew she needed them. She had Eunie, Simon's wife, but no one who knew of her shapeshifting abilities. He suspected Abby and Alex knew. How soon until they shared that information with Sam and Jake? How soon until the wolf seeks to quiet them? And they had a son. Sara would be putting him in danger, too.

He heard the screen door open. Seconds later he smelled her skin as she wrapped her arms around his neck, felt the silk fabric of the floral shirt she wore with the cropped jeans. She had a gym bag packed in every vehicle he owned, along with undies, shoes, and toiletries. Always prepared.

"Come see the fry bread cooking. It smells just like my gram used to make."

What he couldn't deny and what made him even more jealous was how much Sara seemed more at home here.

They were gathered around the dining room table, platters of food lined up buffet style. Each had claimed the same seats they had the night before. "You must have come over pretty late, Sara." Sam dropped several roasted potatoes on a plate in front of Dillon. He quickly grabbed with both hands.

"It was spur of the moment."

"Please, try the fry bread." Abby motioned to Dagger who had the unfortunate position of again sitting across from Alex.

Dagger obliged but found the sugar to be too sticky.

Sam had to reassess her impression of Dagger. Sara obviously had him wrapped around her finger. Unlike Alex, Sam didn't feel Sara was being forced or coerced by Dagger. She was definitely independent. "We know Sara is from Montana, but where are you from, Dagger?"

"That's none of your concern." Dagger leveled his dark eyes on Sam but could feel Alex's own stab of distrust.

"It just seems your past is about as fake as the information in our background check." As she studied his face, Sam realized the cut by his eye was completely healed. How was that possible? His cheek still showed a bruise and his eye was developing a ring of dark purple. But where was the cut?

"It's a talent."

Sam smiled, not wanting him to get to her. "I'm sure you are a man of many talents."

"Not all legal, I assume," Alex said.

"I apologize, Dagger." Abby turned to Sam and Alex. "It isn't our intent to make you feel uncomfortable."

"It isn't?" Alex muttered under his breath. "I kind of enjoy it."

"Did you talk to your captain?" Dagger preferred to get right to the point. "We have to move quickly on this if you want your killer identified." He took a sip of his Bloody Mary, realizing his first sip had been a long slug. He had emptied half of the glass.

"He would first like your source because it isn't the FBI, CIA, or Interpol. We've already checked those out."

"Really? Well, that's not going to happen."

Abby looked from Dagger to Jake. She had always been the mediator at reservation Council meetings and could usually get those with opposing views to compromise. Something told her Dagger wasn't going to bend. So, she tried another tactic.

"That settles it then. You each keep your own information and delay a resolution by weeks, if not months. Perhaps after a few more deaths, someone will be the bigger man and capitulate."

Dagger wasn't moved. He poured a cup of coffee, then had another helping of eggs and potatoes.

"It is better to have less thunder in the mouth and more lightning in the hand." Alex stabbed a glare at Dagger. "An Apache proverb."

"My grandfather spoke in proverbs a lot," Sara said. "The one he liked was 'those who have one foot in the canoe, and one foot in the boat, are going to fall into the river.' That's from the Tuscarora tribe."

Dagger stabbed another sausage patty. "My favorite is 'trust no one.' A saying from the world-renown seer, Chase Dagger."

"Dagger, really?"

"This whole thing is giving me a headache." Sam placed two pieces of bacon in front of Dillon who pointed at the plate of fry bread. "So, we have the video which you want." She cut a piece of fry bread in half and handed it to Dillon.

"And we have the killer's name, which you want."

"Isn't this all a moot point?" Alex turned to Jake. "The question is what organization or government is involved? It shouldn't be that hard to figure out."

"And you have friends in high places," Abby reminded Jake.

"Retired," Sam clarified.

"With connections," Abby added.

Dagger's phone rang. He excused himself, walked into the kitchen and out onto the patio. Sara tried to listen to his conversation, but Dillon was pointing a piece of bacon at her.

"She's pretty, isn't she, Dillon? Can you say Sara?"

Dillon looked at Sam, then at Sara. "See-See" was as close to Sara as Dillon could get.

Dagger returned but remained standing. "We have to go. This conversation isn't over. We need a copy of that tape."

"It's here when you are ready to deal," Jake said. "Talk to your client."

Sara stood. "Do we have to leave so soon?"

"Sorry, babe. We've been summoned."

"Summoned. What do you think that meant?" Sam rinsed the plates while Abby put them in the dishwasher.

"Sounds like they have a very high-profile client."

"Probably a mob boss, someone you don't say no to." Alex set the tray of dirty cups on the island counter.

"Alex, I love you, but you are so dramatic. I doubt Dagger would put Sara in a dangerous situation." Sam grabbed the cups and added them to the top rack of the dishwasher.

"He is private for a good reason." Abby caught Alex and Sam staring at her. "And which you know better than to ask."

"The dangerous part is all I'm concerned about. He was in our house, near your grandson," Sam reminded her mother. "And did you notice the cut on Dagger's face has completely healed. He needed stitches. How could that happen? It isn't natural."

Jake entered from the study carrying a cleaned-up toddler. He set him down and Dillon quickly ran to the patio doors, pounding to have them opened.

"Wait until we are finished, Dillon. Come, finish your juice." Abby held out his sippy cup.

"Hey, Sam. How would you like to take a trip?" Jake tried to hide the smile.

"Where to?"

"Carl wants to see us, in person, about this case."

"Hilton Head? Really?" Sam beamed, then frowned. "Another plane ride?"

"He's sending a private jet for us. We need to be at the Gary Airport by eight tomorrow morning."

"Great. We can catch up with Mossy and her son and Milla." They had met Mossy Belden and Detective Milla Boles with the Heyward Bluff Police Department several months ago. Carl had awakened next to a dead woman and had no idea who she was or how he had ended up in a seedy motel. The victim had used Mossy Belden's name, a woman who was anything but young, white, or dead.

"Unfortunately, no. Carl said we can't let anyone know we are in town. Didn't say why but it was the one stipulation."

12

"I appreciate your seeing me on such short notice." Captain Lamon Robinson examined the wooden chair in front of Sergeant Martinez's desk. The distance between the two armrests would barely accommodate one of Robinson's butt cheeks let alone both. He moved several framed photos from the side credenza and leaned against it. To his credit, the detective sergeant made no comment about the captain's size.

"Play a lot of football?"

"Notre Dame, til I blew out a knee."

"I played soccer on the All Saints seminary team."

"Ahh, now I know how you got the nickname Padre." Robinson had explained the twenty-five-year-old case over the phone, as well as the conflict between Dagger and Jake. Seeing that the public and police profile of Chase Dagger was sketchy at best, Robinson thought the Cedar Point police department could fill in the blanks.

"Interesting old case," Padre said. "Puzzling seeing how the killer is dead."

"Not only that, but I just had a forensic forgery expert compare the photo of the drawing from one of the earlier ones. He says he's ninety-five percent certain they were sketched by the same person."

"The five-percent, I assume, is because he couldn't compare the actual drawings in the flesh."

"Right. All we have are pictures and he's looking at strokes, pen pressure, and whatever else these experts check. And, as I mentioned over the phone, the drawings left on the victims of John Wallace Baker were never made public."

There was a knock on the door, then a young woman entered carrying a tray.

"Thanks, Janet." Padre moved papers from a section of his desk.

Once the woman departed, Padre said, "I assumed you drank coffee. Help yourself to cream and sugar."

After doctoring their java, Robinson returned to his perch and waited, sipping his coffee which was black, not too strong, just the way he liked it.

"So," Padre said with a smile, "you want to know about the pain in my ass."

"Would help to let my people know what to expect. Information online is laughable."

"I'm pretty sure his psycho sidekick changes it up weekly, just for the fun of it."

"This is Sara?" Robinson had learned about Dagger and Sara from the little time Jake and Sam had spent with them.

"Oh no. Skizzy Borden, a bona fide schizophrenic, believer of aliens and every conspiracy known to man. Thinks Big Brother is spying which is why he takes labels off of food cans so the government can't poison him. Don't get me wrong, he is a genius when it comes to computers and electronics. Even has drone bugs. Owns a pawn shop but manages to get his hands on a lot of weapons, some you and I have never heard of."

Robinson's eyebrows slowly crawled north. "That's his circle of friends? Sara and a nutcase?"

"No. There's also Simon, an aging mailman who was a sharpshooter in the military." Padre refilled his cup, then stirred in cream and sugar. "I, too, am in the dark when it comes to Dagger's background. He blew into town several years ago and brought a shitload of trouble with him. Some of the strangest cases have been dumped at my doorstep. And I mean strange. Most I couldn't even write up in an official report."

Robinson said nothing. How strange was strange? If Padre ever saw what Sam could do, he would re-assess his definition of strange.

As if reading his mind, Padre said, "I have read about your former Sergeant Sam Casey, how she can solve cases using some kind of Native American mysticism. Sorry to say, that's nothing."

It wasn't that cold in Padre's office, but Robinson felt a chill. He walked over to the desk and refilled his cup.

"Where should I start?" Padre settled back, warm cup in hand. He checked the door to make sure it was closed. "We had a thief who stole a camouflage suit developed by a research scientist. When worn not even a security camera could pick him up. In another case there were two clones, and I don't mean twins. These clones were in town to kill Dagger."

"How could you tell the difference between a twin and a clone?"

"Couldn't. But my medical examiner and I spent hours scraping remains of one of the clones out of a quarry. A bomb of some type had been planted in the guy's neck, set to go off at a certain time after the clone's death. Luckily Skizzy and Simon had noticed something flashing in the guy's neck, realized it was a countdown clock, and tossed the body into the quarry or the bomb would have claimed them, too."

Robinson was sure his eyes were the shape of ostrich eggs. He probably resembled a cartoon character.

A slight smile crept across Padre's face. His visitor obviously thought his cases were stranger than Padre's. "In another case…and if I hadn't witnessed it myself, I would have never believed it…an arms dealer was selling a vaporizer to the highest bidder using my town to demonstrate it."

"A vaporizer?"

"A high-tech rifle. When pointed at someone's head, it heated the brain so hot it literally vaporized. I saw steam coming out of the victim's eyes, nose, and ears. Almost wet myself."

Now Robinson's gaze searched the ceiling of Padre's office. Who had Jake and Sam involved themselves with? "How the hell have we not heard of these cases?"

"Like I said, no paper trail. I didn't dare write anything down and my M.E. is very tight-lipped. Believe me, the press and public were the last people I wanted to get wind of these. It was bad enough Dagger's ex-fiancée dogged me endlessly for any scrap of detail for her daddy's newspaper. I trust everything I tell you today goes no further, other than what you plan to share with your detectives."

"Trouble certainly seems to follow him. You have your own Mulder and Scully. It's a wonder they haven't encountered aliens."

"Close to it. Ever hear of a parallel universe?"

"Do I want to?"

"This ex-fiancée of Dagger's decided to spend a night in a haunted mansion with some local ghost hunters, all for a story. She went missing, car was still there, her purse, keys, but not her. Next time we saw her she was chased through the wall back into the mansion by a guy dressed in turn-of-the-century garb. I watched the guy disintegrate right before my eyes. As long as he stayed in his era, he stayed his true age. But once he stepped into the current century, his body aged and disintegrated. The guy had been a serial killer back in his days."

Robinson tried to steady his hand as he set the cup down. Suddenly, what Sam and her mother could do seemed like child's play compared to what circled around Dagger. "You said she was a reporter. How was that story not a headline?"

"There were no other witnesses. Sheila Monroe, the reporter, had hit her head when she was tackled. Passed out. Dagger and I told her we found her in a room under the stairs. She had a concussion, had hallucinated. The house mysteriously caught fire after that event. I have to tell you, even I had some sleepless nights afterwards. Our explanation was plausible."

"And you never questioned what happened? Found it all believable?" As a cop, Robinson liked unquestionable proof.

"Sheila recounted some weird things. Said she met a little girl, that she had shared some of her bracelets with her. They were bands with shapes of animals on them. Something they gave out to school kids when they held tours at the newspaper. Sheila had given the little girl ten of them. When Dagger and I walked through the rubble the next day, we found skeletal remains of what looked like a little girl several yards from the property. Those bands Sheila said she shared with the girl were on the wrist of the remains. You tell me what conclusion you would have come to."

"Shit," Robinson whispered.

"Our thoughts exactly."

"Well, I'm not sure your Sleepy Hollow-type town is my cup of tea. And I have to admit, I'm having a hard time believing any of it."

"Don't blame you."

"What I don't understand, though, is how this young woman, Sara, got all caught up in Dagger's life. Sam says she's this shy introvert, quite a few years younger than Dagger."

"Don't underestimate that innocent persona. I witnessed her spin in the air, grab a knife headed for Dagger's throat, grab another knife from Dagger's waistband with her other hand, and while still spinning in the air, throw both knives at the fleeing art thief with such force they impaled the suspect to a tree. Well, by his clothes, not his body. She didn't kill him, surprisingly. And I wasn't the only one to witness it. The FBI, NSA, CIA, and every other alphabet were there to arrest him. He was the same guy who had stolen the camouflage suit. Every one of those alphabets wanted to recruit Sara after that."

"Well." Robinson was at a loss for words. "Not sure my people will be glad I asked for information." He rubbed a hand across the back of his neck. "I'm having a hard time digesting it all."

Padre pushed away from his desk and stood. "Not to make you too unsteady, but those are Cliff Notes from the more believable cases. There are others I cannot in good conscience share." He made the sign of the cross. "*Santa Maria Madre de Dios.*"

"Oh, shit," Robinson whispered as he left the office.

13

"How did Carl get his hands on a Gulfstream?" Sam ran her hand over the soft tan leather seats. Mahogany desks and state of the art electronics made the eighteen-passenger jet feel more like Air Force One, not that she had ever ridden on that prestigious set of wings. A full-service bar was in the back by a door they assumed was the kitchen. "I could get used to this."

"Looks like the seats fold down into a bed. Carl's pension must be larger than I thought." Jake took a seat next to Sam. They had only packed one suitcase since Carl said to pack for two days at the most. Sam wished they could stay for a week.

"I don't know why Carl couldn't share the case details with you over the phone."

"Guess he doesn't trust our phones." Jake set his laptop under the seat.

They heard rather than felt something being loaded into the luggage compartment below. Footsteps pounded up the stairs. The first person they saw was Sara followed close behind by Dagger.

"You have got to be kidding." Dagger glared at the couple, but Sara was delighted.

"What a wonderful surprise to end up on the same flight." Sara took a seat across the aisle from them.

Jake ignored Dagger's attitude, instead focusing on the two people following Dagger.

"Okay kiddies. Time to strap in." The bulky figure was dressed more for golf than piloting a plane. A bright orange belt held up a barrel chest which surprisingly looked firm rather than doughy. The woman was dressed for the boardroom in a black pantsuit. Her short blonde hair and fresh scrubbed face made it difficult to determine her age. "My name is Stan Cazlewski. I am your pilot. Kelly will tend to your every need. Traveling with us today is Jake Mitchell, his lovely wife, Sam Casey-Mitchell." Stan checked his clipboard. "Do you hyphenate, darling?"

"Not normally."

"Very good. I usually go by Casey but we don't want to confuse things so call me Stan." He caught Dagger's eye and smiled. "Then we have Chase Dagger and the beautiful Sara Morningsky."

"You can fly a plane?" Sara's question dripped with suspicion.

"I watched two YouTube videos last night. I'm more than ready to take this baby out for a spin."

This elicited the slightest of smiles from Kelly.

"Really, Stan? I don't see a co-pilot just in case you get a bullet in the back of your head." Dagger's comment amused Stan.

"Why, Kelly here is my co-pilot. She watched four YouTube videos. Right, sweetheart?"

Kelly rolled her eyes and turned to the passengers. "Ignore him. We will be departing in twenty minutes. Arriving in Hilton Head Airport at ten-fifteen Eastern Time. As soon as we are airborne, I will set out a buffet on the bar in the back. I will be serving mini-quiche, sausage muffins, fruit, pastries, juice and coffee. We also have mimosas and Bloody Marys."

"They are great," Stan yelled as he retreated to the cockpit. "I've already had four."

"Is he for real?" Sam asked no one in particular. He was entertaining but Sam was a nervous flyer. If she had her choice she would rather have driven. And why did it appear Dagger and Sara knew Stan? Did they also know Kelly?

"Unfortunately, yes. Stan owns a bar in Cedar Point called The Hideaway. I have an office above the bar." Dagger caught the look Jake and Sam exchanged and could easily guess what they were thinking. He felt the plane taxiing toward the runway. Why did he not know that Stan had a pilot's license? Then again, he shouldn't be surprised that he knew little about the guy. If Mother arranged for the plane, why were the

Mitchells on it? Dagger was certain Jake brought the video, or at least a copy of the video with him. If either Jake or Sam were concerned, they weren't voicing it, but he could feel it radiating from their side of the plane.

"Good morning, boys and girls," a voice blared from a speaker. "We are ready for takeoff. Kelly, please keep our skydiving equipment ready. Sorry, we only brought two parachutes."

"He's kidding," Kelly mouthed.

"We will be flying at fifteen thousand feet with a maximum airspeed of, oh I don't know, two hundred, three hundred. We'll be going fast. With a good tail wind, we should be at our destination in less than two hours. I have brought my emotional support boa constrictor today, but he appears missing from his cage. If you find him, please bring him up to the cockpit. Thank you."

"Hell, do we have to listen to two hours of this?" Dagger said as the engines roared and the jet hurled down the runway.

"Here we go. Wahooooo!" Stan's voice echoed through the cabin.

Sam's hands wrapped around Jake's arm as she buried her face in his shoulder. "We should have driven." She kept her eyes closed and her hands in a death grip until she felt the plane level off. "Have we landed yet?" She looked across the aisle and saw that Sara had her hands wrapped like a vice around Dagger's arm.

"So." Jake glared at Dagger. "How did we end up on the same flight? This have anything to do with the call you received yesterday?"

"I'm as much in the dark as you. If I had my druthers, I would have flown commercial."

"Did your contact say why you were summoned?" Jake used the same term Dagger had used at breakfast.

"Did yours?"

Checkmate.

Twenty minutes later, wonderful aromas drifted from the back of the plane. Jake noticed a panel to his left under the window. He pressed a button and suddenly a solid mahogany tray unfolded and slowly settled in front of them. "Huh, it's a desk." Jake reached under the seat and pulled out his laptop.

Stan emerged from the cockpit and strolled down the aisle. "Um, Stan, who's flying the plane?" Sara asked nervously.

"Auto pilot. I'm going back here for breakfast. Maybe even take a little nap while I'm at it." Stan heard a gun cocking. "Come on, Dagger. Where's your sense of humor? Oh wait. You don't have one." He continued walking toward the back of the plane. Dagger put his gun away with a sigh.

Now that Jake was able to fire up his laptop and use his phone, he sent Carl a quick text to find out what was going on. After five minutes Carl had not replied. "Okay, Dagger. I'm pretty sure we don't have the same contact."

"Mine's a woman."

"And mine's a man. He told me he was sending a jet for us so we can have a meeting in Hilton Head regarding the case. And since you don't know him, I'm still puzzled why you are on this plane."

"Yes, it has piqued my curiosity since our contact also said she would send a plane for us."

"If my contact knew yours, he would have told me."

"Same here." Although Dagger wouldn't put it past Mother to be light on details.

Kelly appeared in front of them. "Ladies and gentlemen, the buffet is now available at the bar. You may sit back at the bar to eat or eat here. I see you have discovered the desks. We also have a bench seat behind you. I can turn on the television set if you wish."

Stan walked past with a tray containing two plates and a cup of coffee. "Great job, Kelly, but not enough Irish Cream in the coffee."

"He's kidding, really," Kelly said quickly. "Please ignore him. However, if you would like an adult beverage, just let me know. Now, please. Help yourselves to the buffet."

"I think I could use a Bloody Mary." Jake folded the desk up and stood.

"I could use one, too," Sam said. They made their way to the back with Dagger and Sara close behind.

With plates filled and drinks made, they returned to their seats. Jake checked again to see if Carl had replied. Still no word. He then opened an email from Captain Robinson from a secure login, thanks to their friendly nerd. They ate as they read the lengthy note regarding Robinson's meeting with Sergeant Martinez of the Cedar Point, Indiana police department. More than once they each glanced over at Dagger and Sara, then re-read the detailed information. Jake deleted the email. He glanced at Sam, and he could almost read the same thought in her eyes: What had they gotten themselves into?

14

"I have to get to work, ma."

"Work? Last time you held a job was three years ago. Another lie, Jess?"

"It isn't a lie." If she was headed to a job, she wasn't dressed for it. Her dishwater hair hung in grimy strings. Clothes looked slept in and gym shoes missing laces. She clung to the hand of a toddler who looked as disheveled and emaciated as its mother.

"Ma, I need you to watch Matthew for only a few hours," May Haslen mimicked. "You didn't come back for two weeks last time. The time before was seven weeks."

"I was in rehab. You know that."

"And how many times is that? Five? Six? They kicked you out last time. I have a job, too, you know. I always end up paying for day care."

"I'll pay you back."

The argument was being carried out on the lawn in front of a row of townhomes. Since most of the neighbors worked, May Haslen was confident there wouldn't be any complaints to the Association Board. At least not like the last time when Jess was dancing naked on the front lawn at midnight singing Joy to the World, all hopped up on pot and God knows what else.

"Ma, I'm trying to get clean. All I need is a job and a chance to show I can care for my kid. I have a disease. Aren't there laws to protect people like me from being fired?"

May folded her arms and leaned against the railing. Maybe it was their genes. May's mother was a flower child, regretting that she had been born too late to enjoy Woodstock. She had named her daughters April, May, and June, each from different men. May had been determined to go a different way, went to a junior college, had a head for numbers and now had a great accounting job at a local business. All three of the sisters were divorced and determined to never marry again. One nephew was in prison for assault, two nieces were kicked out of junior college, both liking bar hopping a little too much. Yes, the family genes were not the best.

"Disease? Really? You know that term just gives people an excuse. It's disgusting." May sat down on the front stoop and held out her hand. "Matthew, come to gram." The toddler pulled away from his mother's vice grip like a frightened kitten fleeing from a pit bull. What terrors had Jess subjected Matthew to with the number of men coming and going like a revolving door and drug dealers hunting her down for their money?

She gathered her grandson in her arms. Such a cute, innocent face, but May could feel the bones in his thin body.

"This time, if you don't straighten out, keep a job, and stay clean, I'm filing for guardianship."

"This time I will, I mean it. Things are gonna be different. Promise." Jess fidgeted, the same way she did when she was younger and had to bring up courage to ask for something…candy, a certain toy, or as a teen, to stay out late. "I just need gas money to get to my interview. I will pay it back. It's a good paying job." Jess stared at her son for several seconds longer than normal. May knew this time Jess would never return. "Stay here Matty." May disappeared into the house and several seconds later came out with a twenty-dollar bill. "Last time, Jess." The bill was snatched so fast it was a wonder it hadn't torn in half.

As she watched her daughter dash to the rusted beater of a car, the Watcher observed the scene from the front seat of a rental car. It wasn't the first time he had followed Jess Haslen. He had even witnessed a Hispanic-looking man barter for her son. It had appeared to him that Jess had given it serious thought. There wasn't any need to follow her. He had done it too many times, knew her haunts, where she scored, as well as the different places she slept and how she paid for her drugs.

The Watcher's attention to detail had always been his greatest asset. That's how he knew that Jess's mother had taken out a life insurance policy on her daughter to assure that her grandson was taken care of when and if Jess did something stupid. He had followed May to the park where she had met a friend. As usual, she had Matthew with her and while he played May commented how she was glad that she had taken out the policy the day after Matthew was born. Most policies weren't effective for one or two years after the policy was signed. It shouldn't be hard to make Jess's death look like an accidental overdose.

As long as he focused on the victims, he could drown out the other voice in his head, the one who questioned his motives, his actions. One thing he could get the voice to agree on was that the innocents were the ones being saved, innocents like Matthew and May.

Life had given Jess more chances than anyone deserved. It was time to put her loved ones and society out of their misery.

15

While Kelly and Stan stayed with the plane, the four adventurers discovered a Lincoln SUV reserved in Jake's name waiting by the hangar. He gladly grabbed the keys. Dagger looked like someone who easily broke too many speed limits. The last thing they needed was to be stopped by the police.

It was a quiet twenty-minute ride, at least in the front seat of the SUV. The women, however, chatted in the back seat all the way from the airport. Sam described in detail the case that had brought her and Jake to Heyward Bluff several months ago. Sara was especially interested in the ghost of the Indian boy who had helped Sam solve the case.

"And that doesn't scare you?" Sara asked. "To see people who aren't really there?"

"Oh, they are there. They just have something to say and are waiting for someone to listen."

"Must have been hard for Abby to try to believe you weren't making things up when you were younger."

Sam laughed. She was sure Abby wouldn't appreciate Sam's disclosing family details, but it didn't stop her from blurting it out. "You forget. Abby is *wicasa waken*. I may pick up clues by touching a body or something the victim or killer touched. But mom only has to shake your hand and she knows every detail of your life."

Dagger's head slowly raised. And did Sara's olive complexion appear a few shades lighter?

They drove the rest of the way in silence. Dagger preferred to study the expanse of water under the connecting bridge while Sara looked for wildlife. Sam had checked her phone to see if Carl had replied to her text since he had yet to reply to Jake's. And unanswered questions still swirled in her head. Why were Dagger and Sara here? Were they also connected to Carl in some way? Why didn't Carl give them a heads up? The only recent text they received was from Captain Robinson informing them that it wasn't the FBI that had confiscated the evidence and the body which made the silence from Carl even more puzzling. If anyone would know what the FBI or its many special task forces were doing, it would be Carl.

"I'm curious, Dagger, why you aren't questioning your visit here. Are you sure you don't know Carl Underer?" Sam asked.

"I can assure you, I never knew, nor never would be involved in anything to do with the FBI. We have obviously been kept in the dark about this trip as much as you."

Jake took the first light after the bridge. Everything looked familiar to Sam, just the same as the last time they visited, minus the tangle of tourist cars and motor homes. Sam couldn't take the silence anymore.

"Too bad we couldn't take a quick tour of the island. The shops there are great, Sara. How long do you plan to be here?"

"Since Jake's driving, I guess as long as you are." Leave it to Dagger to give a sarcastic response.

"You can always take a cab." Sam was starting to tire of Dagger's irritating mood.

"I'm sure a cab or Uber driver could drive a bit faster than you. You drive as fast as your lard ass moves."

"Dagger, really? You're suffering from separation anxiety more than me," Sara said. "Why the vitriol?"

"I'm sure he's as happy to be spending time with us as we are with him. You are excluded since you are a pleasure to be around." Jake turned into the drive to Carl's house. "Looks like Carl did build a garage."

"How did he go from a carport to a three-car garage?" Sam figured someone must have twisted his arm.

"Remember, he did buy that blue '57 Chevy Belair convertible that was involved in that case we worked," Jake reminded her. "He probably needed the garage to work on it."

"Nice house," Sara said. The two-story cobblestone structure had a red metal roof and a screened in porch overlooking an immaculate array of perennials. They climbed out of the SUV then grabbed suitcases from the back.

"You should see the inside." Sam studied the landscaping and the terrace on the side of the porch. The lot next door was still empty, and she wondered if Carl had purchased it for additional privacy.

They climbed the steps to the front porch. The door opened before Jake had a chance to push the doorbell.

"What the hell? Did you take a camel to get here?"

"Please, Carl. We had to listen to two hours of Grumpy Gus." Sam motioned toward Dagger. "And look at you." She studied Carl's yellow shorts with red lobsters imprinted on them and the short-sleeve yellow shirt with various images of palm trees. "Not afraid of showing those knees."

"You learn to dress for the weather down here."

"Helps you to blend in with the locals, too," Jake pointed out.

"The plants look beautiful, Carl. Your landscaper obviously convinced you to build the garage."

"Well, Sam, he was a pushy ass. Kinda reminded me of you." He studied Dagger's bruised cheek, then Jake's. "I see you two are getting along admirably. Come in. I am Carl Underer for those who don't know me." He held open the door and the four filed in, the men toting the suitcases. "You must be Dagger and Sara. I've heard a lot about you." He didn't give them time to ask the how and why questions. "Let's get everyone settled first before we have lunch on the deck. Dagger and Sara, I think you'll be comfortable here in the sunroom." He stopped at a doorway just off the porch. It had a wall of windows, a shelving unit against one wall, a desk, buffet that would serve as a dresser, a television on the wall as well as paintings of wildlife. "The shelving unit is hiding a Murphy bed which is quite comfortable. There is a full bath across the hall." His gaze traveled over Dagger's choice of wardrobe. "I trust you brought clothes for the tropics.

"Dagger never wears anything but black cargo pants and black shirts."

Carl shrugged. "You'll be sorry. If you change your mind, I have extra shorts that might fit you."

Dagger dropped their suitcase off in the room, then noticed a worried look on Sara's face. Carl Underer definitely looked like an agent— steel-grey hair military cut, posture ramrod straight, eyes that appeared to take in everything. They didn't know this man, so how did he know them? They hurried to catch up, rushing through a kitchen that looked more like something found in a culinary school.

"Jake, Sam, you two can take the bedroom just off the living room. It has its own bath."

"But I like the bedroom upstairs across from yours."

"Of course you do, Sam. You probably want the master suite, too. Now, everyone freshen up. We have a light lunch planned, then a lengthy meeting. Tomorrow we will go to the island. For now, feel free to go down to the shore if you like or just sit out on the porch until lunch is ready."

"Sara doesn't eat red meat," Dagger started to say.

"I know. We have shrimp salad as well as chicken salad."

We? Dagger thought. And who told him about Sara's eating choices?

"What about the case, Carl?" Jake set the suitcase in the designated bedroom. "We didn't come all this way just for lunch."

"And how do you know anything about us?" Dagger demanded.

"In good time. There's a lot to discuss after lunch. Now, go. All of you."

Dagger watched Carl walk back to the kitchen. "Is he for real?"

"You have no idea," Jake said. "He probably set a stopwatch."

"He's not telling us anything," Sam said.

"If he has anything to do with the case, he could have done this over the phone. What does he know and how long has he known it?" Dagger's suspicious nature never appeared to take a breather.

"In good time," came a yell from the kitchen.

* * * *

It took less than twenty-three minutes for everyone to freshen up and change into clothes more suitable for the tropics. Sam and Sara were in shorts and sleeveless tops, Jake in a shirt and shorts. Dagger looked miserably hot in black pants and black tee shirt. They congregated on the screened in deck off the living room. Sam immediately noticed there were six place settings. A pitcher of iced tea and one of lemonade were in the center of the table.

"Look at all those birds." Sara could see the bridge to the island off to her left. Carl's house was just a few blocks from the bridge to Hilton Head Island. Tall reeds protected the shore where egrets searched for food. Kayakers were in the distance maneuvering away from the shore. "Is that the Atlantic Ocean?"

"No, it's the Harbor River," Sam said. "Then there's the Intracoastal Waterway and May River and all these other bays and inlets. Can't keep track of them all."

Dagger also studied the extra place setting. "Who else do you think is joining us?"

Jake shrugged. "If our captain claimed the FBI did not take over the case, then I would major a guess that Carl is working with someone behind the scenes."

"Thought he was retired."

"Never know with Carl."

"Are there alligators in this river?" Sara had never seen an alligator.

"They can tolerate a few hours of salt water, but you'll mainly see them in ponds and lagoons. Sometimes crossing a street," Jake said.

Carl appeared carrying a large tray of bowls filled with a variety of salads. "Please sit, everyone. Lunch is served."

Behind him trailed a slim woman wearing a floral tunic over yellow palazzo pants and rhinestone-studded sandals. Short hair had just a hint of grey. The tray she carried contained bread and large tomatoes cut out to fill with the salads provided.

Sara gasped. "Mother?"

"I thought your mother was dead?" Sam said.

"Please sit," Carl ordered. "This is Sophia Milonas."

"No, she isn't." Dagger glared at the woman he and Sara knew only as Mother, the head of AlphaTec.

Sophia smiled as she set the tray on the table then claimed a seat next to Dagger's. "It is nice to finally meet you in person. Please sit. Let's have lunch first."

Dagger threw his napkin on the table. "Let's not. We just spoke to you yesterday. You said nothing, not even a hint, as usual."

"Oh Six-One-Seven. You always were impatient." Sophia placed a hand on Dagger's arm as he tried to back away. "I'm sorry, Dagger. Old habits are hard to break. Carl, perhaps we can fill them in on some of the preliminary details." Dagger reluctantly sat down.

Jake glared at Carl. Numbers? Jake was used to FBI secrecy, but now he wanted answers as much as Dagger. Dagger, however, seemed far ahead of the rest of them since he knew this woman.

"Guess I can do that. First, though, we have chicken salad and shrimp salad. You can stuff a tomato or make a wrap. We also have fruit salad. Help yourselves to refreshments."

Sam eyed Sophia curiously as she filled a tomato with shrimp salad. With plates and glasses filled, the deck grew quiet, but all eyes were still on Carl, waiting.

After several more minutes of uncomfortable silence, Carl spoke. "Sophia was a pain in my ass growing up. Would follow me around like a puppy dog. In my third year of college, this skinny thirteen-year old was accepted into my college. She was so pissed because she couldn't join the Bureau until she was twenty-one even though she graduated at sixteen. Unbelieveably smart."

"Carl, you two are related?" Sam asked. "Is she your sister?"

"Cousin."

Dagger waved a hand in the air as though cutting off their words. He turned to Sophia. "Wait, you are with the FBI? Let me guess. It's one of those unspecified, undisclosed, under-the-radar agencies that Skizzy keeps warning me about." He grabbed his fork and stabbed an olive with such force the pimento fled off the platter.

Sam gave Jake's knee a slight nudge. She stared at Dagger's eyes. Something strange was happening. If she didn't know better, his pupils almost covered up the whites of his eyes in a demonic way.

"Dagger," Sara whispered. "Give them a chance."

"Thank you, Sara. As usual, I can always count on you to keep him in line," Sophia said with a sigh. She again placed her hand on his arm, this time patting it like someone would a pet.

Maybe Sam had imagined it, but Dagger's eyes suddenly looked normal again. She glanced at Jake, but he had never noticed since he was too busy shoving a chicken salad wrap in his mouth.

"Anyway," Sophia continued, "it doesn't seem necessary to go into all the details now because it will just be too confusing. There is a lot of back story, all part of the dog and pony show we have planned. So, let's just eat and get acquainted. Sam, how was your plane ride? I understand you despise flying as much as Sara. Did Stan behave himself?"

"Depends on if making me even more nervous by telling me he learned how to fly by watching two YouTube videos, then I would say no."

Sophia laughed which sounded strange to Dagger and Sara. She had always been stoic and business-like when they communicated via the Internet.

"Stan was a riot," Jake said as he grabbed another wrap. "Asked Kelly to keep the parachutes handy. Which one of you owns that plane? I doubt it's you, Carl, although it seems that I'm learning new things about you as the day goes on."

"It's on loan from the Bureau." Carl glanced at Dagger whose suspicion was growing by the minute. He could practically read the young man's mind. Was the plane bugged? Why would the Bureau loan out a plane? How much did the FBI know about him and Sara?

Another ten minutes of uncomfortable silence hung like a thick haze on the deck.

"Did you really stay at our house on Martinique, Carl, or were you surveilling someone?" Even Sam was feeling like she never knew him.

"All part of the dog and pony show. Now eat up. We have about three hours of explaining to do. We will let the four of you relax while Sophia and I study the video." Carl held out his hand to Jake. Sam sighed, opened her medicine bundle, and retrieved the memory stick.

<h1 style="text-align:center">16</h1>

Carl hooked up his laptop to the fifty-four-inch television screen displayed on the wall. With everyone comfortably seated on the couch, loveseat and chairs, the dog and pony show commenced. A photo of a distinguished-looking man appeared on the screen. "Jonathan Keyes is the Director of a company called BettaTec. He is very elusive, somehow always avoiding having his picture taken. Very little personal information on him because he isn't in any database. Doesn't have a Social Security number, driver's license, or employment history. We have no idea of his parents' names much less if he was hatched somewhere. We doubt Keyes is his real name. Aliases pop up in other countries who would love to have him extradited and tried for manipulating currencies, shakedowns, illegal corporate takeovers, bribery, you name it. He is known as Enrique Mendes in Spain, Jean Rouseau in France, Konrad Schmidt in Germany. Just pick a country where governments have been disrupted, elections influenced, economies ruined, and he is suspected. Can't do anything without proof, though. He always has his minions doing the dirty work while he collects the money."

He looked around the room at the attentive faces of Jake and Sam. But it was Dagger and Sara who appeared bored. Of course, they knew all this. "Before I continue, did anyone want a drink?"

"No thanks," came the collective response.

"We shall continue then. At lunch Dagger was partially right. There is a separate investigative department within the Bureau. Only a handful know about it and, yes, it was under my direction when we worked together, Jake. Keyes had been on our radar for some time, but we could never get close to him." Several images appeared on the screen next. Men, women, all ages and ethnicities. "We started to see a pattern where certain people with exceptional abilities were disappearing. Scientists, doctors, inventors, ballistic experts, people working on the cutting edge of technology. If they had given talks, written papers, anything that put them in the limelight, it wasn't soon after that they disappeared. Some died, allegedly, or made to look like they died as a cover for their disappearance."

"We discovered," Sophia interjected, "that doctors and medical examiners were being bribed, quite handsomely, to falsify information. That's when we suspected these experts in their field were being recruited for BettaTec."

"But it wasn't just adults who were recruited, was it, Sophia?" Dagger's glare prompted a heavy sigh from Sophia.

"No, it wasn't."

"What on earth would he need children for?" Sam turned to Carl. She could feel Jake stiffen next to her. "He wasn't experimenting on them, was he?"

"The short answer is, he was building a special army. That's when we knew we had to put someone on the inside."

"Keyes built an actual city one mile below the surface in an abandoned city in Nebraska. I was able to take these videos undetected but had no way to get them back to Carl. Matter of fact, we lost all communication with each other for years. I'm sure Carl thought I was dead."

"Never. You were too clever, and I knew eventually you would find a way to get in touch."

"Although the city was self-sustaining as far as growing vegetables, we still had to have other necessities brought in. Some of the guards were sent out for supplies every month. I altered the trackers in their necks to send out a signal, a Morse code so to speak, which communicated only with the base computer…Carl's. Eventually I was able to add photos. The technology is complicated so let's just say I had one guard study photos on my computer which then transferred them to the chip in his tracker. So instead of a message via code, Carl also received images. Sorry, but it's very high tech."

"So the FBI knew where the city was. Why didn't they swoop in and close it down?"

"Dagger's right," Sara said. "You could have shut down Keyes' operation and saved a lot of children."

"No." Carl studied his hands as though some viable explanation was written on them. "We had no way of knowing if Keyes was there. He could have had more than one training camp. If he eluded arrest, he'd just set up shop somewhere else. Even with all the messages Sophia was able to get out, we were still seeing proof of him in other cities."

"He wasn't always at the training camp," Sophia explained. "He had others overseeing the camp while he was out finding other ways to create havoc." Sophia nodded to Carl and he flipped through several slides of the training camp. It showed children of various ages dressed in white for self-defense classes, then in black for warfare and ballistics. One image was of small toy tanks armed with live ammunition in what looked like an exercise in kill or be killed. The camera appeared to focus on one boy, around fourteen years old. The similarity was striking. Sam and Jake slowly turned their attention to Dagger. Could it have been him?

"Did any of them try to escape?" Sam knew that would be her first reaction, to find an exit.

"No. The implants indoctrinated them while they slept. They only saw images of Keyes as their father, their only home as the underground city, then me as their mother. Guess you could call it brainwashing."

"But," Sam started. Was that how Dagger knew Sophia? From the training camp? "Were there kids who didn't show promise, didn't make the grade? What happened to them?"

"Keyes only wanted the best," Sophia explained. "Those who didn't meet the required potential were released."

"Just like that?" Sam said with a hint of doubt.

"Their memories of their time there were erased. They were driven, I was told, to some remote area far from the training camp, and released. Their trackers removed because detailed physical exams might have detected them. I can only assume, and hope, that their memories prior to the camp slowly returned."

"Then why don't I have any recollection of my life before the camp?" Dagger's fingers clenched until Sara cupped her hand around one of his fists.

Sam and Jake were finally aware how Dagger knew Sophia. He definitely had been raised in the training camp. But from what age and when did he escape? Dagger felt their stares and drilled them with his own.

"The Director had a separate group he called sentries. They were clones, programmed for one purpose only...assassination."

"I have a fond memory of two of them," Dagger said. "If I remember correctly, they also self-destructed after their mission."

"Yes, something that was actually one of the few mistakes the Director ever made."

"Why was that?" Jake asked.

"It's not a pretty picture when they self-destruct." The slight smile on Dagger's face told Jake he was probably the few people who enjoyed it. "Any witnesses would bring unwanted attention."

"By this time," Sophia continued, "I had already recruited a number of people to my side. When I discovered that Keyes was moving his operation offshore and evacuating the training camp, we planned our escape. I had already been there for fifteen years and heard that the Director was suspicious of my allegiance. There were several underground tunnels. He, fortunately for us, blew up the wrong one. That's why he believed we were dead."

"And, thus, AlphaTec was formed." Sara's voice was barely a whisper.

Sophia took the remote from Carl. "In case you aren't convinced that Keyes was working on cutting edge technology, let me show you a few films."

The first image showed the art thief who wore a camouflage suit to hide his existence. Next was the clone who easily jumped the fence around Sara's property. Sara tensed as she wondered if Sophia was going to show the film of her shapeshifting when the identical clone fell from a hotel window. But Sophia didn't. Next was the crater left when the training camp self-destructed.

"We made sure news reports blamed it on an earthquake," Carl explained.

The next film showed the weapon Keyes tried to sell to the highest bidder. "This weapon is called a vaporizer. It literally vaporized the brain rather quickly." The video showed steam coming from the eyes, nose and ears of the victim Keyes had used for a demonstration.

Sam realized she had grabbed the pillow next to her on the couch and was mangling it. She had never heard of such a weapon. Jake edged forward, elbows on his knees. Robinson had explained some of these cases in his email but seeing them was entirely different.

"As I said, Director Keyes was into cutting edge technology. This next video you will think has been doctored. But believe me, it hasn't been." Sophia pressed the play button and let the video speak for itself. It was from the case Dagger worked with William Sherlock, the case of a shapeshifter. It showed a man changing into a mythical beast, then into a bird and flying out of a basement window. It showed the carnage it left behind. A young cop left in a tree, a biker beheaded, a teen disemboweled.

Sam turned away. "This can't possibly be true. It's like a horror movie."

"It definitely was," Sara said.

Sophia froze the screen on the image of the beast, its odd-shaped yellow eyes, sharp teeth. "The killer was named Paul Addison. It was believed the men in the Addison family born during a full moon on a Friday the thirteenth had the ability to shapeshift. The first was Nathan Addison in the 1800's who was believed to be a witch. All men afterwards inherited the same curse. Dagger and his friend were able to incinerate Paul Addison. We thought that was the end of the family line, but Paul had a twin and his girlfriend gave birth to a boy on a Friday the thirteenth. Now, I'm sure you are wondering what this has to do with Director Keyes. The thing is, he was able to kidnap the baby and also took a vial of the baby's blood in case we got to the baby first. How the

Addison men were able to be on his radar, we don't know, but you can just imagine what might happen should Keyes find a way to create an army of these killers."

The next image was of a ship. "Once the underground city was vacated, this was where Keyes set up his lab."

"Off the coast of Martinique, I assume?" Sam received a curt nod from Carl.

"Right. But then it moved north and we lost it."

"So you thought," Dagger said. "They camouflaged it."

"Now you see it," Sophia said as she moved to another image of a large explosion in the Atlantic. "Now you don't." The next image was of communication satellites with the BettaTec image of the betta fish on the side. "We used BettaTec's own satellites which were armed with lasers to destroy the ship where he took the baby and the vial of blood."

"Why a fish?" Sam asked. "The image is on the satellite and part of the company name. What does it all have to do with a betta fish?"

"It's the aggression hormone in the fish. If you put two male bettas together in a fish tank, they will kill each other. Keyes injected certain skilled operatives with the hormone. When triggered by anger or the fight or flight response, the hormone is triggered giving the operative unusual strength."

Everyone was silent for several seconds. Jake and Sam locked eyes. Dagger clenched his fist. "You killed the baby?" Sam gasped, as though not caring about the betta fish explanation.

Sophia rewound to the image of the beast. "Baby then…this in eighteen years. Which would you prefer?"

The stern look of Mother that Dagger had always seen on his office monitor was evident now. Strip away the fancy clothes and rhinestone sandals and you have the head of AlphaTec.

Jake stood. "Carl, a word, please, in private."

"We don't keep secrets here, Jake. You can talk freely."

"I think I need that drink now." Jake walked to the bar and poured himself a shot of whiskey. He downed it in one gulp, then grabbed a beer.

Everyone decided that was a good idea. He mixed a vodka and tonic for Sam as everyone else fended for themselves. Now he knew why Carl couldn't explain anything over the phone. It was obvious that Sergeant Martinez had not shared the shapeshifter case with Captain Robinson. It was too bizarre to believe.

Jake found Sam on the outside deck. He handed her the drink and noticed the color had drained from her face. "You okay?"

"I don't know. It's all a bit…"

"Yeah. I know."

Sara joined them on the deck, a clear drink with a slice of lime floating on the top.

"How old were you when you first met Dagger?" Sam asked.

"Eighteen."

"Please tell me this wasn't one of your first cases and you are still with him."

Sara gave a half smile. "No. It was the second."

"My god. How did you handle it?"

"Guess I've seen worse in my life, Sam. Nothing surprises me anymore. Weird cases just seem to follow Dagger. I had trailed him to Nebraska when he went on his search for the underground city. There was a fake sun and moon there, a computer system that heard every command. If we needed a scooter to make our way around, a garage door opened and there was a line of scooters. But there were also the armed toy tanks and Star Wars-type robots armed with these weird plasma guns. Dagger was shot and almost died. Then the whole place was set to self-destruct because we had breached the system."

It was amazing to Sam and Jake how easily Sara spoke of such bizarre occurrences. Was there anything in her life she found shocking?

"Shit. I think I need another shot of whiskey." Jake turned and made his way to the bar.

"Are you safe with him?"

"Dagger? Absolutely. I know he seems overly protective, but it's what I need. And in a way, these cases are exciting." She said the last part with a smile.

Sam tried to ignore her comment that she needed protection. "You are hopelessly in love."

"Is there any other way to be in love?"

This time Sam smiled. "No, there isn't."

17

They reassembled in the living room so the dog and pony show continued.

"Can you explain, first," Jake said, "how a communications satellite can be armed for defense and how you discovered that these BettaTec satellites had the ability?"

"Not all were for communications. A couple were armed with high powered lasers," Carl explained.

"Like a Star Wars death ray. That makes me comfortable." Sam took a long swig of her drink.

"Wait, we only now were able to develop lasers for military use," Jake said. "I read about it a few weeks ago."

"BettaTec developed it twenty years ago. Dagger finding the underground city wasn't difficult." Sophia looked at Dagger who wasn't too happy she was describing his capabilities. "His chip was unique, something I invented. I wanted to make sure he could find the training camp to destroy it so I put the coordinates on the inside cover of the chip. He asked a doctor friend to remove it, but it was impossible. It was wired to his brain. So he could only take the outer cap."

Dagger could feel eyes on him. His scowl appeared to be ignored by Sophia as she continued.

"The doctor planned to take it to a friend in California to discover what was in Dagger's head. Unfortunately, that's when one of the satellite's moved to a lower orbit and destroyed the plane right when it was flying over Lake Mead killing all on board and assuring that it would be impossible to locate the wreckage and confirm how it was destroyed."

"So they don't know Dagger is still alive." Sam's comment hung in the air.

Jake asked, "What does this chip in his head do?"

"He literally has access to a myriad of information. He could look at you right now, and I bet he has already done it, and access any data on your history."

"Well." Jake drilled Dagger with his own death ray. "Now we know how you spouted all that history on Sam and me."

"He can see in the dark just by thinking it."

"What about healing?" Jake asked. "He had a serious cut that needed stitches when we had our altercation. Now it's nothing more than a bruise. The cut healed almost immediately."

Sophia took a deep breath. Sara tensed. After all, it was Sara's regenerative blood that saved Dagger after he was injured in Nebraska, which gave him the ability to heal quickly. Sara, being a shapeshifter, can heal quickly as well as regenerate limbs.

"Let's just say Dagger is exceptional, something I noticed in him immediately, which is why I chose him to carry this unique chip. More importantly, every change, every keystroke the Director makes on his computer is downloaded to Dagger's chip and ends up on my computer." Sophia smiled at Dagger, as though he were a prize pupil.

"Speaking of keystrokes, have you found out why the Director hasn't been on his computer in weeks?"

"I was saving this for last, Dagger." Sophia pressed the remote and a video of Director Keyes in an office appeared. "We obtained this video from an operative. One of the Director's residences, we discovered, is in Vancouver. The man you see entering is Doctor Levitt Crane."

The room was quiet for several minutes as the video played, revealing how Keyes had died. Finally, Dagger said, "So, he's finally dead."

"Yes. And now we know what other types of drugs he was making and distributing."

"What did Keyes mean when he mentioned that Crane sold organs?" Jake asked.

"He bio-printed organs and sold them on the black market," Carl replied. "And not to make a profit. He just wanted to do good."

Jake grabbed Sam's empty glass and moved to the bar where he refilled her drink and grabbed himself a beer. He looked over at the rest of the group. All glasses were still filled but Dagger's beer bottle looked empty, so he grabbed a beer for him. He set the bottle on the coffee table in front of Dagger and returned to his seat just as Sophia clicked another image onto the screen. It was the video from the salvage yard that was on the memory stick Sam had given to Carl.

"That's Crane, isn't it?" Sam looked to Carl for confirmation. The image only showed a profile of a man in a dark coat, the collar pulled up, but it was definitely Levitt Crane.

"Yes. It appears he went from killing Keyes to somehow appearing at this crime scene. We do know his weren't the only prints there. However, both were only partial prints."

"He isn't a violent man, anything but," Sophia added. "So it's a bit confusing for me to understand."

Carl studied Jake as though he were a specimen. He took a sip of his own drink and kept staring until Jake met his eyes. "Do you want to fill me in on what you are holding back?"

Jake thought after being retired Carl would have lost his edge. But he hadn't. He could still spot when he was being deceived, when someone wasn't forthcoming. With a sigh, Jake pulled a piece of paper from his pocket, unfolded it, and handed it to Carl.

"The victim in Chicago had this drawing on the inside of his wrist."

Carl and Sophia studied the drawing, then passed it over to Dagger and Sara.

"I have a feeling there is a punchline somewhere." Dagger handed the paper back to Sophia.

"This is the identical image used by John Wallace Baker. He killed over thirty people, mostly prostitutes, and dumped their bodies along I-80. He was a truck driver so that route was convenient for him."

"You keep using the past tense," Sophia pointed out.

"He was killed in prison five years after his incarceration."

"Copycat, obviously," Carl said.

"Different M.O.s. The victim under the overpass was a homeless alcoholic. The reason Captain Robinson had us check it out was because the drawing was a match to the one drawn by Baker. He had a forensic handwriting expert compare the current one with the ones Baker drew. They are almost identical."

"The drawing looks like a demon of some sort. Is that significant?" Sara asked.

Jake nodded. "In an interview Baker said the reason he killed was to release the demon from his victims."

"Have his former cell mates been interviewed? Someone who has been released and now doing the copycat killings?" Dagger asked.

"Captain Robinson is doing that now."

Carl had a unique way of scrutinizing pregnant pauses. He stared at Jake and waited.

Jake took another long swallow of his beer. "A partial print at the scene belongs to Baker."

Sara shivered unexpectedly.

"You okay?" Sophia asked.

Sara shook her head. "Dagger and I have worked enough strange cases that it wouldn't surprise me if John Wallace Baker rose from the dead and is back on his killing spree."

18

Dinner was late. Carl never did like eating before seven o'clock. The conversation avoided anything to do with the case. Carl talked about past and memorable cases when he was with the Bureau. Jake surprisingly found it easy to talk about his kidnapping. And everyone had a good laugh as Sam described how she had first met Jake when she worked undercover at a politician's illegal gambling party and Jake moonlighted as a bodyguard. Sam had been able to retrieve a video the politician was using to blackmail the governor and managed to flatten Jake in her getaway.

Dagger and Sara appeared to relax more around their new team members as well as Carl and the in the flesh Mother. It had been an exhausting day, so everyone retired early.

But not everyone. Sara had that look in her eye and Dagger recognized it. She wanted to explore, survey the area. Was the ship the real reason Carl chose to live here? If the ship had been destroyed, why were Carl and Sophia hanging around? Sure, the house had a scenic location. The weather was beautiful. And the island offered just about everything a person could want. The city itself was four hours away from Myrtle Beach; Atlanta, Georgia; and Walt Disney World, give or take a half hour.

There were few streetlights. Hell, the entire town didn't appear to care for streetlights, preferring that people guess what street to turn on and assume the dark blob crossing the street was a shadow and not a bicyclist. There were rules on the island about turning lights off during certain months when baby turtles were hatching. Dagger thought if hatchlings were too stupid to decipher the moon from a streetlight, they deserved to be run over. Sara wasn't amused.

Both the gray hawk and gray wolf were fearful of humans, even keeping a safe distance from Dagger. A shadow emerged from the doorway as if testing the surroundings. The gray wolf rushed from the house and bounded down the stairs into the darkness. No sooner did the hawk disappear then Dagger heard the whoosh of giant wing beats. A gray hawk's broad wingspan allowed it to reach speeds from seventy to ninety miles an hour.

Darkness appeared to stretch forever as the hawk made its way east. The hawk's eyesight at night wasn't as strong as daytime but it was enough to tell the direction it was headed. It veered east with powerful wingbeats and propelled itself toward the lighthouse. Its UV capability allowed the hawk to view the power lines as popping lights. Its vision was eight times more powerful than a human's. It soon landed on a railing at the top of the lighthouse.

Can you tell where you are? Dagger had discovered after first meeting Sara that they could communicate telepathically whenever Sara was in one of her shifted forms.

According to the map I studied on the plane, I think I'm on the lighthouse on Hilton Head Island. I first went south and thought I was on Hilton Head but now I think that was Daufauski Island. There are a lot of empty tracts of land which I think are golf courses and lots of boats. And I mean big boats. People are partying on them.

Just be careful.

The grey hawk took in its surroundings, then stared into the darkness of the Atlantic Ocean. In the distance were lights from a boat, probably a cargo ship waiting for access, to what? A harbor? With powerful wingbeats, the hawk took flight and headed over the Atlantic. It circled the cargo ship, then continued east while keeping its eye on the lighthouse.

Talk to me, Sara. I need to know you are all right.

It's really beautiful at night. It's a clear sky, full moon. I circled a huge cargo ship. It's just sitting there. I can see a shipping harbor further west.

That's probably Savannah. There's supposed to be a large harbor there.

Hmmmm. That's interesting.

What?

I'm about three or four miles from Hilton Head and there's a small island sitting out here all by itself.

Inhabited?

Don't know yet.

I read there are several islands closer to shore both in Georgia and South Carolina but I don't know about that far out.

How cute.

What? Dagger couldn't think of anything that could be cute in the middle of an ocean.

This island has monkeys on it. The gray hawk swooped down for a closer look. There was something familiar in the way the monkeys moved. At the last moment the hawk swerved to avoid hitting an object. It landed on a nearby tree limb and studied what it had almost crashed into.

Strange.

What?

Sara wasn't sure.

Did you bring your binoculars?

I have them in my head, Dagger joked. He actually did have the ability to read a tail number on a plane flying overhead. A gift from Mother.

I forgot. Didn't Mother mention we were going to have lunch on the island tomorrow?

Yeah. And?

We can visit the lighthouse. Maybe we can climb to the top and you can look at the island and tell me what you see.

Okay. If we can find an excuse to get away.

We're sightseeing. The hawk pushed off the tree limb and circled the island one last time to get its bearings. A sign just off the beach behind a No Trespassing sign had a partial name on it and a design. The island should be easy for Dagger to find. How many islands in the ocean have monkeys?

He followed closely, confident the young woman was wallowing too low in her own drug hazed world to hear the footsteps or aware that she was being tailed. The Watcher had followed Jess from her mother's house to a decrepit building surrounded by discarded furniture wading in a six-month growth of grass and weeds. Fellow addicts had staggered in and out of the dwelling clutching bags or stuffing their purchases deep into jacket pockets. How thrilling it would be to eliminate every one of these losers if only he had enough time. Can't stay in one place too long.

Jess had practically skipped out the door like a kid with a birthday present, probably having sampled the goods first or sold a part of her body for the daily special hot off the back of a truck fresh from the border. She had stopped and talked to whomever she saw. A real chatty Cathy now that she was enjoying her drug-filled high. But it wouldn't take long for the high to level off, then collapse into the world of withdrawal. And he would be there to help her sink into the abyss.

<h1 style="text-align:center">19</h1>

"Nice place." Sam took in the huge patio with umbrella covered tables. Beyond a short wall the beach appeared to extend for blocks. The Coast Restaurant had indoor and outdoor seating as well as a tiki bar. Few sunbathers were on the beach since tourist season had ended when the school year resumed.

"One of our favorites, Sam. Carl and I come here often." Sophie had selected a secluded table in the corner of the patio.

Dagger, dressed in shorts and a sports team tee shirt, had surrendered and accepted Carl's wardrobe selection. He had to admit, he did feel much cooler. Besides, dressed in all black, Sophia had thought he looked more like a hit man. "And why are we here?" Dagger's dark glasses hid his glare as he addressed Sophia.

"Why, to eat." Sophia opened her menu and began suggesting sandwiches and dishes she felt were exceptional, based on her previous visits.

The temperatures were still summer-like in South Carolina, so the women had dressed in shorts and sleeveless tops, except for Sophia who was in a long skirt and floral blouse. She could feel Dagger's eyes on her and smiled. "It doesn't work on me, Dagger. My stats won't be in any files you try to access, neither are Carl's."

Dagger had tried yesterday during lunch to find information on Sophia and thought it was a glitch in his internal computer. Of course, Sophia would keep her background inaccessible. He shrugged as if it was no big deal but inside he was fuming.

Sam set her menu down. "Order for me Jake." She removed her wide-brimmed hat, closed her eyes, and lifted her face to the sun. The waitress made her way around the table writing down orders before retreating.

"You'll be burned in ten minutes, hon."

"You're right." She put her hat back on wishing she had lathered her arms in sunscreen before leaving. Sara on the other had had Abby's olive skin, a true Native. Although she also wore a hat, Sam doubted Sara ever burned, nor Dagger for that matter. For always wearing slacks, Sam thought Dagger would exhibit white legs under the shorts, but he was just as naturally tan as Sara.

"Is it crowded here in the summer?" Sara asked.

Carl chuckled. "We avoid the summers. Traffic moves at a crawl and tourists are everywhere. Not your kind of atmosphere, Sara."

The waitress returned with a pitcher of iced tea and one of water. "Your meals will be up soon."

Dagger watched her leave then turned his mirrored sunglasses toward Carl and Sophia. How much of Sara's background did Sophia share? He saw Jake and Sam exchange puzzled looks. Not good. Sara had a fear of large crowds, a holdover phobia from when hordes of townspeople burned down her parents' house with them in it.

"I saw several shops as we drove through the area. Will those be crowded?" Sara's apprehension was palpable. Another exchange of puzzled looks between Jake and Sam.

"There are a few locals, but as I said, tourist season is over. It shouldn't be crowded at all." Carl moved his drink aside as the waitress returned and distributed their meals.

"Shopping. Sounds like fun." Sam sprinkled salt and pepper on her chicken Caesar salad.

"Actually, we were going to climb the lighthouse, take a few pictures." Dagger hoped this would discourage their cohorts.

"I'd rather look for seashells, take some home to Dillon," Jake said, much to Dagger's relief.

"We should buy some souvenirs for Abby and Alex, though."

"Try the shops in Coligny Plaza, Sam, or had you already shopped there the last time you were here?" Sophia squeezed lemon onto her cold shrimp.

"Actually, there are a couple closer to Carl's house that I liked." Sam said.

Carl was staring at his phone, reading a text message. "You kids finish your lunch. We can all meet back here at the tiki bar in about an hour. Sophia and I have a meeting to go to."

"Without us?" Anger rolled off Dagger like a sandstorm. Why fly them all to the East Coast if they were going to be shut out of any information they could learn from a meeting?

"Does it concern this case?" Jake was also not happy about being shut out.

"Might. Might not. But we'll be taking the car so enjoy your time on the island for the next hour. Now, enjoy your meal."

20

Skizzy's pawn shop was situated in a narrow brick building on a once bustling downtown street. Shoppers now preferred the indoor mall and outlet centers. Less foot traffic was fine with Skizzy, whose shoppers had to buzz to get in or call for an appointment. Skizzy Borden had few friends, which he considered an asset. The fewer the better. Chase Dagger, Simon and Sara were some of those rare creatures.

The narrow building was deceiving from the front. Few people knew how far it stretched back, affording a living area, kitchen, bathroom, and a bookcase which opened to a stairwell. It was in the basement where Skizzy was maestro to a wall of outside and inside surveillance monitors.

Clothes hung on his five-foot eight-inch frame. He hunched over a keyboard like a mad scientist working out an experiment. Tufts of short gray hair wrestled free of a ponytail. The paneled basement had shelves of canned goods, all marked with dates and contents, as well as cases of bottled water. When, not if, the apocalypse started, Skizzy was prepared.

His attention was drawn to three seedy looking characters peering through the front window. Alarm bells clanged like mariachis in his head. They looked too much like the two punks who had been guarding the warehouse the other night, although older. Hispanic drug enforcers? Dealers? Cartel hitmen? Why come to a pawn shop? Skizzy didn't like it one bit.

He pressed a button for the outside microphone. "State your business."

The three amigos jumped back and searched for the disembodied voice.

"I don't sell weapons or ammunition so scram." Skizzy wondered why, of all the shops in town, these three picked his. Had they asked around town for the most knowledgeable person in high tech explosives?

How would anyone know since Skizzy doesn't socialize? "Well? State your business," he repeated. "This isn't a taco stand. Hold your immigration papers up to the cameras." That oughta get them, he thought.

Instead, the tallest of the three with a mangy goatee and eyes that were too close together started pulling on the grating in front of the shop window.

"You don't want to do that." Skizzy picked up the phone and called Padre. A cop would normally be the last person on his contact list. Padre, though, was a somewhat friend of Dagger's, and besides, Dagger was out of town.

Padre answered on the second ring. "How did you get my number, you squirrely nut job?"

"Hi yourself, Padre. I can get anyone's number, didn't you know? And right now I have three guys trying to break into my shop."

"You've got the best security system known to man. Besides, what on earth would someone want from your store, that suit of armor?"

"These look like drug dealers or hitmen from south of the border."

"Whoa, getting a little racist there. Watch your words."

"Fine. How about you just send an ambulance." Skizzy slammed down the phone and checked the monitor. Now the goatee was tugging on the door handle while the other two were attempting to pull the grating off the window. One had a shaved head and the other had hair slicked back in a man bun. Skizzy hated those ugly knobs of hair that made a man look like a sumo wrestler. He wanted to rip it right off their heads. "Okay, boys, you asked for it." Skizzy flipped a switch on the wall. Immediately eight thousand volts of electricity shot through the gratings and metal fixtures sending the three men sailing past the curb. The current lasted for less than a nano-second. Last thing Skizzy wanted was to kill the guys. Course, worse thing would be to make them fighting mad. They could torch the store with him in it. Or wait for him to leave, follow him, string him up and use him as a piñata.

Skizzy scrambled up the stairs to the shop, then peered through the window. He hadn't had a cause to use sparky before so wasn't sure what to expect. Maybe smoke rising from the three bodies? Their bodies jerking in the gutter? Was he imagining it or did he smell skin roasting? Now he wondered if a nanosecond of juice was too much. What if he actually did kill them? Goatee started to move, much to Skizzy's relief.

A black sedan dented in too many places to count pulled toward the sidewalk at a forty-five-degree angle followed by a patrol car. When were they going to give Padre a better car? Course, the disheveled figure that exited the sedan looked as dented as the vehicle itself. Thankfully, the patrol car didn't announce its arrival with sirens blaring. Last thing Skizzy needed were gawkers.

He unfastened all the multitude of locks on the front door and stepped out. "I warned you it would get ugly."

"What the hell did you do?" Padre looked down at the three men who were just coming to, their eyes blinking in their surroundings as two officers exited their vehicle.

Skizzy stood over the thugs as they tried to scramble to their feet. "Warned you. Told you not to touch the grating."

"You wired the building?" The detective pressed palms to his head and stared up at the sky for inspiration. "*Senor ayudame.*"

"Nah, only the metal."

"Same thing." Padre motioned for the officers to help the three men to their feet. "Well, well. Let's see if they have any identification."

"*No hablo inglés,*" Goatee spit out.

"*No hay problema. Yo hablo espanol.*" Padre smiled as the men realized that the detective spoke Spanish.

"No wallets, Sergeant," one rookie officer said. The other officer shook his head after searching the other two men.

"Check their shoes."

"Hey," Padre barked at Skizzy. "Who's running this?" He turned to the disheveled men who still appeared dazed. It was a wonder they could still stand. "Take your shoes off."

Too outnumbered to argue, the men kicked off their scuffed boots.

Not wanting to be injured by weapons hidden inside, the two officers turned the boots upside down and shook each one. A piece of paper floated out of one of Goatee's boots.

Padre slipped on latex gloves, then pulled an evidence bag from his pocket. He unfolded the tattered paper. "Well, well. This little map looks like the location of a warehouse explosion the other night. Now why would you be interested in that?" He looked at the three men who were starting to tilt to one side as the officers stood on either side of them. "Let's have the boys checked out by a paramedic at the precinct, then get them something to eat and drink. After that, we'll have a little chat, okay, amigos?"

Padre turned to Skizzy as the officers loaded the three men into the back seat. "Want to tell me why, out of all the people in Cedar Point, that they came looking for you?" He placed the map into the evidence bag and slipped the bag into his pocket.

Skizzy's eyes wobbled as though not tethered together, sending one eyebrow shooting upward. "Well, gee, I don't have a badge but even I know a pawn shop is one of the first places a ne'er-do-well from out of town would go in hopes of finding weapons and ammo. I told them when I saw their mangy mugs on my surveillance camera that I don't carry nor sell weapons."

"Yeah, right. Except for that flame-throwing weapon I've seen you use."

"Don't know what you're talking about. Besides, it ain't for sale." Skizzy folded his arms, his shirt hanging on him like a hand-me-down from Simon's portly frame.

Padre shook his head. Skizzy was almost as tight-lipped as Dagger. "By the way, why call me and not Dagger?"

"He's out of town."

"Dagger, out of town? Really. And Sara?"

"On business, Dagger told me. I'm taking care of Einstein while they're gone."

"And when will they be back?"

Skizzy realized he had already said too much. "Guess we'll know when he shows up."

21

"Are we crazy or are they crazy?" Sandals dangled from her fingers as Sam slipped her other hand into Jake's.

"I feel like we're in someone's nightmare. Nothing is logical. Carl has done a complete one-eighty on me."

They stopped to stare at a trio of fins in the water a half block offshore. They dove and bobbed in unison. "Sharks?"

"No, Sam. Dolphins. Sharks skim the surface. Course we could always take a dip in the water and find out."

"Funny." Sam pulled on him and they continued walking. Warm sand felt good under her feet as she kept her eyes on the ground. Crabs were known to hide in the sand as well as in seashells so she wasn't about ready to be bitten.

"There's a starfish." Jake bent down, picked it up and studied it. "It's all in one piece. That's rare considering all the foot traffic." He placed it in his shirt pocket.

"Doesn't seem to be a favorite part of the beach. The restaurant, snack bar and rental chaise lounges are back by the hotel so not many beachgoers to trample on the shells."

"Then we should be able to find more undamaged souvenirs."

The sun felt good, temperatures still beach weather. The odor of decaying vegetation wasn't strong, nothing like the pungent rotten egg smell of pluff mud in the brackish marshes near Carl's house. Dunes topped with tall grass lined the beach on the left. Dead fronds from palm trees, blown leaves, and dead fish had been pushed from the ocean by tides.

Sam came to a halt, her hand squeezing Jake's. "What do you see?"

"What?"

"In front of us. What do you see?"

Jake studied the beach, the foamy waves gently slapping the shore, sand that stretched as far as the eye could see. "The usual. Sand, shells, a grass-covered dune. Why?"

Sam's eyes took on a glaze he had seen numerous times before. This time was similar to a case in Indiana where Sam gingerly walked through property following the directives of nature…a squirrel that scratched at the worn grass, then looked up at her; reeds of grass bending in a certain direction. Sam had studied it all and placed evidence flags to mark a spot where a body would be found. The back property had been a body dump site.

"Sam, what are you seeing?"

Her hand slipped from his. "Body parts."

"What?" Jake knew it was fruitless to imagine what his wife was seeing.

Sam cautiously moved forward, still not believing her eyes. "Arms, fingers, pieces of skulls, leg bones, ribs. They're all over the place, clinging to seaweed, and more washing up as we stand here." Somewhere in her vision three letters popped up. "BRL."

"What?"

"The letters BRL. Do they mean anything to you?" She also saw a shape of some sort in her mind.

Jake made a mental note of the letters as Sam again came to a halt.

As she tried to take in everything in front of her, a hand with three fingers clinging by tendons and dragging bloody tendrils slowly clawed across the sand, clamoring over her feet, the sensation sending chills up her spine. The mangled hand headed toward a pile of twigs and brown-colored seaweed. It moved with a purpose, as if searching for something, and then it found it. Two fingers reattached to the hand. It continued its search, scratching at the sand like a cat in a litter box. And then the rest of the body parts started moving. Partial foots scrambled haphazardly. What looked like arm and leg bones rolled through the sand and over other remains in search of their missing parts. As far as Sam could see bloody and torn stumps moved in a rhythm, like a choreographed dance.

A partial skull located one of its eyes. It paused on its side allowing the eye to crawl back into a socket.

What was this from? Had there been a plane crash? What year did it happen? Sam knew from experience that visions she had were not necessarily current. And these definitely weren't drowning victims, not how the bodies were blown apart. She paused to listen. Victims always spoke to her, pleading for her to right a wrong or to find their killer. They had always been gentle souls, taken too quickly. But somehow this was different. Voices weren't pleading, weren't searching for answers. She remembered the ghost hunter-type television shows she and Abby liked to watch. There were always two types of spirts, the kind ones and the evil ones. These voices were anything but kine. *We weren't done.* Those were the words that echoed in her head, not gentle, but angry and threatening. Suddenly the body parts stopped moving as though the music had stopped. As far down the beach where they scattered she watched as each dismembered body part turned, slowly moving at first, then picking up speed…toward her. She sucked in a loud gasp.

"Sam?"

She turned away and grabbed Jake. "I want to leave. I want to go now."

"Okay." Jake stared over her shoulder, but he still saw nothing more than beach, waves, and dunes. "But we have to wait for Carl to return."

"Uber. We can take an Uber, please." Sam pulled on his arm and fled, away from the cemetery of body parts.

"These stairs aren't for the unhealthy." Sara led the way up one hundred fourteen steps to the top of the Harbor Town Lighthouse.

"As long as it's less than the steps to the underground city in Nebraska."

"But you were going down. We took the elevator up."

"An elevator I didn't know existed or I would have taken it."

They reached the top of the lighthouse and stepped out onto the deck. The structure was ninety feet above ground and offered a panoramic view of the area. All they were interested in, though, was the view east, the direction where Sara had seen the island with monkeys. If there were telescopes they either were in for repair or hidden away somewhere. Dagger didn't need a telescope. Sara's hawk vision allowed her to see just two miles. The island, though, she was sure had to be three or more miles offshore.

"What direction, Sara?"

Sara turned toward the south. "I saw an island not far from here. According to a map it's Daufuskie Island and it's about three miles from where we are standing. When I headed east I'm sure I stayed equal distance between Hilton Head and Daufuskie and out at least three or four miles."

Dagger searched the horizon. "I see it." He not only could see the island, but the internal chip also told him the distance. When he first discovered this ability, he was able to read a tail number of an airplane. Just by thinking it, his vision zoomed in. He studied the island giving his onboard computer chip time to calculate the size. "Looks a little over three miles out, around a mile across. I don't see anything but trees, and you're right. There are monkeys running on the beach, jumping tree limbs."

"Can you tell what kind they are?"

"Not sure. Look like the kind in that pandemic movie, *Outbreak.* Hope these guys don't swim."

Sara noticed a man several yards away using binoculars. "Sir, can I borrow your binoculars for a minute?"

The man looked like a professor with his close-cropped grey hair and beard and sporting a business suit. Certainly too warm for this weather.

He turned and smiled. "Sure. Looking for sharks?" The professor had a distinctive British or Australian accent. They were too similar for Sara to decipher.

"Are there whales here?"

"Probably not until November."

"How about Russian submarines?" Dagger interjected.

The professor laughed as he handed Sara the binoculars. "If you see one, let me know. Looking for anything in particular? The Intercontinental Shelf extends ninety miles to the Continental Slope. From there it drops off to the ocean floor."

"You aren't from around here, yet you seem to know a lot about it." Sara was impressed.

"Just a hobby of mine to research places thoroughly before travelling."

Sara scanned the horizon, then adjusted the focus rings. Soon the island came into view. A few more adjustments and she could see the monkeys. She concentrated on the trees and noticed a strange shimmer. The same with the monkeys. For some reason, the images looked familiar, but she couldn't put her finger on it.

"I'm sorry, miss." The professor was suddenly joined by a woman dressed for the Kentucky Derby, complete with hat and long, floral dress. "We have reservations and have to leave."

"Sorry. Thanks for your help." She handed him the binoculars and watched them walk away. Sara turned back to the still waters and the horizon. "Something strange about that island."

"Other than the monkeys?"

"Well, the monkeys, too. It will come to me."

Dagger's phone beeped. It was a text from Carl and another from Jake. "Carl's meeting is over and Jake and Sam returned to the house."

"That's strange."

"Maybe they got tired of waiting."

"But they don't have a car."

22

Jess Haslen raked shaky fingers through hair as dingy as her appearance. Although the air was warm, she tugged a tattered sweater around her shivering body. She could feel eyes on her as she stumbled down the alley to a door behind a boarded-up hardware store. Trying the door handle proved fruitless. With both fists Jess pounded relentlessly until finally the door was yanked open.

"You again." The man spoke with an accent, more European than south of the border. A deep scar ran from his left eye to his chin. "Until you have cash, we have nothing to talk about." He poked his head out far enough to make sure she was alone in the alley. A dumpster next to the door reeked of rancid food and garbage.

Jess reached out and touched his hand. "I can pay in other ways."

He recoiled from her touch. "Not worth it." He slammed the door leaving the young woman shaking and weeping. "Please." Her plea was nothing more than a whisper as a limp hand made one last open palm slap on the door. The money her mother had given her hadn't lasted long.

Jess glanced around the alley, checked the ground as she walked away, hoping for a discarded needle, a few dropped pills.

The scene hadn't gone unnoticed by the Watcher. He had a way of blending with the scenery, going unnoticed as though part of the brick building. Knowing the young woman's haunts, he could anticipate her every move, knew where she scored or sold her body. Earlier she had found a way into an abandoned building and left several blankets and bottles of water. Now he knew where to visit her tonight.

They were quiet as Sam described what she had seen on the beach. She didn't expect anyone but Jake and possibly Carl to believe her. Sophia even had her repeat the events as if Sam were being interrogated in a police station.

Carl cut a gaze toward Sam's laptop. "Who were you emailing, Sam?"

"Abby. I always ask for her insight when I have a vision. She's totally discreet, Carl. You know that."

"What about clothing? Did you see any? Maybe names on lapels or names you might have heard?" Sophia asked.

Sam shook her head.

"Don't forget the letters," Jake reminded her.

"What letters?"

"More like initials, Carl. BRL, right Sam?" Jake asked. Sam nodded.

"Interesting." Sophia nodded, and slowly a smile crept across her face.

Sam looked from Sophia to Carl. "Wait. Was this a test? Were you testing me? You hoped this was what I would see?" She turned on Carl. "Is this why you suggested we walk the beach?" Sam started to stand but Jake pulled her back down.

"Carl, is that true?"

Dagger barked out an uproarious laugh and clapped his hands. "I love it! Welcome to our world."

Sophia shot Dagger a caution. "It was necessary." She turned to Sam. "The initials stand for BettaTec Research Lab. That was the name of the research ship we blew up several months ago. We weren't sure, depending on storms and tides, where, if any, debris might land. We did satellite imaging, designed models, checked coastlines. Although we hoped most of the debris sank, we weren't sure. It was the South Carolina coast that collected most of the debris, mainly the coast of Hilton Head. But we still weren't sure it was from the ship. Not one piece of the ship itself was found and body parts were too obliterated to even do fingerprint or DNA analysis. When Carl told me of your abilities, you were our last hope to confirm what we had found."

"You could have just told me."

"We could have, Sam," Carl said. "But for some reason Sophia wasn't quite convinced and thought by telling you what we needed ahead of time might have…"

"Tempted me to make it all up? Really, Carl? How long have we known each other?"

"I didn't need the convincing, Sam. Sophia is the scientist who always needs absolute proof."

"What about the words I heard?"

Jake jerked his head toward Sam. "You heard words?"

"Yes, I forgot to tell you because I was too busy running away from scrambling body parts. *'We weren't done.'* That's what I heard." Sam glared at Sophia. Sam felt used but the case was starting to intrigue her. "What does it mean?"

Sophia checked her watch. "I think it's five o'clock somewhere. Let's grab a drink."

"This is getting tedious, amigos." Padre preferred to interview all three men at the same time. The door opened and a large figure entered. Red-faced, red hair and a bulbous nose his mother once said could put candles out in a church. John Wozniak had been a fellow seminary student with Padre. Wozniak, chief of detectives, closed the door and leaned against the wall.

"We know our rights. You either charge us or let us go. But you got nothing."

"He is so right, Sergeant Martinez." The chief walked behind his star detective, pulled out his phone, and started taking pictures. "Since they haven't been officially charged, we had no need to take booking pictures." The chief checked the three pictures he had taken. "Damn. Moe, Larry, and Curly. These will work nicely. I have a press conference in a half hour. Press is always looking for meat. If it bleeds it leads. I'll give them a vague story about a warehouse full of drugs and money being blown up by these three. Of course, after they had stolen everything inside."

The suspects practically shot out of their seats. "You can't do that," they yelled in unison.

Wozniak smiled. "You know the press these days. They don't check for accuracy."

Two heads swiveled toward Baldy, a look of fear on their faces. "You wouldn't dare."

Padre studied the three, then settled his gaze on Baldy. "Well, well, Chief. It appears we had it all wrong. Baldy is the head honcho. Don't doubt my boss, amigos. You are not in a sanctuary state so one phone call and you are back in…oh, I don't know…Tepic, Toluca, Guadalajara or maybe Sinaloa."

"NO!" Baldy briefly showed fear, but quickly composed himself. "You're bluffing. Our bosses, they know we weren't in the states when this warehouse blew up. We had nothing to do with it." He leaned back with a satisfied smile.

"Maybe. Maybe you hired others, had them grab the money and drugs and planned to split the bounty. Since bodies weren't found in or near the scene, they have probably fled. Maybe you were in town to find them." When that didn't solicit responses, Padre tried another tack. "We could throw another bone to the reporters, like how you three tipped off the DEA on that tunnel in Arizona that blew up." The tunnel had been one of the cartel's largest distribution points. "According to the DEA, they waited until the shipment was deposited on our side of the border. Almost two tons of meth, over one hundred thousand pounds of fentanyl pills, all worth over ninety million dineros, amigos." Padre emitted a long whistle and shook his head. "Mi amigos, you are in so much trouble back home." Were those beads of sweat forming on Goatee's forehead?

Man Bun opened his mouth but Baldy lasered dark eyes on him, then turned to Padre. "We have nothing to say."

"NO!" Man Bun ignored Baldy. "We can't go back empty handed. He has people everywhere, even in prison."

"Well." Padre pushed back from the table and stood. "Prison is probably the least of your worries." He walked to the door, opened it, and motioned others in. "If he, whoever he is, has people everywhere, then you probably won't even be safe walking outside of this building." Two burly men entered, DEA emblazoned across their chests. "These men will try to keep you safe on your trip to their offices. It will certainly look to the press like you are cooperating fully because these two babysitters are going to be smiling and fist bumping all the way to the van."

"We need protection." Baldy didn't sound very blustery this time. "New names."

"Maybe plastic surgery," Man Bun said hopefully.

The DEA agents burst out laughing.

23

The weather was pleasant as they gathered around the table on the deck. Sam and Sara had cut up cheese and filled a basket of crackers. Sophia brought out a bowl of grapes and strawberries. Once everyone was seated, Sophia explained the situation.

"A couple weeks ago two boys were searching for seashells along the beach and came across a finger and partial skull. Terrified, they ran back to their parents who had stayed on the beach near their timeshare. My people searched the beach for remains after every high tide. Lucky for us the winds had pushed all remnants to a remote section of the beach. By the time the parents arrived, along with a curious crowd, our people had gathered all they could find. A few remnants washed up for the next two days, but nothing since."

Sam set her drink down and stared across the table at Carl. "So that's it? You just needed me to confirm your suspicions?"

"We made this trip for nothing?" Dagger's glare was directed at Sophia.

"No." Sophia's irritation at her prize pupil was growing, but she kept it at bay. "The meeting Carl and I had after lunch confirmed my suspicions. We use what is called an M-Vac."

"That's the microbial vacuum used for DNA testing, right?"

"Something I'm sure your Captain Robinson would like to get his hands on, Jake," Carl said.

"But all the remains had been in water for weeks, though." Sara grabbed several crackers and cheese slices.

"It works on soaked items, even bullet casings. We found debris that looked like parts of a 3D printer. The M-Vac identified Doctor Crane's DNA."

"But, Sophia, that could have been left any time." Sam wasn't sure if she should be writing down notes.

"Wait. Just wait a second." Dagger's aggravation was building with the drip, drip, drip of information. "What exactly was Crane researching on that ship? Besides, we already know he wasn't on it since he's out killing people."

"Allegedly, since Carl only has a partial print," Jake clarified.

"And a partial of a dead guy," Sam added.

"Carl, what was it they were researching on the ship, and Crane specifically?"

Carl looked to Sophia to reply to Jake. She slowly stirred her vodka and tonic as she sat back for what appeared to be a lengthy explanation.

"On a positive note, the ship contained one of the largest seed banks. Although, knowing Director Keyes, he'd sell the contents to the highest bidder while the world starved. The negative, however, outweighed the positives. Scientists were developing new viruses and plagues. Actually, kept a supply of small pox, the black plague and other horrific diseases in a vault."

"Good riddance." Sara's previous disgust at blowing up the ship was waning.

"Doctor Levitt Crane, however, was doing some noteworthy work. From what I understood, his father developed the first 3D printer twenty years before we ever even heard about 3D printing. He taught everything he knew to his son. Levitt Crane was a genius. Graduated college at thirteen, went on to earn a doctorate. His love was actually creating robots and that is what attracted the Director to him."

"He created those robot tanks in the underground facility?" Sara asked. She remembered how utterly intelligent those little pieces of machinery had been. They hadn't been much larger than a Rumba vacuum.

"Yes. But in his spare time, without the Director's knowledge… which I found highly unlikely, nothing got past the Director…Crane was making organs and selling them on the black market."

"3D organs?" Jake asked. "That hasn't been perfected yet."

"Bio-printing. As I said, his father was twenty years ahead of today's technology. And Levitt was about twenty years ahead of his father." Sophia opened a folder which was on the table next to her.

"The meeting we went to after lunch brought us up to speed on the latest that Doctor Crane had been working on," Carl explained. "Since Sophia has been away from BettaTec for several years now, her emissaries, planted in the Director's organization, keep us apprised of new developments."

"As I mentioned, 3D printing has come a long way. We can now produce musical instruments; the military has made shelters in hours rather than weeks. They are 3D printing houses. Regenerative medicine is a high point. Inject extracted cells into a knee and the body grows new cartilage. It can grow new bone tissue, muscle, a human ear, or nose. Think of neurotransmitters which can help patients with Parkinson's. So much is possible with bio-printing. Even I don't know all the ins and outs of this technology, but, as a scientist, I find it utterly fascinating. Think of paraplegics being able to walk again. Soldiers missing limbs can grow new ones."

"Question," Sam said, feeling awkward holding up her hand. "If Doctor Crane was so far ahead in this technology, why are there still long waiting lists for kidneys, livers, and lungs?"

"Greed," Dagger blurted.

"Says the man who probably helped himself to some of that money in the warehouse that blew up." Carl knew quite a bit about Dagger from Sophia.

"I'm more a Robin Hood. After all," Dagger turned his gaze to Sophia, "I'm sure some of the Director's emptied offshore accounts found its way into your account."

"AlphaTec's account, and for a good cause, but touché."

"Anyway." Carl steered the conversation back to the topic. "Guess everyone has a bit of greed and there is a lot more money in the black-market sales. Plus, the Director didn't want the outside world to know the strides his organization was making in this technology. In today's world it takes ten days to print a liver and the last working kidney lasted just under four months. I'm sure Crane's expertise could have literally erased the waiting lists."

"If only we could have gotten our hands on Crane's notes." Sophia sipped her drink as she scanned the rest of the notes in the folder.

Sara tried to digest all that Sophia was saying, but also trying to remember articles she had read on the same subject. She grabbed more cheese and fruit as she tried to jog her memory. "Wasn't there a group in Europe that hinted at the future of creating an entire human body?"

"Yeah, it's called a clone, and we've already met some of those." Dagger reached over to the patio fridge and grabbed another beer.

"My contacts did hint at a secret project he was working on, and I remember a similar article on the study."

"They had trouble with the brain though, didn't they, Sophia?" Carl asked.

"Yes. The brain has a complex nerve system of close to eighty-six million nerve cells. From what I read, it was Doctor Crane's pipe dream, to bio-print a human body. And preferably his own."

"A very big pipe dream," Carl added. "He never married, probably wanted to create another genius before he died."

"Problem is, he'd have to use some of his brain cells. Little hard to do if you're the sandwich maker. Can't kill the cook." Dagger took a long swallow of beer, thinking back to the bio-print technology and how it would be just as dangerous in the control of our government as it would under the Director's. "Imagine they can bio-print the head of any country. No need for some dictator to use a double. He can just bio-print a duplicate. He'd be dictator until the end of time."

"That's frightening." Sophia thought about the procedure necessary for such a task. "He would have had to take only some of his brain cells, I would guess, but that might take time, unless he used another component."

Sam slowly lowered her empty glass and looked across the table at Sophia. "Like part of a dead serial killer's brain?"

24

Sophia continued pacing in front of the monitor. After Sam's entirely incomprehensible comment about the serial killer's brain, Sophia had asked her staff to research the location of John Wallace Baker's brain tissue. Did it go to one laboratory or was it dissected and shipped off to various research labs? Did Doctor Crane achieve his dream? And did the fingerprints on the bio-printer parts found on the beach prove he had been on the ship and died in the explosion after he had created his replica and sent him off to kill Director Keyes?

"How much have you told Captain Robinson?" Carl asked, looking at Jake.

"Nothing as far as what we have discovered today. I believe Sergeant Martinez from Dagger's neck of the woods filled Robinson in on the cases he has worked with Dagger."

"Padre Martinez. Used to be in the seminary," Dagger said. "I don't know if it's a good thing or bad for our cop to be commiserating with Jake's."

"Is that a problem?" Sam asked. "For us to fill Robinson in on Crane?"

Carl looked at Sophia who shrugged. "As long as it goes no further and that they keep their findings within our tight circle. And he was the one to discover the identical sketch on the victims' wrists."

"Well, if Doctor Levitt is actually the killer and John Baker is along for the ride…hell, I don't know what to call him." Jake pressed fingers to his temples, trying unsuccessfully to make sense of it all. "That would explain the fingerprints."

"How do you figure?" Dagger asked.

"I worked a case once. You remember, Carl. A guy was convicted of murder yet he had a full-proof alibi. Was on the other side of the country at the time. Ended up several years prior he had donated a kidney to someone. It changed the recipient's DNA. The recipient was the actual killer. What if, by using tissue from John Baker's brain, it's slowly changing Crane's DNA and fingerprints?"

Sophia stopped her pacing. "Oh my god. Of course. That would explain finding prints from both of them at the crime scene." The monitor beeped and the robotic face of Connie appeared. "Talk to me."

"It is confirmed, Mother. A couple of the brain samples went missing from a lab in New Jersey. It appears to coincide with the year Doctor Crane started his experiment."

"Thank you, Connie." Sophia pressed a button on the keyboard and the connection was cut. "Well, that settles it. We will have dinner tonight, then pack your bags. You are returning home tomorrow morning. Carl, make sure the plane is ready." She turned to the team whose faces appeared disappointed at their short trip. "We can't let anyone stumble onto Doctor Crane. No one can discover that he is a bio-printed replica."

"Why?" Sara asked. "How can anyone tell he is bio-printed?"

"That's the six-million-dollar question now, isn't it?" Sophia smiled at Sara. She had grown fond of the young woman over the past couple days and marveled at her effect on Dagger. "I do know that when they experimented growing an ear, they used the patient's cells and a polymer structure. Once it was transplanted, over time the ear shed the polymer and new cartilage grew. What we don't know, because creating fully functioning lungs, heart, an entire body, has never been accomplished, is if there are any telltale features. Would a medical examiner, when doing the autopsy, discover something not quite right with the organs and start to ask questions? Doctors and scientists are curious creatures, and they won't stop until they figure out if and why something isn't quite normal about Crane. That's why it is important that we find him first." She smiled again at her pupils. "I have a special dinner prepared. Now go pack."

25

"Oh, what to do, what to do." Skizzy wandered in a circle in front of the monitors where the face of a baby punk was pressed against the front window of his shop. The hoodie hid most of his face, but the finger tats and swagger spelled drug dealer wannabe.

He didn't believe in coincidences. Why so soon after the three amigos does this kid show up? Skizzy turned away from the monitors and stared at the gym bag in the corner. It had been upstairs the day the amigos showed up. So for safekeeping he decided to store it in his bunker.

He took a seat in front of the monitor. The kid was checking out both sides of the street. Was he getting ready to break the glass? Skizzy jabbed a button. "Don't even think of it," he warned through the microphone.

The kid jumped back and jerked his gaze around to see where the voice was coming from.

"The glass is bulletproof."

With that, the kid took off.

"Yes!" Skizzy spun in his chair in triumph. He figured he was just nervous after the last visitors. Still, they all appeared after the incident at the warehouse. Were there cameras they had failed to detect that night? Had someone been watching? No. Dagger and Simon had made sure not one other person was in the area. Besides, Skizzy's drone would have discovered any onlookers. Still…

A noise caught Skizzy's attention. It was coming from upstairs. The backdoor? Then a doorknob jiggled. He checked the camera outside the backdoor. There was the snot-nosed kid. He had pulled his hoodie back and now Skizzy could see the punk couldn't have been more than thirteen or fourteen.

"What the hell?" Skizzy punched the mike button. "Hey, didn't I tell you to scram? I'm one minute away from calling the cops."

Dark eyes scanned the roof looking for the camera. He may have been in his early teens, but his eyes showed a fierce disregard for rules, much less life.

"I want it back," the punk yelled.

"This is a pawn shop. If your baby daddy pawned your mama's ring, microwave or television, you ain't gonna find them here. Now get the hell out."

"I want it now or I'll burn the fuckin' place down with you in it."

Skizzy pressed another button. On a billboard at the end of the block he had placed a siren. It wasn't screaming loud, just moderate enough to make it sound as though a squad car was a few blocks away.

The kid jerked back, slamming his hand against the door, then kicked it for good measure. "I'll be back old man, later, while you're sleepin'." Like a jackrabbit, the punk scurried out of sight.

26

"Chateaubriand, lobster, stuffed crab. It's like our last supper, Carl. I feel like you're sending us to our doom."

"Not really, Sam. Sophia likes to show off her cooking skills from time to time."

"Maybe we should have had a taste tester." Dagger pushed his empty plate away with a satisfied sigh.

"We did. We waited for you to take the first bite."

"Real funny, Sam."

"You've been quiet all through dinner, Jake." Carl poured himself a cup of coffee, then passed the carafe across the table to Jake.

"Still trying to digest it all. I thought the story of the haunted house and parallel universe couldn't get any weirder, but now we have a genius twenty years ahead of any scientist who has bio-printed his own body."

Sophia poured three small glasses with Tia Maria liquor. She handed a glass to Sam and one to Sara. "Actually, there are many unexplained things in the world which the greatest minds can't comprehend. Take Albert Einstein for instance. How does a boy who didn't talk until he was four, dropped out of school at fifteen, flunked an entrance exam for a polytechnic school, suddenly produce the theory of relativity? Did he make a miraculous transition, or did he exchange himself with his doppelganger in the parallel universe? Some scientists believe there are ten dimensions in the universe. In one dinosaurs still roam the earth. Then there are those who believe the worlds are layered, super-imposed on ours. This might explain ghosts. Lost souls have found a tear between the universes."

"Okay, stop, before you go into teleportation. My head is going to explode." Jake rubbed at his temples, as though trying to erase everything he had heard the last three days.

"We just go with the flow." Dagger made it sound like a badge of honor. "It's like a surprise a minute, a chuckle an hour."

"What happens to Doctor Crane when we find him?" Sara looked from Sophia to Carl. "Are you going to kill him or isolate him on an uninhabited island somewhere?"

"We are hoping to talk to him first, provided he is still mostly Crane and not Baker. I'm especially interested in knowing the whereabouts of his research papers on bio-printing. Hopefully, they weren't destroyed on the ship."

"And second?"

"What?"

"You said you were hoping to talk to him first. So, what's second?"

"We haven't thought that far ahead, Sara."

"I doubt that," Dagger said none too quietly.

Sophia ignored his comment. "Would be nice if Doctor Crane could continue his work. I fear Baker may become the predominant personality and could care less about doing good. Remember, this is new territory for us, too. We haven't encountered an experiment like this before." Sophia looked around the table at their guests, then finished her Tia Maria.

"Well, aren't we a happy foursome." Dagger found Sam and Jake on the front porch after dinner. They had finished packing and wanted to get one last breath of the Lowcountry.

The sun was taking its last gasp before sinking below the horizon. "Hate to leave this place," Sam said with a sigh. "Carl did mention there is a tropical storm west of Africa that's headed this way. I don't think I care to be caught in that."

"This is a nice vacation place and Carl's house is beautiful." Sara took a seat next to Dagger on the sofa. The screened-in porch saved them from a deluge of mosquitos.

"It appears the whip-poor-wills are still around. Those damn birds kept me up most of the night, just like during our last visit."

"I kinda like the sound, Jake. It's like the hoot of an owl or mourning dove."

"Really, Sam? Don't your ancestors consider the owl a sign of death?"

"That's comforting." Dagger's phone rang. He dug it out of his pocket and checked the screen. "Great. It's Skizzy." He pushed the speaker button. "Have you been staying out of trouble?"

"They are after me. Yesterday three cartel guys tried to break in. Now today a Jamaican wannabe drug lord kid says he's comin' back tonight to burn the…"

"Whoa. Slow down, Skizzy. What the hell are you talking about?"

"I had to zap the three amigos with my electrified grating. Almost killed the sons-of-bitches. Even had to call Padre."

"You called Padre?"

"What else was I gonna do? You abandoned me."

"Okay, take a breath. Start from the beginning."

"The three cartel guys had a map with the location of the warehouse. How did they know we were the ones who blew it up?"

Dagger glanced toward Jake and Sam who were getting an earful, but it was too late to turn off the speaker. He could see questions lining up in Jake's head.

"Did Padre get anything out of them?"

"Nah. He called ICE, but I haven't heard if the thugs told them anything or even if they were released."

In the background Dagger heard a scraping noise, as if Skizzy were moving a piece of furniture.

"What's that sound?"

"I'm moving the coat of armor closer to the window with a musket in his hands to ward off the child arsonist. After I chased him away from the front door, he tried getting in through the back door."

"There isn't any way your building can be torched. The walls are lined in lead for crissake."

"The kid says I have something that belongs to him. What's he talking about? I never saw the punk before in my life."

Sara pulled Dagger's arm to bring the phone closer. "Skizzy, why don't you stay at our place tonight. We'll be home tomorrow. Besides, Einstein, I'm sure, is getting lonely. You probably forgot to fill his food bowls and there are leftovers in the fridge you can eat."

"Really? I can? But how do I get out of here with him watching?"

"Says the guy with an underground garage filled with unregistered cars and accessible from his bunker," Dagger reminded him. "Get out of there now. And take your meds." Dagger punched the off button, then looked over at Jake. "Did you really expect us to have normal friends?"

27

"Interesting place." Jake studied the camera hidden under the gutter and the grating over the windows and door.

"You could have waited in the car. Besides, one look at you and Skizzy will size you up as a cop in one second."

"No thanks. After the way you drive, we needed to get our feet firmly planted on the ground."

Dagger pounded on the door again. He knew Skizzy was back because he had called him from the airport. "You could have called Cochise or an Uber, you know."

A silhouette of a suit of armor and musket could be seen through the grimy window, but there wasn't a hint that anyone had tried to torch the place. The sound of locks slamming open echoed in the still air, then a slight tug as the door was pulled open a few inches.

"'bout time." Bulging eyes wobbled in opposite directions as Skizzy's gaze settled on Jake. "Fed? You brought Elliot Ness?" Skizzy started to slam the door shut but Dagger shoved his way in, sending the waif of a man tumbling back.

"He's with us and he's no longer a cop."

They piled into the pawn shop and watched as Skizzy slammed bolts and chains up and down the door, which seemed to Sam and Jake as overkill. Skizzy scurried around the four and sought refuge behind the main counter. Dagger made the introductions which did nothing to quell Skizzy's nervousness around strangers.

"So, what were you doing in South Carolina with Girlie? Getting married? Oh, wait. I already married you two."

Sara turned to Sam. "Online license. He practiced on us. Now thinks he's a legitimate pastor."

"I'll fill you in later, Skizzy. Now tell me why these guys are showing up. And do you think the kid was one of the ones guarding the warehouse that night?"

"Nah. The kids at the warehouse were late teens. This kid was more like twelve or thirteen, and he had a Jamaican accent. The three brutes who were here never had a chance to tell me what they wanted but had a map with directions to the warehouse."

Jake was half-listening as he studied several items displayed in one of the showcases. Pocket watches, switchblades, jewelry, doorknobs, old postcards. Maybe collector items or Skizzy ransacked a hoarder's domain, or he bids on storage facilities, cleans up the items and calls them collectibles. He looked up when he remembered Skizzy had mentioned a warehouse.

"So, what other trouble have you taken part in besides blowing up that warehouse I heard about?"

"Oh shit, shit shit. I said too much."

Sam placed a hand on Jake's arm. Just can't take the cop out of the man. Even when Sam was a detective, she crossed into questionable territory due to her own curiosity or to gain information on the Police Chief's enemies.

"If you were there and you claim no one saw you so no one should have followed you. Did you take anything out of the warehouse before it exploded?" Sam asked.

"Oh, no," Sara said. "Tell me you didn't take some of the money. Mother pays you quite handsomely, Skizzy."

"Sophia?" Sam wondered how far Sophia's influence reached.

"This is getting better and better," Jake mumbled. "They probably placed a tracker somewhere."

"Skizzy, what the hell were you thinking."

"But, Dagger, the walls in here are lead lined. They can't track it."

"Girlie's right."

"The tracking device worked up to your front door, so it isn't a hard guess as to where it ended up, whatever it is you took." Jake shook his head. What idiots did they get themselves involved with?

"How much?" Dagger demanded. "How much did you take?"

Skizzy disappeared behind the curtain and returned with one bundle. He slammed it on the counter. Dagger cocked his head and glared at the skinny guy. With a sigh, Skizzy disappeared and returned with a gym bag. He tipped it out and bundles of cash piled out.

"Oh, Skizzy." Sara used the same tone she used on Einstein when he would tip over one of his food bowls.

Jake picked up a bundle and fanned through the cash. "All twenties. Has to be about twenty thousand in each bundle, but I don't see a tracker."

"Maybe it's inside the bag," Sam suggested.

Jake checked inside the bag, then the zipper and handle. "Nothing."

Sara picked up one of the bundles. The band around it had a symbol that appeared to glow. She turned it around to show Dagger. "Do the colors look right to you?"

The fact that Sara was showing it to him meant that it couldn't be seen by the normal eye. But Dagger's internal computer spotted it. "It's like a QR code but can probably be tracked by satellite. Pretty sophisticated."

"Skizzy, we agreed. It's drug money and we were going to burn the money and the drugs in the warehouse." Sara shook her head in disappointment.

Sam studied Sara. There was certainly more to the young woman than meets the eye.

"So, you torched a warehouse full of drugs and money. Anything else you want to fill us in on since we now have a working alliance?" Jake wondered what else Carl had kept from him. He could at least have given him a heads up on everything Dagger was involved with that were borderline illegal.

"A half-mile tunnel at a border out west was destroyed. I know it hardly makes a dent in the cartel's operation but it's a start," Dagger replied. He turned to Skizzy. "Here is what you are going to do. Rip the bands off every bundle, place them back in the gym bag. Then, go drum up a bunch of bags, any kind. The girls will put some money in each of the bags and drop them off at food kitchens, food pantries, homeless shelters, women's shelters. I'm sure there are a lot around here and back in the slums where Jake lives." This brought a raised eyebrow from Jake. Obviously, a jab at the massive house where he and Sam lived. "Then the first semi headed to Canada, or a garbage truck headed to parts unknown that you see, toss the gym bag filled with the bands into it."

"Yeh, yeh." Skizzy started ripping the bands off the bundles.

"We'll do that," Sam said. "You go find us more bags."

Jake braced his arms against one of the showcases and stared at the items on display. The old eyeglasses looked like something Ben Franklin might have worn. The pocket watch had the initials WE engraved on it. Wyatt Earp? It couldn't be, could it? If it were, collectors would be lined up at Skizzy's door. If squirrely guy were able to get his hands on these treasures, he wouldn't doubt the suit of armor came from Buckingham Palace. Then he noticed a tea set with a descriptive label...Queen Elizabeth's First Reception.

Dagger sidled up to Jake. "I can read your cop mind. Skizzy must be fencing stolen goods."

"He isn't? A pocket watch with Wyatt Earp's' initials? A silver tea set from Buckingham Palace? If these are authentic, why isn't Skizzy living in a mansion on the lake front? Why doesn't he advertise to collectors?" Jake thought about that. "They're all fakes, aren't they?"

"I don't ask. Before Simon introduced me to Skizzy, the schizophrenic never left the shop, lives in the back, paranoid about everything and everybody. He wouldn't have let you and Sam in the shop if I hadn't been with you. Lately, he only eats the food Sara makes."

"Okay. Are you happy now?" Skizzy held up the gym bag. "Now I'll go find a truck stop or garbage truck somewhere and then spend some time picking through dumpsters for my next meal since Dagger is leaving me broke and destitute."

28

No sooner did the Lincoln Navigator make the turn around to the front door and expel its two passengers, then Dagger tore rubber back down the driveway.

"Was it something you said?" Alex asked when he rounded the corner from the backyard.

The back door opened, and the toddler charged toward Sam. She scooped him up in her arms.

"I missed you." She gave Dillon a squeeze and a kiss. "Were you a good boy while Daddy and I were away?" Sam caught a knowing look on Abby's face. "Did you have fun destroying things?" She looked again at her mother. "Did he break something?"

"Only painted the dog. Alex isn't very happy."

"What color?" Jake carried the suitcase into the house as everyone followed. They found Poco hiding under the kitchen table. She had pink blotches on her front legs and back. "Wow. I'd hide, too, Poco."

"I'm taking her to the groomer this afternoon," Alex said. "They have some remover that might work, but I fear they will have to shave her."

"Did you tell Poco that you're sorry, Dillon?" Sam wiped dirt from the boy's face. Dillon pointed at Poco, then buried his face in Sam's shoulder. "How did he get ahold of paint?"

Alex shrugged. "I was painting a flowerpot for Abby and turned my back for one second."

"Go unpack, Jacob, then come down and tell us all about your trip," Abby said. "It must have been a surprise to see Dagger and Sara on the same trip."

"Oh, you have no idea."

* * * *

Alex and Abby sat silent as Jake and Sam filled them in on Sophia's relationship to Carl and the company called AlphaTec as well as BettaTec and the Director.

"Why aren't you shocked?" Jake asked the two after he described some of the unconventional cases Dagger and Sara had encountered.

Abby shrugged. "Definitely not something you hear every day, but not surprising."

"Nothing surprises us," Alex added. "We find the older we get, the more life reveals. The military is now admitting to the existence of unidentified flying objects. A woman believed she saw a baby dinosaur in her backyard. People still believe in Bigfoot and the Loch Ness monster."

"The operative word is believed. But if you had seen this man who changed into a werewolf creature and then a bird…the video was literally impossible to believe if Dagger and Sara hadn't been eyewitnesses." Jake refilled his coffee cup, the images still clear in his mind. "Then there's this parallel universe and an underground training facility in Nebraska where Dagger was trained to be God knows what…a hit man?" He heaved a sigh. "Now we have to find a doctor who bio-printed his own replica which he merged with the brain of a serial killer." A slight smile crossed Jake's lips. "Never had this kind of case in the Bureau."

"Come on, sweetie, admit it. You are intrigued." Sam handed Dillon a cheese stick. He hadn't left Sam's side since she had returned.

"How do you plan to catch this doctor?"

"Not sure, mom. Unfortunately, we have to wait for the next body to drop and see if my spidey senses can pick up clues. We just hope he stays in the area. Carl is doing his best to keep this case hush-hush, but if the killer moves on, then too many people will be sticking their noses in, the press will get curious. It's going to be hard to keep this under wraps if we can't find him fast."

"Should I invite Sara and Dagger to dinner?"

"No thanks." Jake shook his head. "I can only take that guy in small doses."

"I take it Jake and Dagger did not exactly bond during the trip."

"Quite true, mom. I also got the feeling that there was little trust between Dagger and Sophia. There's a lot of history there. Not all good from what I could tell." Now that he finished his cheese stick, Dillon squirmed off Sam's lap and charged for the kitchen.

"How did Dagger treat Sara during this trip?" Alex had never warmed up to the man he considered dangerous.

"No worries, Alex. She has him wrapped around her little finger."

"And you?" Abby settled her gaze on her daughter. "Any more visions after the beach?"

"Nothing. That was enough," Sam added with a shiver. "I thankfully haven't seen body parts chasing me in my dreams either…yet. It was really weird."

"Not very friendly spirits." Alex checked his watch. "Poco and I have a date with the groomer. Are you coming, Abby? I will buy you lunch while they try to make Poco presentable."

"Go, mom. We'll feed Dillon and put him down for his nap. I also have some laundry to do."

29

The Watcher changed clothes in his hotel room. When he had first arrived in town, he thought a secluded motel would be best. However, there were too few people so he would be easy to remember. Instead, he had picked a four-star hotel near the expressway, which catered to conventions. He would be hiding in plain sight. Too many people and too much going on for anyone to pay him any attention.

He had several fake driver's licenses and credit cards, thanks to one benefactor, so he had made good use of them. Even rented a compact sedan, nothing flashy to garner attention.

Doctor Levitt Crane, The Watcher, sat down at the window where his room looked over an atrium of shops and kiosks two floors below. He felt more comfortable being closer to the ground. One of his many phobias. He guessed it was because he had lived a secluded life, in a lab carved out of a mountain out West and then a ship in the middle of the Atlantic Ocean. He didn't like the noise or the crowds, having always worked in a quiet lab where people spoke in whispers. The bustle of activity in the hotel was too much, even for him, but it provided the obscurity that he needed.

In the atrium, men and women in suits gathered in groups waiting for the next meeting or maybe deciding where to eat. His thoughts turned to his father, Russell Crane. In Levitt's mind, his father had been a genius, the smartest man Levitt had ever known. Even smarter than the Director. Levitt had been sixteen when he and his father had been recruited by the Director. The offer had been too great to pass up for the ordinary man. But money wasn't a motivator for his father. He wanted freedom to do his own research, not follow some mad man's pipe dream. The main sticking point had been the inability to leave for a lab located in parts unknown. Not being able to grow old with his childhood sweetheart or watch his son grow up was a non-starter. "But you misunderstand the Director," the recruiter had said. "He finds a lot of promise in your son and wants him also."

But not the wife. Russell Crane had respectfully declined. Regrets didn't haunt him in the least. Yes, they had a nice home in a nice neighborhood. But certainly not a mansion with three classic cars in the garage. The elder Crane had taught Levitt that it was more important that his work help people, not benefit him financially.

Levitt had been suspicious of his mother's car accident. She had been a good driver, even on rain-slicked roads. The police said the brakes had locked up and the car had skidded over a guardrail and down an embankment. His father had been too filled with guilt to see the obvious. But Levitt wasn't fooled. The Director got the scientist he wanted within two months after trying to recruit him. "I was supposed to take the car in for a checkup," his father had cried. "It's all my fault. I thought the brakes had been sticking." There was no consoling him, even though Levitt had driven the car multiple times and didn't think anything had been wrong with the brakes. Yes, Levitt knew exactly who was responsible and it proved to him exactly how dangerous Jonathan Keyes really was. Levitt Crane was a gentle man without a malicious bone in his body, so why did it feel so good to kill the Director?

Crane was tired. He moved to the bed, kicked off his shoes, and laid back against the pillows. There were times when he worked in his lab that he could live on four hours sleep. The research was too exciting to rest. Work had been so exhilarating. Killing was exhausting. But it's so much fun, a voice in his head blared. Rest now. We have more killing to do, the voice continued.

30

"Something on your mind." Carl made it a statement, not a question. He set a glass of yellow liquid in front of Sophia.

"Limoncello? Thank you, Carl."

He set his glass on the table and took a seat. The back deck faced east. Car lights could be seen in the distance headed to the island.

"You've had that look on your face since our guests left."

Sophia flashed a weak smile, then took a sip of her drink. "What look is that, Carl?"

He studied her over the rim of his glass. His choice was bourbon, and not the cheap kind.

"You're uneasy. You pace like you're waiting for the other shoe to drop. And I don't think it has anything to do with Doctor Crane. My people are good, as are yours. I have confidence that they will find him, especially since it appears he is staying in the same area for now." A whip-poor-will started his calling somewhere nearby. Carl was sure it had a nest in the lot next door. Fear was one emotion he had never seen on Sophia's face. Worry, maybe caution, but never fear. This was something else.

"It's too easy."

"Sorry?" Carl studied her face in the darkness.

"Keyes would never make it that simple to kill him. That's what bothers me. Over the years not one of his guards could be bought. Very few people knew of his suite in Vancouver. I didn't even know."

"So you think the video was doctored?"

"With events unfolding as quickly as they were with the research ship being destroyed, to me, it was just a matter of time until his empire collapsed. He was overly cautious. It shouldn't surprise me that he had a residence in Canada. When he would talk about one day retiring, his dream was to buy a private island somewhere. *Mon Petit Refuge* is French Canadian for My Little Hideaway. But Jonathan Keyes retiring? I can't see it. Too much power and money to give up."

The whip-poor-will continued its call as the couple looked out into the dark marsh. It stretched for miles without one boat light in sight. Just the beams from the vehicles on the bridge.

With a sigh, Sophia rose and repeated, "It was just too damn easy."

31

Jess gathered a ratty blanket around her body as the uncontrollable shakes rattled her teeth. It had never been this bad before. She felt too sick to even work the streets. The empty building she was using for shelter was scattered with debris from what might have once been a real estate office. One corner of the office had a blackened wall and leak in the ceiling. She could still catch a hint of soot from what must have been the results of a fire. An array of for sale signs were strewn around the floor. Windows were boarded up, but the three skylights provided some light. Jess, though, at least had her candles and a couple lighters. She took deep breaths to calm her body. At one time Jess had been into yoga and meditation. It wasn't doing much now to quell the withdrawal. Maybe she could try breaking into a pharmacy, if only her legs could hold her up that long to walk five blocks. Fellow drug addicts were avoiding her lately since all she did was steal their stash.

Another wave of the shakes rattled her bones and threatened to bring on a bout of the dry heaves. She was so busy fighting the nausea that she almost missed the scraping sound from the back door. Had another squatter found her hideout? Just as she thought of yelling for her intruder to go away, the thought hit her that it might be someone with drugs to share.

"Hello?" she called out.

Soft footsteps slowly approached. The light from the candles and skylights gave off enough light to see him clearly. Shoes were shiny and probably expensive. Clothes were clean and pressed. Obviously not a squatter, but maybe a possible customer she could service for a fee. Maybe someone who could buy her the drugs, so she didn't have to leave the building. As her gaze climbed to his face, she was sure her disappointment showed. "Oh, it's you."

* * * *

Crane tossed the pen against the wall and pulled out another one. Jess's eyes were locked on a wall across from her, not seeing or comprehending anything anymore. How someone so young could throw her life away, and with a child to raise, too, just baffled him. Doctors have been studying the brain for decades. They have documented what these horrific drugs do to the body, and yet some people don't seem to care. If it feels good, do it. Wasn't that the mantra?

"I believe the last straw was when you attempted to sell your child. If that kind of desperation didn't get you to stop, then nothing would. You are a hopeless wretch, Jess. I'm doing your son a favor." Crane studied the young woman who could hardly be recognized as in her twenties. More like in her forties. Dirty hair and clothes, eyes deep set and surrounded by dark circles, teeth that were beyond the aid of even the best dentist, and a stench from her clothes and body that repulsed him.

Crane studied his handiwork, snapped the cap on the black marker, and shoved it back in his pocket. He couldn't get away from her fast enough.

At a seedy part of the neighborhood, far from the high-priced hotel, two teens crept up to a singlewide, side-stepping beer cans strewn in the yard. One dim light at one end of the trailer cast little light through a torn curtain. Freshmen in high school, the two boys had been friends since sixth grade. Ebony and Ivory had been labeled by the other students because Darius was black and Eddie was white. They had heard about the weed wagon from some kids on the basketball team. Neither one had ever tried pot before, but everyone was doing it, so the other kids claimed. If they wanted to fit in, they had to get some weed. And not the legal way, not that pot was legal. They were told to steal it and bring back proof. It had been a dare, and Ebony and Ivory were never ones to pass up a dare.

"I bet there's a back window that might be easy to break into," Ivory suggested.

"What if he's home and calls the cops?" Ebony asked.

"I doubt a drug dealer is going to call cops and risk them finding the drugs. He might have more than pot."

Ebony had to be talked into things. His grandmother was strict. A transplant from Alabama, she didn't take shit from him or any of the kids and ruled the roost with a wooden spoon. But she was good to him, and fair. She had raised him since his parents died in a car crash when Ebony was three years old. The thought of disappointing her didn't sit well with him. And there was that wooden spoon.

Ivory only wanted to fit in. The tractor company his father worked for had transferred him five times since Ivory was born. It was like starting over every time, trying to find friends, trying to fit in. And he wanted desperately to fit in.

The trailer was a loner, just like Ivory. It sat at the end of a dirt track, swallowed up by a small forest in the middle of nowhere. The abandoned trailer could barely be seen from the nearest main road, which made it the perfect place to deal in unsavory business. It resembled a construction trailer set up for a building site that never took off.

"What's his name again?" Ebony whispered.

"Kenny something." Ivory peered through the window. A dim light was above a sink. All he could see was a small table and one chair. "Maybe no one's home or he's passed out. Let's try the doorknob."

Ebony scanned the surrounding area. "Did you hear something?" His eyes were playing tricks on him. The moon was full creating shadows that darted between trees. Maybe there were deer in the woods. Or maybe there were others looking to score. "Let's leave. My mee-maw will be totally pissed."

But Ivory already had his hand on the doorknob. The sooner they got this over with, the better, he thought. The knob turned easily in his hand. "It's open," he whispered, and slowly pushed his way in.

"Let's just find some and get out of here." Ebony saw dirty dishes on the counter and paper plates on the kitchen table. The place smelled of garbage and rotting fruit. It reminded him of the time apples had spilled out of grocery bags in the back seat of his grandmother's car. Two had rolled under the front driver's seat and hid there for a month until his grandmother found the mushy, moldy remnants.

Ivory stepped over discarded newspapers and knocked into a coffee table where empty bottles almost tumbled to the floor. Ebony joined him wishing they had brought a flashlight but then remember his phone.

"Don't," Ivory started to say, but the flashlight came on and spilled over a body lying on a tattered couch, foam dried around the mouth, eyes sightless. They both screamed and charged out of the trailer.

32

Skizzy hardly slept since the three amigos and the cartel brat showed up. He kept hearing someone jiggling the back doorknob and a rattling sound at the front door. His OCD had him checking the doors every five minutes. No wonder he wasn't getting any sleep. What made matters even worse was the call he received from Padre. He had discovered that the motel the three men had stayed at was near the Illinois border. Although there weren't any personal effects or papers left in the room, the motel manager confirmed that four men had checked in. So where was amigo number four? Cameras inside and outside of the motel were only for show so Padre couldn't even give Skizzy a description of the fourth man.

With pressure from Dagger, he had disposed of the money and, more importantly, the bands which had allowed the money to be tracked. But still they were hounding him. It wasn't his imagination, he knew positively. Well, maybe not quite one hundred percent.

He paced in a tight circle, the meager living quarters in the back room hampering his movements. A small twin bed was in a side room and his pacing area consisted of a microwave, small refrigerator, cabinets, and a table and two chairs. A doll house had more furniture.

Skizzy stopped and glared at the clock on the wall. It was almost midnight. Anger tamped down his anxiety. He finally made a decision. No longer was he going to be hounded or be a sitting duck in his own establishment. Skizzy scampered down the stairs into the bunker, grabbed night vision goggles and the keys to a black truck he had stowed away, then headed down a narrow hallway to another door…his escape route.

The moon was barely a sliver which worked out well. With the night vision goggles on and all lights off on the truck, Skizzy inched the vehicle toward the quarry and the remnants of the burned-out warehouse. The dirt road was one hundred yards from the warehouse but afforded him a view of two other buildings nearby. Simon and Dagger had checked those vacant buildings for occupants and any working cameras. They hadn't found evidence of people or surveillance equipment. So how could there have been witnesses? Could the trackers have been their only way to find him? One side of his brain told him it had to be because Dagger and Simon weren't being harassed. Then again, Simon was out of town and Dagger had been in South Carolina with Sara. Skizzy knew, though, that Dagger's sophisticated security system would have alerted him if anyone had been anywhere near his property since the night of the torching.

The other side of his brain screamed louder. They had been observed and the someone or someones connected to the warehouse were still in town wanting their pounds of flesh. The two youths guarding the warehouse perhaps? Maybe they were threatened with death unless they brought back information on the men responsible for destroying their local distribution operation. If they had been killed in retaliation, wouldn't the police have been notified? Not if their bodies were hacked up and burned, one side of Skizzy's brain said. Not if their eyes were gouged out and their lifeless bodies posted on the Internet for other cartel members to be warned about what happened if you lost the cartel's precious cargo and money, the other side of his brain argued.

"Shut up," Skizzy whispered as he turned off the truck and quietly exited, careful not to slam the door. How stupid, his left brain whispered. No one here. Why whisper? What's with the stealth creeping?

He ignored the taunting as he maneuvered in a crouch through tall weeds and thick underbrush, trying not to twist an ankle on the cans, bricks and other debris scattered around. Skizzy wished he had Dagger's high tech night vision goggles which eliminated the sickening green glow he was seeing through his cheap knockoffs.

The weeds were so thick he needed a machete to cut a path. He could see the fence surrounding the quarry to his left. It was the same quarry where he and Simon had tossed the clone armed with a bomb in his neck rigged to go off a certain time after his death. This had been on the opposite side of the quarry where a section of the fence was broken.

The tall underbrush he fought through served a purpose. Skizzy was so well hidden he should have left breadcrumbs to find his way back. His breath came out in billows like a snorting dragon. Although the day had been warm and sunny, here in the forgotten lands it was damp and chilly. Dressed in all black, he resembled a Ninja with only a slot for eyes in his balaclava. He took another step, disturbing something on the ground that scurried so quickly Skizzy almost screamed out. "You sissy," he whispered.

The weeds closed in on him, bringing something else which creeped from the quarry to his left. It crawled like steam from a lab experiment, spreading across the ground and circling his feet. "What the…" Skizzy lifted the night vision goggles to witness a sea of fog wrapping around his body. If he had been in a cemetery, Skizzy would have run screaming like a banshee. Someone should turn the spigot off, he thought. Another sound echoed from a tree, a cry from a bird of prey, he wasn't sure. Then it took flight, screeching over his head in warning to what or whom? He shook off the feeling of watchful eyes and continued as the fog foamed up around his waist. Up ahead something else was foaming up, taking shape like a corpse, dead and buried and emerging from its grave. It floated from its resting place.

Skizzy was frozen to the spot, his head barely above the weeds as the shape took form and rose to full height. It seemed to stare right at him, then turned and disappeared into the growing fog. Skizzy wasn't aware he was holding his breath until a sucking gasp clutched at his throat.

"What the hell?"

I told you this was a bad idea, the right side of his brain said. You should follow the ghost. It's probably a zombie, the left side of his brain countered. Then he heard what sounded like an engine. What kind of zombie can start a car engine? The killing kind, his left brain said. As the fog started to settle, he thought he saw fruits and vegetables floating and dancing. How cool is that? Skizzy thought of running back to the truck and burning rubber back home. But then the dead body/ghost/zombie might hear the truck. That was the last thing he needed trying to break into his shop. But it was better than sticking around. He turned to run, tripped over something, and fell, hitting his head on something solid.

33

"Who found the body?" Jake scanned the area around the trailer, the trampled dirt from the parade of people who had somehow found their way to a secluded, abandoned construction trailer out in the middle of nowhere.

"Two high school boys who would just as soon forgotten what they had seen. Darius Young and Eddie Miller, aka, Ebony and Ivory. Clever, huh?" Captain Robinson said with a grin.

"Hilarious," Jake said with a sigh.

"They wouldn't have reported it at all except Ebony had nightmares and screamed about a dead body in his sleep. His grandmother practically dragged him in by his ears this morning and he confessed it all. One of those initiations boys like to do to incoming high school freshmen. In this case, they had to steal weed from a known dealer, which happened to be our dead guy, Kenny Bracken." The captain glanced over the tall weeds surrounding the trailer. "Where did Dagger go?"

"Around back, checking for God knows what."

A black van slowly backed up toward the trailer, tall weeds scraping the sides of the massive vehicle. It parked next to a black sedan, its windows as dark as the van's. There weren't any descriptions on the van nor were there names on the black Hazmat suits the two men wore. Their hoods and masks prevented anyone from seeing their faces.

"Who's inside?"

"The occupants of the black sedan beat me to the scene, Jake. Don't know how they get to these crime scenes so fast."

The van occupants pulled a stretcher from the back of the van, then carried it into the trailer. As cramped as the singlewide was, Jake wasn't surprised the two early arrivals stepped outside, propping the door open with a brick. They each were dressed in black cargo pants and black sweatshirts which had Jake wondering if the men had raided Dagger's closet. Black shades hid their eyes making it difficult should anyone want to give the authorities a full description of Sophia's people.

Several minutes later the Hazmat twins finessed the stretcher out of the cramped doorway. The body of Kenny Bracken was safely enshrined in a non-porous black body bag. The stretcher was shoved into the back of the van, doors slammed shut, and the van slowly maneuvered along the ruts.

"You might want these." The black-shaded men each held open a gym bag. One contained bag of pills and pot. The other was filled with money. Jake and Robinson each took one.

"You removed evidence?" Robinson was appalled. He and Jake never had a chance to inspect the interior.

"And you might want to move further away." Without another word, the two men climbed into the sedan and followed the van.

"They're gone?" Dagger asked as he brushed weeds and debris from his shirt.

"Yeah, and they said we might what to move further away. Any idea what that means?" Jake asked.

"Oh hell." Dagger started running followed by Jake and a lumbering Captain who swore under his breath that he needed to get to the gym.

The explosion blew the trailer door over their heads as they dove for the ground. Flames licked the sky as billows of smoke and debris rained down on the area. Dagger had his phone out as he rolled onto his back. He didn't have to call Sophia. A text message had been sent to him just before the explosion. "Damn."

"What the hell?" Jake pushed himself into a sitting position. "Don't tell me they planted a bomb."

Dagger shook his head in disgust. "Sophia says to tell Captain Robinson that the deceased had a meth lab and accidentally blew himself up. Remains could not be identified, and the last owner of the trailer was the Ballard Construction Company who vacated it ten years ago. Case closed."

The three men scrambled to their feet, dusting dirt and ashes from their clothes and hair. The burning rubble had been flattened, the remains not resembling a trailer much less any type of structure.

"She certainly covered all bases." Jake sent a quick text to Sam telling her not to bother coming to the trailer and that he would fill her in later.

"No trailer, no crime, no killer. That's how Sophia works."

They walked toward a side road where Robinson's car was parked. He opened the trunk and the two bags were loaded. "At least the debris didn't reach my ride. Hope you two were just as lucky."

"I drove my motorcycle. If there's any damage you can be sure Sophia will get a bill."

The captain maneuvered the rutty road as he followed Jake and Dagger back to their vehicles. The explosion had looked more like an implosion...more smoke than fire. As they rounded the curve they could see a long-legged blonde stretched out on Dagger's motorcycle, short leather skirt hiked just short of being obscene, and a sweater that revealed far more than should be seen in broad daylight.

"I smell a reporter," Robinson growled.

"I'll handle it." Dagger drilled her with a look of disgust. "What do you want, Sheila."

She slithered off the bike and stood on heels definitely not meant for walking on unpaved roads. "Saw some smoke and figured where there's smoke, there's fire. And here you are." She closed the distance between them. "Aren't you going to introduce me to your friends?" Her eyes raked over Jake's body, then suddenly drawn to the welts on his neck. She winced and reached a hand toward the scars. But Jake's hand shot out and grabbed her wrist so fast, Sheila took a step back.

"I've met his wife," Dagger said. "You definitely don't want to try that a second time." Dagger wondered if Sheila had followed him here or if there was a leak in one of the precincts. Sheila had a way of finagling information out of officers with a taste for rich, sexy blondes. "Gentlemen, this is Sheila Monroe from the Daily Herald. Her father is..."

"Leyton Monroe? I know all about him. But as Dagger mentioned, your territory is on the other side of the border."

"We have a long reach and this is unincorporated area. So, Mister..."

"Robinson. Captain Robinson of the Chasen Heights Police Department." He turned to Jake. "And this is Jake Mitchell, a private investigator."

"And why would a P.I. be investigating a murder?"

"Who said anything about a murder?" Robinson asked.

"Oh, I don't know. Maybe the two teens who were here last night and saw a dead body."

Dagger knew Sheila was going to be trouble sticking her nose in this case. "Like many other places in the area, squatters search any vacated premise to find shelter. Jake was hired to find a missing person."

"Really?" Sheila tried to keep her eyes on Jake's face, but the scars kept drawing her attention. "And who's the missing person?"

"Client privilege."

"And the dead guy?"

"Haven't identified him yet," Robinson said. "Place was a meth lab. With it being closed up like that, it's pretty unstable. We barely got close, so you'll have to direct your questions to the DEA."

"Now, if you don't mind, back your car out so we can leave." Dagger made a shooing motion with his hands.

Sheila gave a last look but couldn't see much over the tall brush. One long glance over her shoulder to make sure they were watching, and then she was gone.

"Not sure that was one of your brightest ideas, Dagger," Jake said. "She probably has a contact at the DEA to confirm what did or didn't happen here."

"No worries old man." Dagger clasped a hand on Jake's shoulder. "Sophia already has Sheila's picture and all the phone numbers she uses. If she tries calling any department to confirm anything in this case then her calls will be funneled to someone at AlphaTec."

34

"Like what you've done with the place," Sam said, although she had never stepped inside the Hideaway bar before. "I trust you're a better barman than a pilot."

Stan stopped wiping down the bar and tossed a pained expression her way. "Now Miss Sam, I got you there and back in one piece, didn't I? And you won't find entertainment like that on Southwest or United. Gotta admit, too, the food was much better on my plane."

"Well, there is that."

Sam and Sara took a seat at a long table surrounded by six chairs. A pool table was on the far side of the room and a wide-screen television set hung on another wall. The floor looked as though it had been recently sanded and refinished. However, the typical bar smell of beer and cigarette smoke, which usually lingered long after patrons had departed, were lacking, as if the building were strictly for show.

"Why didn't you two tag along with the men folk?" Suddenly Stan had developed a southern drawl. "Lotta excitement there, I hear."

"Your pipeline is fast and thorough."

"That it is, Miss Sam."

Padre entered the bar and took a seat at the end of the table. He placed a small notepad in front of him having been warned not to type anything into a laptop or iPad. "Got coffee?"

"Coming up. Percolating on the bar. Help yourselves. I'll just go and get the sandwiches out of the fridge. I also have iced tea and water."

"Need help?" Sara offered.

"Thanks, but I'm great at multi-tasking. Remember, I could fly a plane and take a nap at the same time."

The door opened and the remaining members of the meeting entered, bringing with them the hint of smoke.

Paper plates were passed down the table. Stan set a tray on the table with a carafe and cups. Sara appeared with two glasses of iced tea since only the ladies were drinking iced tea. Once the tray of sandwiches appeared, everyone helped themselves.

Dagger studied the sandwich as if expected ground bugs or mold. "Really, Stan? One quarter of a sandwich and you cut the crusts off? What is this, a tea party?"

"I was thinking of the ladies. If you wanted something more manly, I could glue the crusts back on." He waved his hand over the tray with the flourish of a waiter at a five-star restaurant. "I have cucumber and cream cheese, pimento cheese, and for meat lovers there's roast beef and turkey." Stan grabbed one of each and put them on a paper plate before sitting down."

Robinson grabbed four quarters and positioned them on a plate to look like a full sandwich. "Do I hold my pinkie up when I eat it?"

"Could be worse," Padre said. "He could have made Spam sandwiches."

"I love Spam. I'll make it next time."

"Next time, we'll be eating in a restaurant, Stan. Don't want you to put yourself out fixing your favorite meal."

"You had it on the plane, Dagger. "Bet you thought you were eating ham."

"It was ham," Sara said. "Even I could tell the difference just by looking at it."

"Okay, back to basics." Robinson had opened his notepad to the first page. "It would have been nice to examine the trailer before it was destroyed." He directed his comment to Stan who simply shrugged. "Sam wasn't even able to take a look-see. Probably not even worth her time assuming the place was a revolving door of users and suppliers."

"You're probably right, Captain." Sam turned to Dagger. "It would be nice if her Highness would give us a few minutes before carting the body away. I'm sure the victim isn't going anywhere."

"Does she plan for her people to blow up every crime scene?" Jake asked no one in particular. "That alone will make the wrong people curious, like reporters and curiosity seekers."

"No, this was a one-off," Stan replied. "By making it look like Kenny had a meth lab operating out of the trailer, the killer will think he's out of the clear, that no one suspects murder. You can't take Doctor Crane's picture around hotels. If he catches wind, he's gone, and you will lose your chance to catch him. You'll have to get creative now, which I hear you are experts at. I know Dagger is."

"Someone can always go undercover," Jake suggested. "Maybe hit some AA meetings or hang around park benches or outside liquor stores. This guy is picking out his victims from somewhere."

"Right." Stan passed a tray of brownies across the table. "He seems to know his victims' history." He caught another stare from Dagger. "What? Made fresh this morning."

"What about your squirrely friend, Dagger?" Padre asked. "He would make a perfect undercover addict."

Jake groaned. "Really? He's afraid of his own shadow."

"He liked the undercover work he did in our previous case," Sara said. "He spied on that art dealer and Sheila, used his drone insects."

"The son of werewolf case, full moon and all that other shit?" Robinson's bulk shivered at the thought.

"Drone insects?" Sam wasn't sure she heard right.

"Video and audio." Dagger checked his phone. "I'll send him a text."

"I'm sure he has clothes to help him fit him." Jake remembered when they had first met him that his clothes looked off the rack at Goodwill. "We just have to douse him with alcohol."

"We know he doesn't drink with the meds he's on." Dagger sent the text, placed his phone on the table, then headed to the coffee pot. "If I don't hear from him, I'll stop by the shop. He'll want to be paid, I'm sure. The guy's a leach."

"You just need to make it sound like an adventure. And the chance to use his toys are always a plus." Sara grabbed a brownie and passed the tray to Sam.

"And what are Sophia and her people doing while we chase our tails?" Jake directed his question to Stan.

"CCT footage. They are scanning as we speak. Rental car agencies, hotels, shops, restaurants, take outs, plus any clinics, emergency rooms he might hang out at to catch idiots who overdose."

"I'm not sure he would expose himself that way." Sam thought about that for a moment. "He doesn't have time to search for victims, many who live under viaducts or in tents. I think he eavesdrops on conversations, blends in with the addicts in sections of town where they frequent, follows them probably to get a better picture of their lives. Kenny was a pusher whereas the man under the viaduct was an alcoholic. I'm not certain that his victims are random. According to the boys who found the body, Kenny recruited kids to acquire more users. Maybe the doctor saw him recruiting and followed him to see where he lived. What we need is to give Skizzy a background story, create a past that would really make him despicable. Something that would make Skizzy the perfect target."

The door to the Hideaway blasted open and Skizzy rushed in. Hair sprouted in all directions resembling a mad scientist who might lead a tour through Area 51. Dirt and half of what looked like a forest clung to his black clothing. His balaclava was missing revealing a large bruise on his forehead. Skizzy shot a straight line toward Dagger.

He grabbed fistfuls of Dagger's shirt and shook him like a ragdoll. "You gotta help." Coffee spilled as Dagger set his cup down.

"Whoa, slow town." Dagger pried Skizzy's bony fingers from his shirt. He stood back and tried to take in the grime-covered specimen in front of him. "Where the hell have you been?"

"They are back, the drug cartel, and they, they brought a voodoo witch doctor with them. He rose someone from the dead, right in front of my eyes. He's, he's probably from Haiti, or, you know, New Orleans. I saw Midnight in the Garden of Good and Evil. The body just grew from the fog, and I swear it looked right at me." Skizzy brought his voice down to a whisper. His eyes bulged and wobbled more than normal. "He's probably doing a ritual now, you know, with chicken feet, to put a spell on us because we burned up their drugs and money."

"Well, that answers the question of who," Padre said. Dagger had never admitted to Padre that he was anywhere near the warehouse when it exploded.

There were five sets of eyes watching the exchange. Sara slowly rose and walked over to Skizzy. "Have you been skipping your meds?"

Skizzy turned sharply, suddenly aware they weren't alone. "They make me drowsy, Sara. I don't like them."

"Cut them in half. I told you that might work better."

"I know it sounds crazy, Sara. But I saw the body rise right out of the grave, over by the quarry. It was dragging bits of clothing, like, like, you know, what they wrap mummies in. And then there were floating fruits and vegetables."

Jake shook his head in disbelief. "And this is the man you want working undercover for us?"

"Where did you get my medicine?" Skizzy had finally settled down, washed his face and hands, and was now eating the sandwiches Stan had made. Sara had said she helped make them, so he figured they were safe enough to eat. She didn't admit that she had never been in Stan's kitchen other than to grab a knife.

"I saw the extra bottle at your place, Skizzy, and thought I'd hold onto them for fear you were going to flush them down the toilet." Sara used the knife to cut the pills in half. She set a half pill by his plate and ordered him to take it. She watched him finish his sandwich and wash the pill down with water.

"Did you make the brownies?" Skizzy eyed them suspiciously.

"Of course." Sara didn't like lying to Skizzy, but it was the only way to get him to eat.

Padre and Lamon had left to do paperwork, instructing Jake to let them know what the crew planned to do next. They in turn would give them a heads up the next time a suspicious body cropped up.

"So." Jake let that word hang in the air as he studied the bizarre man sitting across from him. "He would probably fit right in hanging around a burning fifty-gallon drum eating dumpster food. Won't even have to change his clothes."

Skizzy jerked his head up, then looked around the table. "You talking about me? I'd never eat dumpster food."

"You obviously didn't have your phone on you this morning." Dagger brought the coffee pot over and filled everyone's cup. He returned the pot to the warmer on the bar and returned to his seat. "We have a job for someone with certain talents for an undercover job." Dagger had barely finished when Skizzy started shaking his head.

"Uh uh. Not with that voodoo witch doctor putting pins in a doll or raising another dead cartel member to hunt me down."

There was silence in the room while Stan cleared the plates and trays and the others tried to think of ways to put Skizzy at ease and make the job sound like an adventure.

"What if Jake and Dagger go to the quarry and check out if there are any uprooted graves while you channel your inner homeless addict in preparation for a little undercover work," Sam suggested. The two men exchanged glares which easily read as what the hell?

Skizzy was still shaking his head.

"Of course," Sara started, "you did such a great job with the gallery owner case you probably will never be able to be that creative again. You blended in so well with a suit, hat, and wire-rimmed glasses. Your laptop gave you a great cover to use your drone bugs. You can probably never be that creative again. Of course, I guess we could wait until Simon comes home…after a few more people are killed."

"Simon? He can't blend in. He's too big to blend in and he looks too normal. No. What do you need me to do?"

35

Doctor Levitt Crane cradled his coffee cup as he studied the people passing by the upscale coffee shop. He sat at a table outside, an umbrella shading the mid-morning sun. His shock at a seven-dollar cup of coffee hadn't yet settled in his mind. Obviously, he had been sequestered far too long with BettaTec where coffee had been free. Even before working for the company, he remembered his father paying only a dollar for coffee, and it didn't taste any different than what passed for coffee today.

Crane set the cup down and took a bite of a salted bagel, something else that used to cost fifty cents. His thoughts turned to Jess. What bothered and confused him was the lack of remorse. It seemed any remnants of a conscience was missing. Was that part of the bio-printing? The young woman hadn't been a supplier or running a meth lab in an empty building. Crane's fury had grown as he watched her disinterest in rehabilitating herself, how getting her next fix was more important to her than her son. And trying to sell her son? That had been the last straw. She had been on his radar, and he had been compelled to give her what she deserved. How? In the past, sympathy would have been his first reaction. Drugs affected each person differently. As a scientist, he knew everyone's brain was wired differently. Some became hooked so quickly and thoroughly it turned into a craving. Others, like white collar workers, took a hit on their break and went right back to work.

Brain...as a scientist, Crane questioned equations and scientific theories, working each out until they made sense. His brain never rested until all the kinks had been worked out of his theories. Now all he thought of was finding his next victim, the next addict that society could do without. His normal personality had taken a holiday.

Crane didn't understand why so many people buzzed around frantically. What was the rush? Who on earth would want to vacation in Chicago? Sure, it had the lakefront beaches, provided they weren't brimming with feces. And high-end restaurants and entertainment were a draw if your credit cards weren't maxed out. What used to be a caution to stay inside after dark was now a whispered not safe during the daylight either. The sightseers and convention goers he witnessed at the hotel, took shuttles to Chicago during the day and returned before the sun went down. Smart people. He pulled a folded piece of paper from his jacket pocket. It had been on the nightstand this morning. Staring down at the unlined sheet of paper, Crane noticed he had been drawing a map. It had neat lines and X's as well as what might be landmarks with initials. What prompted him to draw it? Lately, some of his dreams had been flooded with identical images. Were they someone else's dreams?

The door to his hotel room had been locked and bolted, the privacy card on the outside doorknob. Only one person could have drawn the image, yet Crane didn't remember doing it. What if…? But any thoughts to addressing that question quickly evaporated as a disheveled man hanging onto the light pole drew his attention. The drunk's hair hung in his eyes and past the collar of a ripped jean jacket. Slacks might have once been a light brown but were now so stained it was hard to tell if they were dark brown or tie-dyed. A beard was scraggly and in desperate need of a razon blade. The addict took a step to the left, still hanging onto the light pole with one arm as he purposely reached his hand into a bypasser's jacket. The man recoiled from the derelict and hurried past. The addict or drunk slipped whatever he had stolen into his pocket. When he started to move away from the light pole, Crane folded the paper, stuffed it back in his pocket, and followed.

<h1 style="text-align:center">36</h1>

"Why are we stopping here?" Jake lifted his sunglasses and studied burned out remnants across a field of brush and weeds. "Isn't that the building you did or did not torch?" It was a stab at Dagger's lack of responsibility for destroying the warehouse. "Shouldn't we be examining the area by the building?"

"Skizzy said he parked on this dirt road and walked near the quarry." He studied a rock on the ground covered in a rust-colored stain. "This might be where he fell. Looks like blood."

The quarry was far from any industrial or residential neighborhoods. It was a wonder some developer hadn't purchased the property, filled the quarry, and built housing or a large outlet center. Jake remembered when he was a kid how the house shook when the rock quarry was being blasted with explosives. Pictures would fall off the walls and his father would stagger to the phone to call City Hall, as if they could do anything about it. Now the quarry was a large empty cavern. The fence kept the kids and curiosity seekers out. One could never tell when loose debris might cause a rockslide.

"There was a lot of fog last night. Maybe the fog was playing tricks on Skizzy's eyes." Jake shoved the sunglasses in his pocket and started walking through the brush. They both took their time looking for God knew what…clothes? A makeshift scarecrow that Skizzy mistook as a zombie? Empty beer cans as evidence teens had been in the area?

"Skizzy can have an active imagination and I wouldn't be here if Sara hadn't promised him. We'll just give it a quick walk through and then take a look at those other two buildings."

"Thought you checked them out before you didn't torch the warehouse?"

"All right, already." Dagger shook his head. "So, we sometimes operate below the radar."

"Against the law?"

"It was for a good cause. There were pallets of drugs and money in there. Besides, we made sure there wasn't anyone inside nor was anyone in the area other than the teen guards. Cameras were non-existent. Sara insisted we double and triple check that. Damn, she's like my hidden conscience." Dagger moved to his right, checking the ground for footprints which was impossible. The brush was so thick he couldn't see how anyone could even hide without leaving an imprint of crushed vegetation.

They were halfway to the burnt warehouse when Jake's shoe hit something hard. He looked down and saw a square piece of metal, larger than a manhole cover. Dagger closed the gap and stood next to Jake.

"Looks like a path here through the brush." The crushed underbrush appeared fresh, pushed aside by someone either very heavy or wearing large boots. The disturbed grass had barely bounce back. He bent down to move the tall grass away. Weeds around the edge looked torn or ripped. "What the hell."

They bent down and pried the grass away, revealing a depressed metal pull tab. Jake grabbed it and pulled the metal hatch up revealing a set of stairs into darkness. "Might be a sewer. Maybe Skizzy saw a worker climbing out and with all the fog, it played tricks on his psychotic brain."

Dagger shook his head. "I don't smell water and I see a large concrete floor about fifteen feet down."

"How can you…?" Jake heaved a sigh. "Right. I forgot. Shall we go down?"

"Wait." Dagger turned and put his foot on the first rung. He descended halfway, turned and looked into the darkness, then back up at Jake. "Ceiling lights turned on the moment I stepped on the ladder." He climbed the rest of the way down, then turned and stared down the tunnel. "Pretty sophisticated. Concrete walls and floor, wrapped pallets as far as the eye can see."

Jake climbed down the stairs and joined Dagger. "Hell, looks like one of those tunnels the cartel would dig. Wonder how long it's been here." There were cracks in the walls, but he couldn't see any water leaks. Overhead tube lighting brightened the tunnel which appeared to have no end in sight. "What do you think? It's been here less than five years?"

Dagger's response was interrupted by a loud bang as the hatch crashed shut and the lights went out. For Dagger, though, it wasn't dark. All he had to do was think it and his night vision kicked in. To him the lights were still on.

"I certainly hope that was the wind that closed the door instead of unwanted company." He walked back to the ladder and climbed up. Dagger looked for a latch or handle but all he found was a keyhole. He shoved at the door, but it wouldn't budge. He paused for a few seconds while he listened for footsteps, voices. Only silence. "Well, there must be a door at the end of the tunnel. They certainly didn't drop these pallets down the hatch entrance." He walked back and passed Jake who appeared to be doing some deep breathing. Dagger pulled at the shrink wrap which covered the boxes stacked on a pallet. Jake's breathing deepened. Dagger glanced his way and saw beads of sweat trailing down the side of Jake's face. He couldn't avoid giving Jake's neck a passing glance. He remembered how Jake had been kept in darkness after being kidnapped; and even after returning to work, could not bring himself to enter dark buildings, much less tunnels. "Do you have your phone on you?"

"Left it in the car."

Dagger dug his phone from his pocket, turned the flashlight app on, and handed his phone to Jake. "Take a picture of the skid while I open one of these boxes. If the products are hidden down here, they can't be anything legal."

The box wasn't taped shut. He opened the flaps and found a plastic bag filled with small blue plastic containers. He lifted the bag and turned it around. "Looks like there's some kind of powder in each of these."

Jake shined the light on the bag. The containers weren't much larger than a pencil eraser. "Those are trash cans. Heard about these a year ago. They fill them with drugs."

"Fentanyl?"

"Anything. Could be Xylazine, which is a horse tranquilizer."

"I don't think they are ready for primetime. No shipping labels if this is a distribution point."

Jake snapped a picture of the bag. "Question is, why are they storing them here and in the warehouse?"

Dagger thought about the ones they had destroyed. "These are different from the ones in the warehouse. Those were pills in different colors. Almost looked like candies for a Pez dispenser. Perfect to tempt kids."

"Maybe wherever this tunnel leads is where they do the packaging and shipping." Jake aimed the flashlight down the tunnel, but the beam didn't go farther than the length of four skids. "Maybe we can see where the tunnel ends as long as we know we have a way out of here."

The tunnel ended up being less than one hundred yards long. At the end was a metal door, wide enough to be a freight elevator. Dagger pushed a large red button. "Here goes nothing." The door screamed open. Jake was relieved to see the bright overhead lights in the elevator. He turned the phone's flashlight off and handed the phone back to Dagger.

The elevator shook as it climbed slowly, then came to a stomach-clenching stop. The door automatically raised. First, they saw two sets of legs. Then they saw the guns. Although they had left their weapons in the Lincoln, Dagger did have a spare gun strapped to his ankle, but he didn't have time to grab it.

"Ah, mi amigos, welcome. Nuh uh. Don't even think about it." The bulky man had a tattoo of a spider on his neck. His partner couldn't have weighed more than eighty pounds. The gun he held looked too large for him to handle. Spider waved them out of the elevator with the sawed-off shotgun he held. "First floor furniture, home furnishing, kitchen and bath accessories."

"I actually wanted the second floor," Dagger quipped.

"We were checking out toiletries and medicines on the lower level," Jake added.

"Ah, Benji, we have comedians here."

"Yeh, real funny."

Dagger noticed the kid's Jamaican accent, but the man could probably be the fourth man on DEA's radar. He gave a cursory examination of the warehouse. Other than stacks of empty pallets and a pallet jack, the building hadn't seen activity in decades, probably since the quarry closed. The odor of oil, dirt and mold filled the air. Walls were pitted and dirty and windows had been bricked up.

"Your bosses know you're stealing their product?" Jake's question only elicited a slight smile on Spider's face. "Or do you have a side business going?"

"Where's the money?" The Jamaican voice didn't fit the choir boy face. It dripped of menace and danger.

It was Dagger's turn to smile. "I've got about twenty bucks on me. Was there a candy bar you wanted?" The skinny legs came flying faster than Dagger could react. It rammed his solar plexus and sent his sprawling. Before Jake could react, something solid hit the back of his head. Lights out.

37

I know a lot of work needs to be done because of the fire. The water damage is more excessive than the fire damage, but that is why the price is so low."

Jill Wagner couldn't wait to get the fifty-pound gorilla off her back. The building was an eye sore and a realtor's nightmare. "This is a prime location just perfect for your business. The locals would finally have a pharmacy within walking distance." She silently hoped those future customers would be packing heat.

She unlocked the door and ushered in the two men, Paul Moser and his son, Paul Junior. A father and son business was perfect. Jill had quickly determined that the son had the enthusiasm and the father held the purse strings. Both were pharmacists and had moved from Iowa several months after the death of Paul Senior's wife. While Junior exuded passion and fire before she had even unlocked the door, it was Senior who had checked the structure of the building, the gutters, the cracked sidewalk and was mentally tallying up the costs of improvements. She hated to think of what Senior would say about the melted floor tiles, poor wiring, and crumbling drop ceiling. I'm getting too old for this, she thought. Selling high end residential buildings was so much more lucrative. Why did she have to come out of retirement? Gardening and her bridge club were enjoyable. But keeping up with the country club ladies had become expensive. Had she really needed a ruby chain to tether her reading glasses? And her dead husband's five-year-old Lincoln was still in good condition. There wasn't a need to trade it in for a Lexus convertible.

The stale odor interrupted her thoughts as she closed the door and forced a smile. "With a little paint, new tile, and a good carpenter, this place will look like new."

"A little paint?" Senior huffed. "And what's with the food bags, trash and that horrible odor? Has someone been using this place as a bathroom?"

Jill waved a hand in front of her face. Damn, I should have checked this building out first before showing it, she thought with a sigh. "Unfortunately, any vacant building, especially one vacated as long as this one has been, does have vandals and teen partying. The police have chased them out and we've cleaned the place up. Then another string of vandalism occurs. We always feel bad calling the police out on a weekly basis. You know how that goes."

By the look on Senior's face, he obviously didn't know. His watchful eye was taking in the bloated ceiling and rotting baseboards, probably calculating how much the repairs would cost. Junior had stars in his eyes, imagining raised ceilings, marble counters and oak flooring.

"Let's check the backroom. It affords generous space for offices, storage, and a work room for compounding. Did you plan on doing compounding?"

"Yes." Junior's eyes smiled as he continued to imagine palatial surroundings and wall-to-wall customers. They were matching bookends…same height, same features, although Senior was growing a paunch and losing some hair. Maybe not the same features. While Junior was bright eyed and bushy-tailed, Senior was dour and suspicious.

Jill led them through the doorway and listened closely for footsteps following and not bolting for the exit. It wasn't the signs scattered around the room or hole in the ceiling which had allowed rain to collect and rot the floor that drew her attention. The footsteps behind her came to an abrupt halt. The next sound was Jill's blood curdling scream as her eyes took in the gray, lifeless body leaning against the wall.

Senior drilled his son with a scornful glare. "Now I'm sure we can negotiate a better price."

<h1 style="text-align:center">38</h1>

"Do you think he'll be okay?" Sam didn't know Skizzy that well so she would have to trust Sara that they weren't doing the poor man's psyche more harm.

"Trust me. I've never seen him more excited. He's a born actor."

"If you say so." Sam had parked her Jeep behind the berm, as Sara had suggested. She had originally planned to drive Sara home until they realized neither had been able to reach Jake or Dagger by phone. Since the quarry was where the men had been headed, Sam decided to take a quick run by the area to see if Dagger's Lincoln was there.

"I don't see Dagger's car." Sam knew it was unlike Jake not to answer a text or phone call. Even when he used to work in Homicide, he would at least rattle off a quick text response if he was busy on a case.

"The auto tracker says he's parked nearby. I think it's behind that tree by the gravel road."

The city fathers and citizens had always wondered why every building hadn't been demolished after the quarry closed. Cinderblock walls were crumbling, windows were broken, and frames rusted. Although the area was off the beaten path, it was still an eyesore and open to nefarious activities.

The door on the first building had a rusted padlock. Not unusual if they wanted to discourage vagrants and thrill-seeking teenagers. Sara leaned close to the door. "There isn't anyone inside." She headed to the next building leaving a puzzled Sam. How did Sara know the building was empty? The men could be unconscious or trapped by fallen debris. Sam hurried to catch up.

The next building was in better shape. At least the windows weren't broken. Matter of fact, they looked rather new and had bars on the outside. The padlock on the door was also new and sturdy. Sara put her ear to the door. "They're in here."

"How do you know?"

Sara shrugged and pulled on the lock. "Do you have a crowbar in the Jeep?"

"Don't need one." Sam reached in her pocket and pulled out a key. After working it in, Sam turned the key and the padlock was opened. She held up the key. "Never leave home without one. It's a bump key. Will open any lock."

"Wow. I want one of those."

Sam handed it to Sara. "I have more at home."

They entered the warehouse to find the men struggling to get out of the ropes tying them to chairs. They approached slowly, not sure if anyone was lying in wait, wishing they hadn't left their guns locked in the Jeep.

Sara stopped and tilted her head. "We're alone."

"What happened?" Sam checked Jake's head. Blood was trickling down the back of his head. Other than appearing groggy, there didn't seem to be any other injuries.

"Damn, I need an aspirin or three."

Dagger didn't look much better. "How about you get these ropes off of us and we'll tell you."

The women untied the ropes tethering them together around their chests and then worked on their ankles. "How did this happen?" Sam asked.

"We wouldn't be in this situation if lardass hadn't left his gun back in the Lincoln."

"You're going to go with that?" Jake touched the back of his head and winced. "If my memory is correct, you're the one who let a pipsqueak of a kid dropkick you to the floor."

"Wait. What kid? Who else was here?" Sara asked. "Would you start at the beginning?"

"You tell them, Jake. I need to call Padre." Dagger pulled out his phone and called the detective.

As Jake gave the women a tour of the tunnel, Dagger filled Padre in on the drugs, Spider and the young Jamaican arsonist called Benji. "I'm not sure what kind of car he was driving. We didn't see any vehicles near the quarry when Jake and I arrived. They could have been riding a motorcycle as far as I know. We were a little incapacitated." After Padre informed him that he would bring the DEA agents with him to the quarry, Dagger hung up the phone.

"That's a lot of drugs," Sam said as they emerged from the elevator.

"So Skizzy was right about some zombie climbing out of a grave," Sara said.

"I just hope he wasn't right about the dancing fruits and vegetables. Don't know how that can be explained." Dagger led them out of the warehouse where they waited for Padre and the agents to arrive.

"They certainly had an elaborate operation. How long do you think it took them to dig that tunnel?" Sam's attention was drawn to a swirl of dried leaves dancing several yards from the warehouse door. The leaves appeared to dance in one place before taking off past the warehouse door, spinning in place for a few seconds as though waiting to get Sam's attention.

"Concrete looks rather recent and it was sealed well. I didn't notice any rain seepage," Jake said.

A chill crawled up Sam's spine and clung there. She slowly followed the leaves.

"Sam, where are you going?" Sara asked.

"I'm following the leaves."

"What?" Sara turned to Jake.

"Doesn't mean anything good." Jake followed Sam to the back of the building. Broken pallets and rusted metal littered the ground. The berm rose forty yards behind the warehouse, but it was a large patch of disturbed ground where they found Sam standing. The cyclone of leaves danced and swirled before scattering over what looked like a recent grave.

She bent down and touched the dirt. With eyes closed she took a deep breath, then slowly stood. "There are two bodies here."

"You're kidding." Dagger stared with disbelief at Jake.

"We need to look for shovels. I think I saw some in the warehouse." Jake turned and walked back to the entrance.

"Never a dull moment with you, Dagger." Padre jammed his fists at his waist and shook his head. The bodies hadn't been buried deep nor that long ago.

"Don't look at me. Sam's the culprit here."

"She was just doin' what she does best," Robinson chimed in.

"So, anyone know who they are?" Jake directed his question to Dagger. "You seem to be the expert on this area. Maybe you saw them on a previous mission."

"Yeah, yeah. That's getting old. Yes, I know them. They were guarding the warehouse that night. Took off after the explosion." Dagger didn't think the two boys were more than eighteen or nineteen years old. "Obviously, Spider and his crew weren't happy after the warehouse blew up on their watch."

Dagger had given the two cops a tour of the tunnel. Padre had arrived with two beat cops and a cadre of DEA agents. Within minutes beat cops had cordoned off the area and the agents were waiting for a couple DEA trucks and crew to remove the contents of the tunnel.

"Oh, and I saw your favorite reporter pull up, Dagger. One of the beat boys is doing a half-ass job of holding her back."

"Thanks for the heads up, Padre."

Robinson's phone rang. He stepped aside to answer the call. "Where at?"

Jake and Sam exchanged looks. They knew that tone in the captain's voice.

"We've got a body. Looks like an overdose. Realtor was showing the old Boyle Realty building to prospective buyers."

"We know where it's at," Jake said as he turned to Sam. "You and Sara meet us there. I think we've left this place in good hands and they will be here for hours."

"I'll wait for the medical examiner. You follow them, Lamon. Maybe you can make sure the boys in black wait this time before carting the body away."

39

"A realtor was doing a walk-through with potential buyers when they found her. They have already given the responding officer a statement."

"Hey, give us a minute this time," Dagger barked at an AlphaTec minion in black crime scene attire. Robinson had been several minutes ahead of the men in black having kept knowledge of drug overdoses to a small circle of police, namely, him and Padre. The black van was parked outside the back door while two more men in black were wheeling in a gurney.

"She's so young, I think." Sam could only tell by her size and taunt skin. It was the victim's face that was deceiving. Dark circles around sunken eyes, hair lifeless and dirty, all added years to her age.

"I think I know her." Robinson did a deep dive into his memory bank, then snapped his fingers. "Jess something. That's it. She has a son and mother. Been arrested before." Robinson looked at the men in black as they hovered over Jess. "Her mother will want to bury her. You can't take her body before we get a positive I.D."

Three black hooded men turned in unison to Dagger. "Take it up with the boss."

"What about her necklace?" Sam pointed at the J initial. It was on a beaded chain with smaller beads forming the letter J. It looked handmade. "Maybe her mother can I.D. her necklace."

Robinson rubbed his chin. "What if she wants to see her daughter?"

"There's an option, Captain," Jake said. "You don't have to tell her mother she was found here. Say she was found in the woods and animals had gotten to her. I don't think any mother would want to see her child in that condition."

"Yeah, guess that would work." He looked at each of his makeshift group of detectives for agreement. One of the black clad men removed the necklace and handed it to Robinson. With a quick nod he signaled the AlphaTec crew to take the body.

The five of them stood back in silence as Jess was bagged up and hauled out like a sack of garbage. Sara heaved a sigh. "I thought Mother would have taught her people to have a little respect for the dead." The back door slammed shut, the sound echoing through the empty building.

Jake asked, "What about the witnesses, Captain? The realtor was showing the building to two men. So that's three people who saw the body here, not in the woods."

"I'm good at giving sketchy details to the press." Robinson turned back to the group. "Okay, have a look around the place. Maybe the good doc left a clue to his hotel or a list of the next victims on his agenda."

Dagger and Sara headed for the front of the building. Jake and Sam stayed in the back room where the body had been found. Robinson opened the back door assuming the good doc had entered from the isolated area. Within twenty minutes they all assembled in the back room.

"I've seen enough garbage and stains to ruin my dinner," Dagger said. "He's too smart to leave any clues, picks his victims randomly and takes the time to study them."

"But that doesn't explain how his victims trust him. There's never a sign of a struggle. Kenny let him into his trailer. Jess didn't try to run away. The drunk under the viaduct shared a bottle of whiskey with him…we all assumed."

"Or the doc gifted him a bottle of whiskey laced with drugs, Captain," Jake said. "Maybe he offered Jess drugs. And Kenny could have thought Crane was a customer looking to buy pot."

"What do you think, Sam?" Robinson asked.

But Sam's attention was drawn to a rotting baseboard where a light appeared to flicker. The sun was coming through the grimy windows but not in that part of the room. She followed the flickering beam.

"Sam?" Robinson called after her. "Jake, tell me this isn't what I think it is."

Sam stooped down and picked up what looked like a pen. The label said it was a permanent black marker, thin point. She stood, turned, and held the pen tightly.

Dagger started to say something but Jake raised his hand. Sam smiled, finally a clue. "He's a priest."

"What?" Sara said.

"The killer. I mean he dresses as a priest. He's wearing a collar when he approaches. That's how they trust him." She held up the pen. "Guess his marker ran out of ink."

40

Skizzy wandered one of the more populated skid row streets, getting the lay of the land. Food pantries, magazines and sundries, coffee shop and liquor store were some of the various snatch and grab shops posing as backdrops to the ill-forgotten stumbling around like the walking dead.

He leaned against the crumbling brick wall of the magazine store, patted his jacket pocket to make sure his bottle was still there, then pulled his cap down low to hide most of his face. His hair, relieved of its rubber band, hung past his collar.

How soon until he was one of the unfortunates roaming the streets begging for change, hoping he wasn't mugged, beaten, and left for dead in a dark alley? Walking these streets made Skizzy realize how much better off he was. He had a business, a roof over his head, money, most of which wasn't from his legal business, and a handful of friends who pounded him over the head if he didn't take his meds. The unfortunates out here, though, were more interested in their next fix or bottle. How many could lead half-way decent lives if they would just seek help, whether psychological or for substance abuse? How many didn't want to change? They had passed the point of no return.

A man stepped out of the storefront next to the magazine store. He wore a white shirt, black slacks, and a priest's collar. Skizzy stared at him for a few beats, then noticed the sign in front of the window announcing a group meeting tomorrow night. The priest noticed him staring and smiled. "Come tomorrow night, my friend. We welcome all who are suffering from the devil's temptations...drugs, alcohol, anger issues."

Skizzy's response was interrupted by the rumbling of a motorcycle. As it growled past, he noticed the Jamaican kid clutching the back of the driver. And was that a spider tattoo on the driver's neck? Spider parked the motorcycle just past the liquor store near a food truck serving something burning the air with hot flaming spices. Skizzy fumbled in his pocket for his phone and called Dagger.

"Now what?"

"Well, that's a fine howdy do, seeing as I'm doing your spy work."

"Sorry Skizzy. We just found the bodies of those two teens who were guarding the warehouse. And we found your walking zombie. There's a trap door in the ground near where you fell. It leads to a tunnel where someone was secreting skids of illegal drugs, probably stealing the drugs to start his own business. Jake and I were caught by some Jamaican kid and…"

"And a guy with a spider tattoo on his neck? The guy and the arsonist kid just rode in on a motorcycle." Skizzy told Dagger his location.

"I'll tell Padre. Oh, by the way, we haven't found the dancing fruits and vegetables." Dagger hung up before Skizzy could respond.

It didn't take long. Skizzy could smell an unmarked squad car a mile away. Spider and the baby arsonist were sitting on a bench eating sandwiches from the food truck, too busy talking to notice the two men casually approaching from behind the bench. Before they could take another bite, a tight grip squeezed each of their shoulders as a patrol car skidded to a halt, lights blazing, but siren silent. He heard one of the cops say, "Sorry boys, lunch is over."

Skizzy fled while the agents did their thing. Hopefully, those were the last of the spider gang left to harass him. He headed toward a dented truck parked down the street. Although his fleet of cars and trucks were in excellent condition, he kept beat up junks which deterred most car jackers.

There was a small section of Cedar Point which catered to visitors. It was close to high-end hotels known for business conferences, sports conventions, as well as little known out-of-the-way meeting places for political back-room dealings and afternoon trysts. Not long after the hotels opened, various shops and restaurants peppered the streets. High-end clothing stores, flower shops, coffee emporiums. Restaurants catered to whatever fad food was in fashion for the month, as well as bakeries serving goodies from all corners of the world.

Skizzy found a small table outside of a coffee shop and took a seat. Gradually he noticed some patrons moving away from him. So, he wasn't dressed high-end enough. Bite me, Skizzy thought. He had dressed the part of a homeless drunk to blend in with the other side of town. This side of town obviously didn't like rubbing elbows with the likes of him. They should see him later tonight after he douses himself with whiskey and staggers like that Cajun zombie. He picked up a menu and studied it. "Seven dollars for a cup of coffee?" he blurted, forgetting he wasn't alone at the sidewalk café littered with tables and patrons.

"Really? Since when does Dagger let you out of your cage?"

"Oh, shit." Cripes, did I say that out loud? Of all people to run into, it had to be Dagger's crazy ex-fiancée, Sheila Monroe.

Sheila pulled a napkin from the container on the table and wiped the chair before sitting down. Couldn't let a smudge of dirt stain her white leather skirt. She flicked the napkin onto the table and took a seat.

"If you're buying, I'll have a cup of something. Can't tell what the hell is in all these fancy names."

With a flick of her finger, a waiter came over and greeted Sheila, avoiding Skizzy, probably hoping he would get the hint. "Miss Monroe, what can I get you."

"My friend and I would like two mocha cappuccinos, Claude. Oh, and see if there are any eclairs left. I'd like one." When Claude dragged his gaze to Skizzy and grimaced, Sheila added, "Can't tell a book by its cover, sweetie. Don't you remember Howard Hughes?" Claude had a blank stare. "Forget it. You're too young."

"Hughes was a head case," Skizzy said as Claude retreated into the coffee shop.

"And your point?" Sheila leaned back, arms folded over a glittering handbag. She gave Skizzy another cursory examination. "So, what on earth are you doing on this side of town out in public, and at Cafe and Pasticcino, of all places."

Skizzy said nothing.

"Oh my god. Dagger has you working on something, doesn't he?"

"Why is he the first person you think of when you see me? Dagger doesn't run my life."

"You don't even run your life. You never leave your junk store."

"High-end antiquities."

"Whatever."

Claude appeared with a tray and distributed the cups of foamy coffee, then set the eclair adorned on a doily-laced plate, in front of Sheila. She handed him thirty dollars and told him to keep the change.

"Thirty dollars? What the hell is in this stuff?" Skizzy studied the cup where a smiley face started to materialize in the foam. "They charge for artwork?"

"You obviously haven't been on this side of town before. So, what does Dagger have you working on? Does this have anything to do with the recent bodies dropping all over town?"

Oh shit, shit, shit. How does she do that? "I will have you know it's about me. Three guys were trying to break into my shop looking for guns. Little did I know the DEA was also looking for them." Skizzy leaned across the table and whispered, "But there was a fourth guy and I happened to see him on Vagrant Alley stopping at a food truck. I called Padre, he called some agents, and I headed back to the shop. Thought I'd stop for coffee first."

"Here? At the most expensive coffee shop in town? And since when do you eat, much less drink, out in public?"

"I didn't know it would cost me a week's pay. Oh, and thanks for buying."

Sheila sipped her coffee as she studied Skizzy. Jittery as hell, fingers scratching at his hands, legs bouncing. She would normally consider this a sign of lying or fudging the facts, but she knew Skizzy's history, or at least knew this was classic Skizzy. She also knew the coffee cup would never cross his lips. Someone in the café might be poisoning him.

"Sooooo…what's Dagger up to these days?"

Skizzy glanced at nearby tables for nosy people. Most were enjoying pastries and over-charged lattes, surprisingly ignoring him since Sheila had arrived. He leaned over and whispered, "They found two bodies this morning by the quarry…cartel people. That couple working with Dagger, the wife, boy is she weird. Anyway, I hear she found them just by…"

"Hearing the dead speak? Yes, I read about her. A little far-fetched, I'd say. But what was Dagger doing by the quarry this morning? I'm surprised he crawled out of his coffin during daylight."

"I did some investigating there last night," he whispered, ignoring her sarcasm. "Saw a zombie crawling out of the fog. Raised by some witchdoctor, I'm sure." His gaze dropped to the smiley face. How long does the image last? Does he have to take a sip before it disintegrates? Skizzy raised his head to see one well-formed eyebrow raised in skepticism. He knew that look. Skizzy was a basket case, needed to be put away.

"A zombie?"

"Saw it, I swear. Tripped and fell trying to run away." He touched the bruised bump on his forehead. "Got this for my troubles. When I woke up, it was daylight. Sara offered to have Dagger check into it."

Sheila winced at the mention of Sara's name. "Of course, he did what he was ordered."

Skizzy ignored her. "But he didn't find the dancing fruits and vegetables." His eyes took on a glaze as the smiley face appeared to place him in a trance.

Sheila snapped her fingers. "Are you still in this world? I didn't see anything this morning. I only heard about the large tunnel with pallets of drugs."

"That was the guy the agents caught on vagrant alley. Spider tattoo number four and a Jamaican baby arsonist."

Sheila closed her eyes and inhaled deeply. Skizzy expected her to break out in a yoga pose to center her inner feng shui. She finally opened her eyes. "I should have known it would be useless to talk to you."

"Well hidey ho. No one told you to sit down. Just minding my own business, sitting here catching rays."

"Are you going to drink that?" She slid Skizzy's cup over. "Of course not."

41

May Haslen wiped her eyes with a tissue. The beaded necklace sat on the coffee table while Captain Robinson watched May intently, his hands folded as if in prayer. He actually was praying, though, praying that May wouldn't ask to see the body even if it had been ravaged by animals, as Robinson had told her. Matty clung to his grandmother's arm, afraid of perhaps being pulled away and returned to his mother.

"Jess made that necklace one of the many times she had been in rehab. Christ, that place was just as bad as being out on the street. The addicts in there could still get just about any drug they wanted. Friends brought them in when they visited. Oh, they were clever in how they hid them...under eye makeup containers, ribbons tying gift baskets. All they did was glue two ribbons together but in between were hidden flat candies like those thin breath strips. Staff was none the wiser." She paused while she stroked Matty's back. "You'll be staying here for good, sweetheart."

"If I remember correctly, you are a bookkeeper for one of the home insurance companies."

May appeared on guard and hugged Matty a bit tighter. "I can still care for him even though I work full time. There are great day cares and I have neighbors who love to watch Matty if I need to work late."

"Oh, I'm not insinuating anything, Miss Haslen. Anything but. Just that there are local agencies who can help financially if you need it."

May breathed an obvious sigh of relief. "No need for that. I took out a life insurance policy on Jess after Matty was born. After Jess's third stint in rehab, I knew she had no plans to straighten out her life and would one day end up like she did." She swiped at her nose again.

"Do you know who the father is who might cause trouble if you gain guardianship?"

"I have no idea and I don't think Jess did either."

So far, so good, Robinson thought. May had not asked to see Jess's body. "What about where she lived besides the..."

"Besides alleys and boarded up shops you mean? She had a singlewide I had purchased for her and Matty. It was in a trailer park on Highland Street. I probably should put a for sale sign on it, maybe put it in the paper. Why?" Another flash of suspicion crossed May's face. "You aren't going to see if she has information on the father in there, are you?"

"No, no. Just like to get an idea of who she might have hung around with, perhaps gave her tainted drugs. People are buying drugs online these days not realizing they are laced with fentanyl. Over one hundred thousand people died last year from overdoses, all attributed to fentanyl. If we can give any clue to the DEA on where they are coming from, we might be able to save some lives, even if we couldn't save Jess's."

Another sigh of relief from across the coffee table. "Stay here, Matty. Grammy will be right back." May turned to the captain. "I have a set of keys to her trailer. Hate to think what condition it's in. I'm sure drug dealers have stripped the place clean." She returned one minute later and handed Robinson the keys.

"Thank you. I'll get the keys back to you later this week."

Outside Lamon Robinson breathed a sigh of relief. He placed a call to Sam. "Hey, witchy woman, are you free to meet me at Jess's abode?"

"Oh my. You sure this is a place where someone lived?"

Robinson scratched his head as he stood on the top stair of the singlewide. The trailer shifted a bit from his weight. "I warned you, Sam. May Haslen said drug dealers might have stripped the place clean trying to retrieve some of the drug money Jess owed."

The singlewide was like a showroom model waiting for the furniture to be delivered. The microwave had been ripped from the wall, as well as what might have been a table and sleeper as remnants of a brace was hanging from the wall. The living area had been stripped of furniture, maybe even a television set. The back bedroom lacked a bed or dresser.

Sam opened a drawer in the kitchen. She had yet to find silverware, plates, or even pots and pans. If Jess had a checkbook or credit cards, Sam didn't find any in the drawers. "If Jess received bills, they must have been sent directly to her mother because I can't find any receipts or overdue bills."

"May is going to put the place up for sale but I don't know how she's going to furnish it. Don't they put the furnishings in before putting the trailer walls around it?" Which made him wonder how they got the furnishings out.

"I think they do that with motor homes but haven't a clue about single or doublewides." Sam grabbed a framed photo of Jess and her son, the broken glass distorting their features. In her other hand she held the permanent marker she had found in the real estate building where Jess's body had been found.

"Anything?"

Sam shook her head. "Crane was never here, and I don't think Jess has been here in months. Dragging her son from boarded up buildings to tents on the sidewalks is pitiful. She definitely doesn't deserve the best parent award."

They exited the trailer and locked up. The structure appeared to sigh when Robinson's weight finally eased off the stair.

"Well, well. I hope that little lady is moving."

They turned to find a rotund woman, hands jammed at an area which previously might have been a waist, and three children in stairstep ages clinging to her legs. Her dark eyes smiled above caramel-colored cheeks.

Robinson parted his jacket to reveal his badge. "Did you know the woman who lived here, Miss?"

Her eyes widened at the sight of the badge. "Cornelia, but you can call me Coozie. It's a nickname because I'm kinda' shaped like a beer coozie." She let out a loud whoop as the two girls and one boy giggled in unison."

Sam smiled. "Did you know Jess Hazlen?"

Her arm shot out in a pushing motion. "Oh, baby. Who don't know that woman. Did she have problems. Men comin' around at all hours, that little boy of hers stuck outside while she did God knows what in that trailer. Sometimes there'd be hollerin' and screams. Other time that trailer would be rockin. Didn't matter what time. That boy, I'd come out and take him over to my trailer so he didn't have to sit out in the dark."

"Ever hear anyone threaten her?" Robinson checked the trailer forty yards away. He could only assume it was Coozie's since it was the closest. It looked well kept. AstroTurf for grass prevented the need for a mower. A shed off to the side probably stored toys and bikes out of site. Potted flowers and even a tomato plant were lush.

"Who didn't, baby?" Coozie shook her head of short black coils. "If she wasn't trading her ..." she looked down at the three toddlers ... "talents for goodies, then she was trying to keep dealers from taking whatever they could get their hands on to sell. She be yellin' she would kill them. They be yellin' back, not if I kill you first." She reached down and patted the older girl's head. Eight braids stuck out in all directions, pastel bows tied on each. Coozie looked up sharply. "Wait. Did something happen to Jess?"

Robinson sighed. "Overdose. Probably fentanyl, which is why we are trying to find out if one of the dealers was passing on tainted drugs."

"Oh, dear Lord. That poor child. What about Matty? That cute thing, all alone."

"Jess's mother has him. Matty will be living with her now."

Coozie's head shook from side to side. "He used to play with my grandkids. So shy, and so thin. Tried to fatten that little boy up. But I wishin' I could help you with names or descriptions. I never went outside when men arrived, never saw make of car or truck. Voices were all types...white, Black, Hispanic. I have the little ones here, so I kept the lights off and shades closed."

"But you went outside to grab Matty, didn't you?"

"Yes sir, but that was when she was having the boyfriend of the hour over. The dealers didn't park nearby. I only knew they was trouble by the way they pounded on the door and yelling for her to open up now or they'd kick the GD door in. Once they forced their way in, they weren't letting the boy out so I can only think Jess hid him in the bathroom."

"Is there a lot of crime here?" Sam nodded toward the toddlers. It wouldn't be safe to raise kids if there were meth labs and robberies taking place every day.

"Mostly elderly here and people like me. No pension, small social security. Trailer is paid for. These little ones are my daughter's. She used to live in Chicago. Husband was a Chicago police officer. Got ambushed on the nightshift, shot in the head two years ago. Died right there on the spot trying to answer a domestic call. He and his partner didn't even have time to open their car doors. Chicago is not a safe place to raise kids. They had some money saved, a bit of survivor benefits. But I wanted Charlene, my daughter, to finish nursing school. So, they moved in. Got them out of that crime-ridden city. We have security here in this park. Jess had been given two notices to move. She was bringing unwanted crime into our peaceful haven."

Robinson handed her a business card. "Thank you for the information, Coozie."

"You tell Jess's mom that Matty can come over and play any time."
"I'll do that."

42

In Chasen Heights, Illinois, the hooting of an owl bled through the screened patio door. Sam hadn't slept peacefully since returning from Hilton Head. One night she could swear she heard whispers and something tugging at the blankets. She dismissed it as REM sleep. Tonight was different. She could hear the owl so knew she wasn't completely asleep. Then the covers started moving, or were they? Was it her imagination that she felt fingers on her leg? Slowly, she lifted her head. Moonlight sprayed across the bed, shining a light on a bony hand pulling its way onto the bed. Trailing behind it was an arm bone. A partial head peered over the foot of the bed, one empty eye socket. The body parts from the beach had followed her home. She slowly pulled back the covers and fled the room.

"Shhh. I have water for you." Dillon whimpered as Sam finished changing his diaper. "Take a drink." The toddler sat up and lifted the sippy cup. He handed it back to Sam, then raised his arms.

Sam was dressed in an oversized Bears tee shirt that hit her mid-thigh. She detested pajamas, even the shorties. The shirt was a little worn so when Jake had purchased a new one, she grabbed his old one.

The bay window was her favorite place to cuddle Dillon when he would awaken in the middle of the night. They would stare up at the ceiling where glow-in-the-dark stars formed the constellations. Jake had taught Dillon constellation names, not that he could repeat any of them yet.

A decorative railing bordered the outside of the window. She felt safe in Dillon's room. Once she had moved from her bed, the body parts had faded. "We weren't done." The same words she had heard on the beach. They weren't done with what? Killing humanity? Creating destructive weapons? And why bother her? She's not the one who blew up their research ship. No, but she was the one who had disturbed them.

Dillon reached up and patted Sam's chin. "Not sleepy either?" He breathed deeply as she held him close. A movement outside the window caught her attention. A hawk had landed on the railing. It cocked its head and studied them with human intellect. How strange, Sam thought. Hawks don't have turquoise-colored eyes.

Dillon raised a chubby arm and pointed. "See-See."

A chill crawled up Sam's spine as she watched the hawk leap from the railing and swoop out of sight. Dillon continued pointing. "See-See, where go?"

Why did Dillon say Sara's name? Did he notice that the hawk's eyes were the same color as Sara's? And how did Sara hear through the warehouse door? And the night she spent in the teepee with Abby and Alex. She didn't have clothes or shoes, not even a car. How did she get to Chasen Heights?

Of course, she flew, a voice in her head said. The chill spread over her body as she carried the sleeping toddler and placed him back in the crib. Sam crept down the hallway and stood outside Abby's bedroom. One small night light was in the outlet by a wardrobe cabinet. Thoughts of her childhood on the reservation flooded back. Elders would tell children stories of shapeshifters. If they were bad, shapeshifters would drag them from their beds into the woods never to be seen again. And if you were really bad, they would change you into an animal and you would never be able to change back.

Elders believed shapeshifters could shift into animal forms to harm and destroy their enemies. As Sam reached her teens, she shook off these stories as nothing more than tactics to give kids nightmares and force them to be good. But wasn't there always a kernel of truth to myths?

Abby's back was to the door as Sam crept around the bed and slowly sat down. Her mother stirred, then opened her eyes. "Samantha? Is everything okay? Is Dillon sick?"

"He's fine. I just had a question."

Abby raised herself up on one elbow and studied the clock on the nightstand. Abby's hair hung down her back in one long braid. "At three o-clock in the morning?"

Sam took a deep breath. How crazy was this going to sound? "Were the stories about shapeshifters true? The ones told to us as children?"

"Stories?" Abby slowly sat up.

"Shapeshifters, they would drag disobedient children into the woods at night and leave them there. Was any of it true?"

Abby gave a slight laugh. "Of course not. Do you know of any friends who disappeared?"

"No, but were the shapeshifters true? Isn't there a bit of truth buried in every myth?"

"There were also stories of good shapeshifters, those who protected and healed their people. The stories were nothing more than today's bogeyman or monsters under the bed. I would say those stories worked."

Abby smiled weakly. Just tired, Sam thought, or something else? Abby had always been truthful or would change the subject if it were a question she didn't want to answer. Sam learned over the years that evasiveness often meant that Abby didn't want to share a truth Sam might not want to hear. Was that what was happening now? And when Sam questioned her about Sara's appearance that morning, didn't Abby avoid answering?

"Why all these questions now, my daughter? What is worrying you at three in the morning?"

"The stories the elder told, I remember he said if any siblings or friends witnessed the abduction, they would be taken, too. He said the shapeshifter never left witnesses." Sam saw a shift in Abby's eyes. She had to see the worry on Sam's face, the seriousness of her question. So why wasn't her mother taking this more seriously? "Are we safe, mom? Is Dillon safe?"

Worry creased Abby's forehead as she cradled Sam's face in her hands. "Of course, we are safe. We are family. We are ALL related."

43

"I don't understand, Padre. How can we have all these overdoses and not one body taken to our own medical examiner?"

Sheila sat with one rounded cheek on Padre's desk. He made a shooing motion, then pointed to a chair in front of his desk. "You are distracting me."

"Am I?" She smiled coyly. "Any particular part of me?"

"Only that I have a report to write on those two bodies found by the quarry and you are taking up my valuable time asking questions. Those two bodies are in our ME's office so why don't you scurry over and watch the autopsies. Should be fun seeing how your days are obviously boring lately."

Sheila moved to one of the chairs and sat down, her skirt riding high as she crossed her legs. "Soooo." Padre glanced up with a heavy sigh. "What's Dagger working on, my cute jalapeno?"

"I'm not his keeper. Other than his stumbling onto those bodies yesterday, we haven't talked much. Bodies tend to drop out of the sky when he's around. You of all people should know that."

"And you just happened to appear together at the trailer that blew up. Did he stumble onto that body, too?"

"Last I looked, you two weren't an item anymore, now that he's joined at the hip with the very lovely Sara." He thought that would make her bristle. Five points for him.

Sheila slowly uncrossed and crossed her legs, hoping his eyes would travel the distance and all areas in between. Not a chance.

"Saw Dagger's psychotic friend today sitting outside of Cafe and Pasticcino, of all places, dressed like a Goodwill reject, not that he's known for shopping at Hermes. The fact that he resembled a derelict and in that area of town tells me he's working undercover for Dagger. Any comments?"

"Did you ask Skizzy?"

Sheila rolled her eyes. "I'm the last person who can decipher what comes out of that idiot's mouth. A headcase mumbling about a zombie climbing out of a grave and dancing fruits and vegetables, I swear the guy needs his meds adjusted, if he's even taking any."

"Well, the zombie turned out to be a cartel member exiting an elaborate tunnel filled with pallets of drugs."

"So, he's not completely off his rocker. Shocker."

"Being the award-winning reporter that you are, maybe you can search for those dancing fruits and vegetables."

"You are no fun." With a sigh Sheila stood with enough speed to cause her girls to attempt an escape from her low-cut sweater. "By the way, if the DEA is so busy in this area, why isn't my contact answering my calls? All his office will say is 'he's in the field.'"

Padre opened his hands, palms up. "Maybe that's why he isn't returning your calls…he's busy."

"I have a fine-tuned bullshit meter, and something smells. You know when that happens, I keep digging." As she turned toward the door, Sheila hesitated. "What about that guy who was with Dagger?" She eyed Padre curiously.

"Captain Robinson from Chasen Heights?"

"No, the detective allegedly looking for a missing teen. Jake something was his name."

"Just like you said…he's a private detective looking for missing kids." He noticed how her eyes lit up when mentioning a new man in town. "I'm surprised you haven't met his wife, Sam Casey."

"Well, that's news to me."

"I'm surprised you haven't researched her."

"I have. Must have ignored the marital information." With another sigh, she left the office.

Padre picked up the phone, the number etched in his brain. "Your nosy ex is a royal pain. Find something for her to do."

<h1 style="text-align:center">44</h1>

"I have been expecting you."

"Really? Mom has been talking to you?"

"No. I just know when something is bothering you. It means you either didn't like or understand the answer she gave you."

Alex sat on a brick wall which surrounded a garden pond. In his lap was a squirrel, its one foot in Alex's large hand. His other hand held tweezers as he appeared to pull what looked like a thorn from the squirrel's foot. Alex whispered to the animal as Sam's presence had startled the squirrel. She remained silent while Alex tended to the injured animal. It wasn't unusual to find a deer or fox peering through the chain link fence in the mornings. Animals with injuries instinctively knew of Alex's ability to communicate with them. He had even installed a door in the fence so he could admit the animals. The homemade salves Alex made had healing agents. And if the injury needed to be wrapped in gauze, the animals knew when to come back so Alex could change the dressing and check on the wound.

Alex set the tweezers down and applied salve to the infected area. He then spoke to the squirrel in his Native language. A few seconds later, the squirrel scrambled over the fence and out of site.

Sam took a seat next to Alex. "Do you have a salve for fears?"

Alex smiled. "Only you have the power to remove your fears. What are you fearful of, Sam?"

She looked beyond the shaded forest, toward the tipi and past the sweat lodge. Alex had brought some of the reservation to Chasen Heights, just as Sara's grandparents had brought their traditions to Cedar Point. Why not believe they had brought something else?

"Do you believe in shapeshifters?"

"Ahh…" He gathered up the salve and bandages, placed them back in a metal tin, then snapped the lid shut. "They are known by many names. The Navaho call them Skin-walkers. Lakota, Iktomi…the Spider trickster. In Japan, Kitsune; Korea, Kumio. It's not reserved for indigenous peoples. Hungary has Ordog. The Norse, Loki. And everyone knows of werewolves and Dracula. Some were believed to live in the dark, communicate with evil. Some were shaman who did good. The Deer Woman was believed to lead adulterers to their death."

"And disobedient children?"

"You are remembering the elder's stories."

"Any of it true? Has anyone ever seen someone who can change into an animal form?"

Alex pulled a pipe from his shirt pocket and tapped out remnants onto the brick. He took his time refilling the pipe with the cherry scented tobacco. He lit it and took a few puffs. Sam recognized his stalling techniques.

"Many stories have been written over the years."

"I know, monsters under the bed, demons in the closet."

Alex eyed her through the scented smoke. "Something has piqued your curiosity. What did your mother not answer to your satisfaction?"

Sam took a deep breath. Alex knew exactly what concerns she had. He was with Abby when Sara had appeared that night. No car, no clothes or shoes. She had curiously appeared wearing an old traditional dress of Sam's. Sam repeated everything she had said to Abby about the hawk, how Dillon had called the hawk by Sara's name.

"I asked mom if we were safe, if Dillon was safe. All she said was that we were all related, that, of course, we were safe."

"Hmmm." Alex puffed harder and stared into the forest beyond. After several minutes he turned to Sam, reading the genuine concern on her face. "There are many mysteries in our culture, some wondrous, some which cannot be explained but must be kept a mystery. Some are made up stories, some myths handed down through centuries. Some would never believe or understand how we communicate with the spirits, how I communicate with the animals, the spirits who speak to you or how your mother has insights into people just through a touch. If any of these gifts were written about in a book, readers would call them myths."

Alex stood and motioned for Sam to follow. "Come. Let's have coffee and you can tell me about these dreams you have been having."

Huh? How did Alex know that the body parts had followed her home? And how like him to give a cryptic response to her question, leaving her just as puzzled as when she had arrived.

45

Sam had never kept anything from Jake, at least not since they have been married. When she was the police chief's eyes and ears and Jake's nemesis, she had not only kept secrets from Jake but had also piled on more than her share of lies. All to cover up the undercover work she had engaged in for the chief. She didn't think Jake would understand shapeshifters, even after watching all the films Sophia had shown regarding the bizarre cases Dagger and Sara had worked. For now, she had to keep it between the few who already knew and understood.

The black marker she had found near the body in the boarded up real estate office was in her pocket, her hand clasping and unclasping as if it were a genie's lamp ready to reveal its secrets. A blur of an image kept popping into her head.

"Foods on." Stan waved at the table with the flourish of a world-renown chef.

"They are nothing but sandwiches, Stan. And still you cut the damn crusts off." Dagger pulled out a chair and sat down. He glanced at Sara who was staring at Sam with a worried look on her face.

"Are you okay, Sam?" Sara asked.

Jake's cop eye noticed Sam's demeanor. She had been quiet all morning, but he hadn't pressed.

The image evaporated the moment she released the marker from her fingers. "Not really." Sam took a seat next to Jake and grabbed a plate. "Not sure any of you would understand. Well, maybe Jake will." She grabbed a corner of a chicken salad sandwich and then a handful of potato chips. "Those body parts from the beach followed me home. I've been seeing them every night and they say the same thing ... 'we weren't done.' They crawl up from the foot of the bed. Arms, skulls, legs. It's just a bit jarring and I keep trying to decipher what they haven't finished."

Stan stared at her for a beat, then took a seat. "Our happy little group of weirdos and misfits. Isn't this fun?"

"No," Jake replied. "Thanks for painting that visual for me, Sam. Lucky for me you're the only one who sees them, but tell me, why now? We've been home for a few days."

"I think it's the marker I picked up. That's the only thing that links me to Crane and Crane had been on that ship."

"Either way, Sam seems pretty calm about it. But it does beg the question, what will it take to get rid of them? Makes me wonder if there's another ship out there we haven't located." Dagger grabbed another sandwich.

"Or an underground facility," Sara added.

"Sophia would have known, wouldn't she?" Sam looked from Dagger to Stan.

Stan shrugged. "Her contacts keep searching and keep her informed, but I'll certainly let her know about your bony visitors."

The front door blasted open and Skizzy charged in. "Food?"

"Lock the door," Stan yelled.

"Yeah, yeah." Skizzy shut the door and turned the dead bolt. He was still dressed in his homeless attire. Lucky for the others, he wasn't doused in liquor.

"Sara made them, right?" Skizzy grabbed three corners of a sandwich, not even bothering to ask what was in them much less waiting for confirmation from Sara. "That nutty ex of yours is always lurking. I don't think I said anything I shouldn't have said, but you know me." He grabbed a handful of potato chips, checked first to see if anyone else was eating them, then grabbed another handful."

"What the hell? Haven't you eaten today?" Dagger wasn't sure if Skizzy was on his meds or off his rocker.

"Have to stock up before going out tonight. Plus, having Sara cook for me twice is a bonus."

Eye contacts bounced around the table. Not one person was going to break it to Skizzy that Stan had made the sandwiches.

"How did you get rid of the body parts?" Sara was more curious than shocked. She had seen her fair share of weirdness.

"Body parts?" The sandwich had barely touched Skizzy's mouth. "What body parts?"

Sam explained about the remains she had seen on the beach and how they had attempted to reattach. Now they were appearing at the foot of her bed, clawing at the covers.

Skizzy stared, blinked a few times. "Want any of my meds?"

"Hah," Stan barked. "That's a good one. Who said the nutjob wasn't quick on the uptake."

A slight smile tugged at the corner of Dagger's lips, a rare sight for anyone who knew him well.

"Down to business." Stan waited for everyone's attention. "Our nosy reporter is going to be a problem. She has made several calls to the DEA looking for details on these deaths. We keep holding her off, but she is like a barnacle...keeps hanging in there. She wants to find a conspiracy, write a Pulitzer-winning story. Probably has made-for-TV stars in her eyes. So..." Stan swung his gaze to Dagger. "What are you going to do about it?"

"Me? Don't look at me. Nothing I say or do will divert her attention from a story. And no, I'm not going to wine and dine her. Ask Jake. Any new face and body in town always piques her interest, and she was definitely piqued when we ran into her at the trailer."

There was silence as five gazes turned to Jake. "Don't look at me. I have little patience for reporters, much less a rich female trolling for attention."

"Ooooh, let me." Sam had heard enough about the reporter to make her curious.

"Sam."

"Don't worry, sweetheart. I'll be gentle."

"Let me help, please," Sara added.

"What are you two planning on doing?" Dagger didn't like the nefarious tones to their voices.

"Not sure yet, but I'll think of something." Sam reached into her pocket finding the black marker and curious why her mind was forming a strange picture.

"What else?" Stan looked around the table.

"When I reconnoitered yesterday I did notice someone in a priest's collar. I think he runs the AA meetings at the shop next to the magazine store."

"Sounds like it's right up your alley, Skizzy," Dagger suggested.

"Nuh uh," Skizzy protested. "Me in a close room with a bunch of smelly guys, their hands all over the cups and chairs with unknown stains on their clothes? I'll do my thing outside, not inside. You go and take the FBI guy with you. You look like a drug addict, Dagger, and Elliot Ness looks like a wife beater." Skizzy looked across the table at Sam. "No disrespect, ma'am." He lowered his voice to a whisper. "It's just that he looks mean."

Jake turned his mean face toward Skizzy. "Really?"

Skizzy scootched down in his chair and focused on his sandwich. "Well, you were looking for someone in a priest's collar, right?"

"Great, it's settled, Dagger. You and Elliot Ness stagger into the AA meeting and see if that priest is our guy." Stan clapped his hands as though he had solved the case.

"Did he look like Doctor Crane?" Sam asked.

Skizzy shrugged. "How should I know? I've never seen a picture of him." He ignored the sighs emitted from around the table. "So, what's for dessert?"

46

"Nothing worse than a woman's constant nagging. Who the hell cares if I want to relax after a hard day of doing nothing?" The other faces around the fire nodded and laughed along with Skizzy. He popped pills into his mouth and washed them down with another long swallow from the bottle he pulled from his jacket. If he swallowed anymore mints and washed them down with soda, he swore his farts would produce a minty odor.

"Where's your woman now?" The face across the fire in the fifty-gallon drum barely had enough teeth to chew noodles.

"With the other three." He lowered his voice. "See the trick is, you use native plants, cover the graves with them cause it's against the law to dig them up. Ain't no way cops are going to touch the area. Course, if that don't work, it's amazing what landfills can hide these days." More laughter erupted. These idiots are too drunk to know if I'm telling the truth, Skizzy thought. Some ignored him, others watched with skepticism. Others eyed the bottle he shoved into his jacket pocket. Maybe he was laying it on too thick with the three dead wives. The killer was looking at drug pushers and hopeless addicts who neglect life and loved ones, not wife killers. This was his first night out and already he could tell which of his fellow homeless preferred liquor and which preferred drugs. There was something in the eyes. One thing was apparent, very few spoke, preferring not to reveal any personal information. Skizzy noticed some had already staggered off to lean against a building or get swallowed up by the darkness. Maybe he shouldn't have mentioned the AA meetings at the church. All he had asked was if anyone had found the meetings useful, other than to get out of the cold and grab a cup of something hot. But most had scurried off as though he were trying to recruit attendees.

He turned away from the firepit and stumbled toward the church.

A man with glassy eyes and long greasy hair partly covered by a dark hoodie bumped into him as he maneuvered past. Jeans were stained and torn in places as was the blue jean jacket he wore. Skizzy bounced off the big guy as if he were a soccer ball. There was pain in his eyes. Skizzy guessed oxy, not meth or party pills. It was difficult to tell the man's age. He moved like a man much older, every muscle in agony. Skizzy watched him for several seconds, then slowly turned back around, scanning the faces in the darkness, the prone bodies buried under cardboard, the forgotten slumped against the building walls.

Skizzy missed the man in the dark suit tailing the pill popper in the dark hoodie.

Dagger and Jake had entered the addiction center. All of the attendees were men, each with cup and paper plate, probably just getting in from the chilly air to grab something hot to drink. The walls were dotted with posters blaring inspirational messages. Dagger and Jake had brought their own drinks in thermal cups, probably not trusting what the good pastor was serving. When the pastor emerged from the back room, it was obvious he didn't look anything like Doctor Crane. Jake watched the door close, noticing first the round table surrounded by men seated, holding cards in their hands.

"Hold on a second."

"Oh hell," Dagger said. He reluctantly followed Jake. When the pastor saw where Jake was headed, he rushed to follow the two men. Jake pushed the door open and entered.

"This is a restricted area," the pastor explained.

"Pastor...?" Jake scrutinized the organizer of what was supposed to be an addiction recovery meeting. Four sets of eyes regarded the intrusion with a combination of fear and irritation. They turned their gaze to the pastor.

'Andrews, Phillip Andrews."

"Really, Jake. Do you have to play cop every room you walk into?" Dagger wavered between escaping through the emergency exit or dragging Jake out through the front door.

"I thought you were supposed to be helping people." Jake towered over the meek pastor.

"This is a new program I'm trying. Rather than going to the casino they are playing a friendly game using vanilla wafers."

"So next they will have to go to Weightwatchers, if they don't get the bug to scurry off to the casino again."

"I can tell the signs if they start to lose control." Pastor Andrews kneaded his fingers in a tight ball as he tried to turn the two men back the way they came. "You aren't with the police, are you? You really have no authority back here."

"No, I'm not," Jake replied. "But I have connections."

Dagger clamped a hand on Jake's shoulder and steered him away from the table. "Sorry for the intrusion, Pastor. My friend is a little over-zealous when it comes to rules."

"Wait. Are you the only pastor who conducts these meetings? We are looking for someone round face, slightly bald."

"Sorry, it's just me but I could really use the help if you could pass the word."

"Thanks anyway." Jake reluctantly left the room, then pounded his way out the front door.

"What the hell?" Skizzy glared at Dagger. "Too many fleas in there? What were you doing in that back room?"

"Jake got an itch to play cop."

"I'm sure they've got pills for that. Now what about the pastor?"

"It's not him," Dagger said. "The guy isn't even close to resembling our guy."

"Well, jeez Louise. How the hell was I supposed to know? All you told me was he wore a priest's collar."

"No harm, Skizzy. Why don't you go stagger over to your friends and see if they have seen a pastor, other than this guy, chatting it up with people." Dagger patted Skizzy's shoulder and hoped the stain his fingers touched was just wear and tear.

* * * *

With Dillon sleeping and the kitchen cleaned, Sam sat at the kitchen table with her laptop reading articles about Sheila Monroe. Most of the personal information appeared in celebrity sighting articles. Sam never thought of herself as rich. It was her grandfather who had built their three thousand square foot home as a wedding present for her father and Melinda. Sam and Abby inherited it after Samuel and Melinda Casey were killed in an explosion. Yes, Sam had a trust fund, but when reading about the wealth of the Monroe family with their mansion and jet-setting lifestyle, Sam felt more like middle America.

Sheila was an only child, probably the apple of her father's eye, and being groomed to take over the Daily Herald newspaper when he retired. Anna Monroe, his wife, looked coifed and dressed by only the most expensive salons and boutiques. Leyton Monroe looked pompous, with a barrel chest probably built by the best restaurants and wineries.

"What are you making notes of Samantha?" Abby leaned over the kitchen table as she set her cup of tea down.

"What?" Sam looked at the notepad next to her laptop. She had thought of writing down details about Sheila, so her pen was in hand; but instead of words, she had drawn a line and X's. She set the pen down and studied the notepad. "I have no idea. I've been seeing this image ever since I picked up the black marker Doctor Crane had tossed. And I didn't even know I was drawing it. Looks like a treasure map."

"What looks like a treasure map?" Jake had entered with Dagger who went straight to the refrigerator and grabbed two beers."

"The derelicts have returned from their AA meeting. How did it go?" Sam closed her laptop and set it aside.

"Your husband had to play boy scout and try to bust a card party." Dagger took a long swallow of beer.

"Nice going, honey. Now you know, Dagger. Jake lives in a black and white world, whereas you are shades of gray."

"Don't even know why I'm drinking this." Dagger looked at the beer can, wondering how it appeared in his hands. "There were enough alcohol fumes in the air that I already feel drunk. Have no idea what this one guy was on, but he was having a serious conversation with some bricks in the front of the magazine store."

"With all the resources available, I have never known why they don't seek help." Abby took a sip of her tea.

"Most don't want help. Powers that be say it's against their rights to admit them into rehab or institutions." Jake took a long swallow of beer.

"I like what China did to get their addicts off drugs. They dragged them into the middle of the street and shot them in the head. No more addicts."

"Nice, Dagger. You are full of so much empathy. Please promise you will never run for office." Sam picked up the notepad with her sketch.

"So, what's this about a treasure map?" Jake moved to the table and took a seat next to Sam. She handed him the notepad.

"I've been seeing this image ever since I picked up Crane's dried up marker. Have no idea what it means. When I saw the X's, I thought of a treasure map. Maybe it's marking where the Director's labs are. What do you think, Dagger?"

Dagger walked closer and studied the sketch. He set his beer on the table, pulled out his phone, and took a picture. "I'll send it to Sophia and see what she thinks. It does look more like a treasure map to me, but the fact that you're getting vibes from Crane, it could mean something else." He emptied his beer and left the can on the island counter. "Crawling body parts and treasure maps. You're a laugh a minute, Sam."

"You're one to talk, exploding clones, full moon werewolves, parallel universes." Sam was certain Dagger's cases were far more weird than hers.

"Later, and thanks for the beer."

After Abby heard the back door close, she rose and picked up Dagger's empty can. She closed her eyes and held onto the can for several seconds.

47

"You were pretty hard to track, not like some of the others." Crane wasn't sure what drug the thief was on. He didn't smell liquor on his breath, so it had to be pills, especially by the slow reaction, the lack of resistance. Oxy maybe? Might be why he was stealing money, but Crane could never find out who was supplying the thief. That's the person who should be held accountable. They were sitting in the back pew of a church. Doors were always locked but somehow in his drugged stupor the thief had found a way in. It was a one-story church with stained glass windows and a small altar. A large crucifix hung on the back wall behind the altar and an organ and chair were against the wall to the left of the altar. He could see hymn books in the pew pockets, ready for the next mass. Several sconces on the walls provided the only light.

The thief blinked slowly, staring at Crane as though trying to remember who he was. His hair touched the collar of a blue jean jacket that was stained and ripped in places. He had a beard that looked hand-trimmed, short in some places and long in others. There was a scar that ran from his left eyebrow to his chin as if someone had tried to carve a crater.

Crane held the bottle up to the thief's mouth. "Have a drink. You must be thirsty." Even that was hard to do with someone so numb of pain he didn't have the strength to swallow. The thief finally tipped his head back and swallowed. "You'll feel so much better soon, my friend. No more stealing money to provide for your habit. Didn't you ever think you might have been stealing food from the mouths of your victims' kids?" He watched the thief's eyelids grow heavy and slowly close. "You probably didn't." Crane pulled the jacket sleeve up, then froze. He pulled the sleeve up further to see the entire tattoo. Crane had seen that motto before, read about it. He pulled back and looked closer at the thief.

"Oh no." He pulled an object from his pocket, placed it under the thief's nose and sprayed Narcan. Next, Crane ripped open the man's shirt, ignoring the buttons flying errantly. With his black marker he wrote four letters on the man's chest. As he hurried away he dialed 911. *The Only Easy Day Was Yesterday.*

Water laps at her feet, waves glistening under the moon's rays. Even in the dark Sam could see the body parts, suddenly aware of her presence. One hand turns, a finger pointing, alerting the other parts of her, the one who had disturbed their resting place, only to discover they would never complete their work.

In unison they turned, then charged. Sam ran into the water, thinking they would never follow. But she was wrong. The ground beneath her feet fell away too quickly for being only several yards from shore. Unfortunately, she couldn't swim. Sam cried out for help until she felt strong hands holding her up. She tried to thank her rescuer, grabbed hold of the hands only to find they weren't attached to arms. The grip around her neck tightened until she couldn't breathe or call out.

Sam pushed at the air as she sat up, gasping for help. Across the bed body parts recoiled, appearing frightened at the force of her sudden response. She turned to see if she had disturbed Jake. Of course not. When she turned back, the body parts were gone. But not for good, she was sure.

48

Crane preferred eating breakfast in his room. He needed time to think after last night. The thought of sticking around to make sure the ambulance arrived in time had not been an option. The burner phone he had used couldn't be traced so he was assured the authorities wouldn't discover who had made the call.

The atrium was filled again with people shopping, eating, checking out at the front desk or conversing on couches, coffee cups in hand. His breakfast tray was already outside of his door, a *Do Not Disturb* sign on the doorknob. The notepad in front of him had new lines and X's. And again, he didn't remember drawing them. The additional lines were thinner, like a strand of hair. And a misshapen circle was near one of those thin lines. It made zero sense. So where did it come from?

"I hate hospitals, hate the smell, the dull paint on the walls, the moans coming out of the rooms." Robinson shook his head. "Spent too much time here over the years. Not as a patient you know."

"I hear you. Can't get out of here soon enough."

Robinson leaned against the wall in the hospital corridor, Padre standing next to him. "I thought you were supposed to be notified?"

"He wasn't dead. According to the doctor, someone used a Narcan spray on him and called nine-one-one. There wasn't anyone waiting by the victim and the call came from a burner phone. I don't know much more so this might be a wasted trip."

"Something must have sparked your interest." Robinson hadn't wanted to call Sam and Jake until he had checked out the victim. Might be a dead end. Padre felt the same about Dagger and Sara. There wasn't any sense in disturbing the victim with a room full of people peppering him with questions.

"Definitely. It's something the responding officer told me, but I'll wait so you can see for yourself."

The doctor emerged from the room and approached the men. He was a seasoned professional by the looks of his age and the weary look in his eyes from long hours and long years. "I'm Doctor Stephens. Sorry to keep you waiting."

"No problem," Padre said. "We are patient men."

Right, Robinson thought.

"He's very lucky that someone had a Narcan spray on him...or her. He's awake now if you want to talk to him. With as many drugs he's been on, and for a lot of years, too, is my guess, I doubt there is much he can tell you."

"Did you at least get a name?" Padre asked.

"Yes. John Smith. You wouldn't believe how many John Smiths we get in this hospital."

They watched as Doctor Stephens walked down the hall, then stopped to speak with a nurse.

Padre entered the hospital room with Robinson close behind. The figure in the bed looked worse for wear. Bedraggled would have been a compliment. His skin was a shade of grey with raccoon eyes at half-mast. Disheveled beard sprinkled with grey. His head didn't move but the eyes followed their entrance.

They each flashed their badges and Padre made the introductions. "Do you mind?" Padre reached over and lowered the sheet covering the writing. Then he lifted John Smith's left arm to show Robinson the tattoo.

"The only easy day is yesterday?" Robinson dragged his eyes to Smith's face. "You were a Navy Seal? What the hell." He checked the inside of Smith's wrist for any sign of a sketch of a demon. There wasn't one. Then his eyes took on the four letters on his chest written with a black permanent marker...*PTSD*. He turned his attention to Padre, wondering if he thought the same thing.

"Do you remember anything from last night, Mister Smith?" Padre pulled out a business card and placed it on the side table. "Someone saved your life. It would be helpful to talk to that person."

"I don't remember much of anything." His voice was dry and raspy.

"No description of the person who applied the nasal spray?"

"No."

"You were found in a church. Do you remember getting there? Were you there to talk to a priest?" Robinson knew friends who had suffered with PTSD. Some recovered, a few had not. Smith remained silent. "Have you thought of going to rehab? There is one I know of that is strictly for veterans with PTSD." Robinson pulled out his business card and wrote a name, address, and phone number on the back. "It might be worth it. You never know."

Smith turned away from them and stared at the ceiling, avoiding the card Robinson placed next to Padre's.

As they exited the room, Robinson stopped a nurse who was carrying a clipboard. Her name badge said she was a supervisor. "Ma'am," he whispered. "Do you still have the orthopedic wing where they have the physical therapy room?"

"Yes. It's on the fourth floor."

"Could you see if Doctor Stephens could find a bed up there for Mister Smith?"

The nurse winced. "There are a few amputees up there."

"Former military, right?"

She nodded. Then the light bulb came on and she smiled. "I'll see what I can do."

"What do you think?" Padre asked as they made their way across the parking lot.

"I think Crane noticed the tattoo when he pulled Smith's sleeve up and realized he was a vet, probably with PTSD which is why he wanted to make sure when the police showed up that they would get him the help he needed."

"I thought the same thing. We have a killer with a heart, it appears."

49

"This is a very popular restaurant. Wait until you have their tea with impatiens flowers floating on top." Sam noticed that Sara had stopped following her. She appeared frozen in place.

"Is it usually crowded?" Sara could feel her heart racing.

Sam weaved her arm through Sara's, remembering the young woman's fear of crowds. "Christian set up a special place for us in the window alcove. It will be fine. Plus, it's too late for breakfast and too early for lunch." Sara followed Sam into Cafe Fleurs Grotte. True to Sam's words, there were only four tables of customers.

"Samantha!" A man wearing a white beret with tufts of sun-bleached hair visible at the neckline, grabbed Sam in a bearhug, then kissed her on both cheeks. "You are looking magnifique." His gaze drifted to Sara. "My, my, Sam. Do you only hang out with beautiful women? Who is this gorgeous creature?" He clasped Sara's hand and kissed the top of it. "Let me guess. Tahiti? No, one of the Polynesian islands maybe?"

Sara glanced at Sam, embarrassed at the attention. "Assiniboine."

"Native? But such gorgeous eyes." He released her hand and waved toward an alcove in front of the window bordered by a privacy screen. "Elizabeth Taylor would be jealous of those eyes of yours."

"Christian Didier, this is Sara Morningsky."

Christian made a slight bow. "Welcome to Cafe Fleurs Grotte. Grottoes are my passion which you can tell by the stone fountain, cobblestone floor and beautiful archways."

Sara's gaze was drawn to an elaborate painting on the ceiling. "That's beautiful. The Libyan Sibyl?"

"Why yes." Christian was always surprised when a customer recognized the painting. "A priestess guarding her writing which foretold the future."

"Did you know that the model for the image was a male assistant."

"Really?" Now Christian looked curiously at the image. "That certainly explains the broad back and muscled arms. You are very knowledgeable. Now come. I have a special lunch planned for you." Christian led them around the hand-painted Venetian style screen, then pulled out their chairs. "Sit, sit. I will bring out your iced tea."

"Wow, so charming."

"Oh, you should see Evan, his partner. Evan Collier has been my shrink, on occasion. He's like a Hermes model."

"Where's Jake today?"

"You don't know? He's with Dagger and Stan. They are in Dagger's office waiting to hear from Sophia."

Christian returned with two glasses of iced tea. "Sorry, I assumed that Sara also wanted unsweet iced tea. I can bring sugar if you need it, Sara."

"I'm fine, thank you."

"Hibiscus, Christian?" Sam had expected impatiens.

"I thought I would mix it up today. And the yellow color looked so brilliant this morning."

"It's beautiful." Sara waited until Christian left to catch Sam's attention. "Did you come up with any ideas?" They were meeting to discuss ways to steer Sheila away from the Levitt Crane case.

"Unfortunately, no. Thought if we put our heads together here, we might come up with some kind of diversion."

"Do you know of any single men, preferably rich, and a bit on the bad side? Sheila has a certain taste. Of course, I doubt it would matter to her if the man was married. She has a one-track mind when it comes to conquering a new future ex." Sara picked up the flower floating on top of her glass. "Are these edible?"

"Supposedly, but I'll wait until you try it," Sam added with a smile. They watched people strolling in front of the window, some appeared sightseeing while a few did seem in a rush. "From what I've gathered, Sheila doesn't appear to me to be sidetracked by a love interest, not if she can find a hot story to make a name for herself. But you probably know her better."

"She doesn't need to make a name for herself. I'm surprised the town isn't named after the Monroe family."

Christian returned with a tray. "I think I outdid myself, ladies." He set a plate in front of Sara. "Blackened salmon petite filet with mango citrus salsa and asparagus." He next set a plate in front of Sam. "And your favorite, Sam, chicken pesto on grilled sourdough. These are small servings because I have a special dessert today...tiramisu cake. So, save your appetites, ladies, and bon appetit."

"This looks wonderful," Sara said after Christian left. "And I bet very expensive. Just look at the decor. I bet that privacy screen is an antique right from Italy."

"Yes, it's expensive but well worth it. It's not like I eat lunch here every day. But no worries, lunch is Christian's treat today."

They enjoyed their lunch in silence as they watched cars maneuver the turn at the end of the street. Christian had an ideal location on a street of upscale apartments and up-and-coming businesses. The restaurant was several blocks from the cafe where Skizzy had run into Sheila.

"How did you know about the painting on the ceiling?"

"I was homeschooled. My grandmother had a collection of books and insisted I study a variety of subjects. Anything I happened across in the papers or magazines, she had me look it up to learn about different cultures, art, you name it."

"So, you didn't want to go to school?"

"Schools are rather large and have a lot of students in it. I didn't feel comfortable."

Crowds, again. Sam had forgotten. "I know how you feel. Abby and I would go back to the reservation when she had meetings to attend or during annual pow wows. I wasn't discreet at a young age regarding my abilities. I thought it was cool. However, kids thought I was a freak. I was basically an outcast, so I had few friends. Abby kept telling me my gift was between me and the spirits so I shouldn't telecast it. I obviously didn't learn my lesson because even now it's difficult to hide how I solve crimes." Sam glanced at Sara's face. Was it shock that Sam might have alluded to Sara's abilities? "What I'm saying is, I know what it's like to feel uncomfortable and to withdraw into a shell." Sara appeared to relax, Sam hoped. Besides, neither Abby nor Alex had confirmed Sam's suspicions about Sara's possible shapeshifting abilities.

A waitress appeared and removed their empty plates. Behind her Christian carried a tray with their desserts. Refilling their glasses, he said, "Let me know if you need anything else."

Sara slowly bit into the cake, either stalling for an answer, Sam thought, or enjoying the cake. It was hard to tell.

Sam stabbed a forkful of cake. "I'm glad I saved room. This is heavenly." It didn't take long for the two women to finish off the dessert. "I think I may have to move the button over on my skirt."

"So? What is the verdict?" Christian placed a tray on the table as a waitress cleared away the empty dishes.

"Excellent, Christian, as always."

"Agree," Sara chimed in. "We don't eat out much, I mean me and Dagger. But I'll have to tell him about your restaurant."

"Well, if you hang around with Sam enough, she will show you some of her favorites."

"Thanks again, Christian. It was so nice of you to treat us today."

"Anything for you, Sam. Just don't be a stranger."

They watched him leave, then Sam pulled a paper from her purse and unfolded it. "As long as we are here, I thought I'd show you the detail that I added to the treasure map."

Sara studied the map which, to her, did look like a treasure map. "You added more X's." She opened her phone and sent a quick text to Dagger. "I wonder if Sophia had anything to say after Dagger showed her your map." A few seconds later, Dagger replied. "Sophia doesn't believe the Director would have had this many additional labs or underground cities. That would be too many to control."

They studied the map which now showed thin vertical lines as well as a small kidney-shaped blob near one of the lines. They sensed a shadow appear over their shoulders.

"My, my, Sara. I didn't know you had any friends, female friends I mean. Your only friends seemed to be the men Dagger hangs around with."

Sam studied the intruder from her platinum hair, short leather skirt and halo of perfume that wasn't overwhelming but definitely smelled expensive. She could only guess by the annoyed look on Sara's face that this charm school graduate was Dagger's ex, although her words were anything but charming.

Not appearing embarrassed by butting in, Sheila hovered close, having snaked around the privacy screen. The two women stared at Sheila as her reporter eye scanned the map displayed on the table. She reached out a hand to Sam, who hesitated at first for fear the multitude of bling on Sheila's fingers would blind her. "Sheila Monroe, the Daily Herald." When Sam didn't reply, Sheila added, "Sorry, I saw you two through the window. Just wanted to introduce myself. After meeting your husband the other day, I just had to look both of you up. You are Sam Casey, right? It was in The Pines where you had discovered all those bodies in your ..." Sheila added air quotes ... 'peculiar way.' Had to look up where on earth this town was so that's why I recognized your map." The stares from the two made her feel like a specimen in a petri dish. "The map," she added with a nod to the map. "Returning to the scene of the crime?"

Sam studied the lines and X's again. Sheila was right. The slightly rounded line at the top was the Lake Michigan shoreline. That made the broader line drawn left to right was I-80. She counted the number of X's. "Oh my God." She caught Sara's eye. "There are eight X's."

"You think there are eight more bodies that you hadn't located the last time?" Sheila dragged the one vacant chair over and plopped herself between Sam and Sara.

Sam had to think quickly. What Sheila said made sense, but how to explain it without revealing Levitt Crane would require creative manipulation.

"Jake and I touch base occasionally with our former captain. He was pretty chatty the other day and told us stories about his early days as a cop in New Jersey. There was a case thirty years ago that really piqued his interest, but he was only a patrol officer back then. All this time he hung onto a file on John Wallace Baker." Sam repeated what Robinson had told her, leaving out the drawing on the inside wrist of his victims, but revealing how Baker claimed there were eight more bodies.

"But how...?" Sheila studied the map. Her reporter enthusiasm was palpable. Her eyes took on an intense hunger.

"I held the folder. I read what few notes Robinson had kept before the case was taken over by the homicide detectives. I've been sketching what I thought was a treasure map. Didn't even know I was drawing it. After rocking my son to sleep, I'd look over at the paper unaware I was drawing anything. Each day I appeared to be adding more detail. We've been sitting here trying to figure out what it all meant."

"If these are the eight bodies Baker was going to reveal before he died, then all that's needed is for one of the university archeology departments to use their high frequency ground penetrating radar equipment to locate them," Sara suggested. "Perhaps using a plane since there's quite a distance between the X's."

Sheila wrenched a thick notepad from her purse and started writing. "I'll have to research this guy. Sounds like his murder spree spanned several states so I'll contact my FBI contact here." She stopped scribbling for a second. "I'm sorry, I mean if you don't mind my butting in on your investigation."

"Not my investigation," Sam said, waving off the comment. "I touched the folder, drew something weird, but this sounds like it needs a lot of investigating which I don't have time for."

Sheila pulled out her phone. "May I?" She snapped a couple pictures then started scribbling again. With a whispered, "wow," she looked at the two women and said, "This could be big. I think Baker is reaching out from the grave."

Sara discreetly placed her hand over her mouth to hide the smile. They had found a way to keep Sheila busy.

50

A shrill whistle echoed off the wall of the aviary. "AWWWKK. COMPANY, COMPANY." A flash of royal blue and red maneuvered from behind a branch in the corner faux tree. One yellow-ringed eye peeked from the side of a frond.

"On my god." Sam stood next to Sara who was tempting the macaw from the tree.

"Look what I have, Einstein." Sara held up a cheese curl. "Come say hello."

Einstein dropped to a lower branch, studying the visitors curiously.

"This room is larger than some apartments." Jake felt the warmth seeping from the room. "Damn that room is hot."

"Humidity and temperature controlled," Dagger replied from his desk. He slammed another drawer shut then shoved the chair against the wall.

"Dagger, you are scaring Einstein. Come here and assure Einstein you aren't directing your anger at him." Sara had noticed Dagger's irritation the minute she had called to tell him she was bringing Sam to the house which then forced him to bring Jake. They rarely had visitors except for Simon and Padre.

"Yeah, it's really irritating when people appear in your house unannounced," Jake said, referring to when Dagger and Sara broke in to look for the video from the salvage yard. "It's five o-clock somewhere so pop open a beer and relax."

"You better break open more cans because Padre and Lamon and also coming."

Dagger glared at Sara, but knew it was a fight he wasn't going to win. Sara had turned a corner having met Sam and her mother. She found friends she could relate to, but he still feared mixing with others could be dangerous.

The buzzer at the gate sounded. Two cars appeared on the security monitor. Dagger pressed the button to release the gate, then walked over to the aviary. "Hey, buddy. Come meet some people." Dagger took the cheese curl from Sara and waved it.

"Why isn't there a lot of bird do-do all over the place?" That had been the first thing Sam had noticed. The room was clean. "And what's that shower head for?"

"Dagger trained him to go in only one place in the room, over there by that floor basin. And the shower over the one perch is where Einstein showers. There's a chain that he pulls for the water," Sara explained.

Einstein moved down to another lower branch. With another shake of the cheese curl, Einstein flew over to the perch by the door. Sara introduced their guests to the macaw.

"Wow, he is beautiful. Wish Dillon could see him." Sam watched as Einstein gingerly removed the cheese curl from Dagger's fingers. "He doesn't bite?"

"He does strangers. Maybe Jake can reach in and show us."

"It's amazing how close we've become, Dagger," Jake commented dryly as the door in the kitchen opened and the two cops entered.

"This is the most people I've ever seen in this house." Padre pointed a finger gun at Einstein.

The macaw returned the finger gun. "AWWKK, UP AGAINST THE WALL AND SPREAD THEM."

"How cute," Sam said with a laugh.

"Okay, buddy. We have business to talk so I'm shutting you out. Go play." Dagger slid the soundproof door across the grated door to close off the aviary.

They assembled on the couch and loveseats, drinks in hand. Sam explained how they met Sheila and the map Sheila had assumed was of more bodies near Pine Lakes. "That's when I realized that the X's represented the eight other victims of John Wallace Baker. It has to be because I started drawing it after I touched Crane's black marker."

"Wait," Padre said, setting his beer can down. "All you had to do was touch the marker and then you started drawing this map?"

"That's what she does," Robinson said, hardly surprised at the revelation.

"Sheila bit so hard on the possible cold case that she almost fell off of her hooker heels running out of the restaurant," Sam said with a laugh.

Padre made a sign of the cross. "*Santa Maria de Dios*. Thought I had seen it all with Dagger's cases. I sure do miss my quiet days of drive-bys, robberies and logical cases."

"How was Sheila?" Dagger directed his question to Sara. He would never forget how in their last case Sara had been injured in a burning building. Sheila had entered the building, but when she saw Sara, she had left, not bothering to call the authorities. Dagger had been furious, but Sara wouldn't let him react because all of her injuries were healed by the next morning. Instead, they kept quiet and let Sheila think she had hallucinated. After all, how else would Sara be able to explain how she had escaped the fire without any injuries?

"Sara showed more restraint than I ever could. She told Sara she didn't know she had friends, then clarified she didn't know she had any female friends. How did you ever get mixed up with her, Dagger?"

"A moment of weakness, Sam. I was new in town and rich people have connections. Next thing I know she's buying a ring and telling me the wedding date."

"I never had grey hair until I met you, Dagger." Padre grabbed the beer can and took a healthy swig.

"Have you spoken to Sophia lately?" Robinson looked from Dagger to Sara.

"I sent her a picture of the map. At first we thought it might be more labs or underground facilities since Sam didn't start drawing the map until after she touched Crane's black marker." Dagger watched as Sara carried empty beer cans to the sink. She was enjoying playing hostess to a room full of guests which was making Dagger nervous. He feared this might be a regular occurrence. "I also spoke briefly with Carl. He said

Sophia thinks everything is too easy. She doesn't believe the Director would let anyone get close enough to kill him so she's expecting another shoe to drop."

"That's reassuring. I mean we all saw it on the video." Not that Jake would think videos couldn't be altered.

"Well, back to the map. Why didn't Sam pick up vibes about Crane rather than Baker? After all, it was Crane's marker." Padre was confused. "I mean, you didn't start drawing the map after touching the Baker case file. It was after touching the black marker, unless..." Padre let that thought hang in the air.

"Baker appears to be getting stronger." Sam thought it made sense. "Which begs the question, how much stronger can he get?"

Padre made another sign of the cross.

Robinson stood. "Well, I'm out of here. Keep us updated on anything you or Skizzy find out. I just hope Crane's mistake of targeting a military vet with PTSD doesn't scare him off. If he skips town, it will make it more difficult to track him."

"I'm right behind you." Padre stood and gave a salute. "Thanks for the unexpected hospitality. Sara finally has you coming out of your shell."

"Don't get used to it." Dagger escorted the two men to the door.

"Nice room." Jake surveyed the sunroom complete with island decor and a fireplace.

"Dagger built it," Sara said. "I, of course, decorated it or we would have ended up with black and grey furniture."

"I'm impressed."

"You probably don't know which end of the hammer to use, Jake," Dagger said as he returned.

"I helped Alex build the gazebo in one of the gardens, but I have to admit, this looks professional."

Sam sighed. "The island furniture has me pining for visiting Carl again. Too bad it's close to hurricane season."

"I agree. I would have liked to have seen that Monkey Island up close." There was still something strange about the monkeys that Sara couldn't quite put her finger on.

"It would have been too long of a ride." Jake took in the view outside the window. Most of the yard was a natural habitat of wildflowers and tall fescue. "We could have gone while we were there, but it was a half hour ride to Beaufort and Lady's Island. Then a one-mile boat ride."

Sara looked puzzled. "No. The island is about four miles east of Hilton Head, isn't it?" She glanced at Dagger.

"Yes. We saw the monkeys on the island from the lighthouse."

"There was an article in the magazine on the plane that showed a map of the coastline, and Jake's right. It's the only one and it's way north of Hilton Head."

"I believe you, Sam, so what on earth did Dagger and I see from the lighthouse? It doesn't make sense."

51

"What do you think?" Carl had been watching Sophia closely. He had heard her a number of nights pacing at three in the morning and doubted she slept more than five hours a night. She was over-thinking the case which wasn't like her. She was detailed to a fault and could think five steps ahead.

"Ferdinand is building up steam." Sophia was standing on the deck looking toward the east as though the hurricane was going to bare down on them any minute.

"That's not what I'm referring to." Carl joined her at the railing. He had no idea what could ease his cousin's mind regarding Director Keyes.

"I know. Something will break soon, I have a feeling. As far as the storm, we will just batten down the hatches and wait it out, regardless if they call for evacuation. We are needed here."

"Another feeling?"

"Of course. Director Keyes was brilliant, in a devious way. The underground facility in Nebraska held the largest seed bank unknown to most everyone. If he could destroy the one in Ames, Iowa, which had been established in 1947, then he would control the future. People would have to pay a fortune not to starve to death. He predicted the powers that be would one day pay farmers not to grow in order to save the planet, such ignorant idiots. And wouldn't you know, he was right. Little did he know, though, that nineteen more seed banks would crop up in the United States, which made his one seed vault pointless. It was just a minor setback. Besides, he saw a more lucrative business in drugs. He was years ahead of China and Mexico. He hadn't survived this long without being more cunning than the next psychopath."

Now Carl understood what was bothering his young cousin. "You never got to see the Director's body so you aren't completely sure it's over."

The sun disappeared in the distance. All that was visible were the lights on the bridge to Hilton Head Island. Although Director Keyes was dead, his tentacles seemed to be reaching out from the grave, settling doubts in Sophia's head that the Director's realm was over. Without the head of the snake, the rest of his body...followers...would die, go into hiding.

Sophia left the deck and returned to the living room. Carl followed, closing the sliding glass door behind him. He went to the bar and poured them both a drink. "What did you think of the map Sam had drawn? How do you suppose she could pull details about John Wallace Baker but not Levitt Crane?"

"I wouldn't have expected Crane to make such an enormous error."

"He didn't know whose brain he was using. I'm sure if he had, if he had even an inkling of what might happen, he would have never taken that next step. But it would have been helpful if she had channeled Crane's thoughts. We would know his next move, especially if he planned to leave town."

Sophia sighed, not even in the mood to enjoy her drink. "If Baker goes on another extended killing spree, if the police get involved and suspicions grow with prints and identical M.O., we won't be able to keep control of the situation."

Nine hundred miles west in Cedar Point, Indiana, Crane was puzzled as to why he was out on the streets again. He had told himself he would stay safely indoors, decide on whether to leave this town and where to go next. Something appeared to be controlling his thoughts and action. So here he was, back on this skid row of derelicts and drunks. How had he gone from surveilling misfits the world would do better without to just picking victims at random? And why this need, this impulse to kill?

With hands deep in his pockets, as if that could keep them under control, he walked the broken sidewalks lined with trash and crumbling buildings. The same addicts appeared to be warming themselves over a fifty-gallon drum. The air around the street had its own odor of burning trash, liquor, body odors, and the disgusting smell of pot. The skinny one who enjoyed bragging about disposing of previous wives was beginning to disgust him. He swayed and stumbled, grabbing onto the derelict next to him who quickly brushed him away as if he had the plague, not that any of them were exactly sanitary. Crane knew nothing about him, not like the other victims. What surprised him though was he didn't care. Just pick someone and put him out of his misery.

The skinny guy moved away from the group. Something had caught his attention, or was it someone? Crane followed, puzzled by how the stumbling gait shifted to rapid, sobor steps. The skinny guy's target appeared to be a semi turning into an alley. Crane quickened his own pace and followed. As the drunk turned down the alley, Crane waited and watched just around the corner.

"Yo, hope I woke you." Skizzy didn't care if he woke Dagger. He was just glad that he wasn't as crazy as people thought him to be. Skizzy walked up to a side window, stood on an empty wash bucket, and peered through a window covered in black paper, seeing little, but enough to know what was going on."

"What is it? You know what time it is?"

"Yeah, yeah. Just wanted to let you know I found my dancing fruits and vegetables. I'm not as crazy as you thought."

"You're supposed to be finding a killer."

"This is important. Call Padre, the DEA, whoever. The semi is parked down an alley just off Marsh Road. This is where they bring those drugs to package and ship. There's a whole bunch of workers in the building packing the shit up. The building is abandoned, a foreclosure sign in front. So get DEA out here to arrest these people." Skizzy stabbed at the phone and ended the call.

Crane was puzzled. Was this supposed derelict a cop? He no longer acted or spoke as though he were a drunk. He had no idea who the skinny guy called but he mentioned the police. Crane slipped passed the front of the building, then turned down the alley on the opposite side. The windows were covered in a dark covering, obviously to prevent any light from seeping out, especially since the building was supposed to be empty. He walked further down and found a window where a corner of the paper had been torn. Tables and workers were lined up in rows. The workers were packing the boxes with plastic pouches containing what looked like pills. Drugs. Crane's anger bubbled to the surface. This was why the skinny guy mentioned calling DEA. This was a pack and ship operation. He heard cars speeding toward the building, no lights or sirens but he was certain they were cops. Crane rushed away from the building and escaped back to his hotel.

After Skizzy's call, Dagger had called Padre. Now he couldn't sleep. He found himself parked near the entrance to Sam's house, not sure why he had gone for a drive much less taken this street. With the engine off he sat in the darkness staring down the long drive and the darkened house. What Sam had said when they were in South Carolina kept creeping into his thoughts. *Abby is wicasa waken. I may pick up clues by touching a body or something the victim or killer touched. But mom only has to shake your hand and she knows every detail of your life.*

And Abby had shaken his hand, held it just a little too long, stared into him as if she were sucking secrets of his life right out of him. And it didn't go unnoticed by him how quickly Abby had grabbed his empty beer can, holding it tightly with a glance that seemed to pierce his very soul.

If Sam was right, what if...? But Dagger let that thought die with a shake of his head. He started up the Lincoln and headed home.

52

Robinson stood as the reporter entered the room. "Miss Monroe." They shook hands. He was surprised someone so privileged and influential had such a firm grip. He had expected her to offer the top of her hand for a kiss. "Please, sit. Can I get you some coffee?" Although he doubted the breakroom brand would meet her high standards.

"I'm fine and thank you for seeing me on such short notice. I take it Sam Casey told you what this was about."

He handed her a folder as he sat down. He had been careful to not include any pictures or reference to the hand-drawn images that Crane was currently sketching on his victims' wrists. "I'm afraid there isn't much in there. As I'm sure Sam told you, I did not investigate the case, being a beat cop back then. I did, however, include the name and phone number of the detective who headed up the investigation. He is still on the force and the captain at his precinct. He is expecting your call."

Sheila picked through the scant items. "You certainly weren't wrong when you said there wasn't much here." She closed the folder then brought out her notepad. "How do you think Sam does it?"

"Excuse me?" That question had been out of left field. Robinson expected her questions to only be about Baker.

"You know, her thing."

"She did tell you to keep her name out of your article, right?" Padre had warned Robinson to be careful around this woman. She had a way of tricking cops into revealing the most closely held secrets, and he wasn't talking pillow talk. This reporter had her own magic tricks and she was an expert.

Sheila flashed a smile, waved him off with an unladylike pffft and "of course. I was just curious after reading about those bodies she found in The Pines."

"I'm as in awe as you, but she gets the job done, all proven and legal. She makes my job a lot easier."

"But with this map she drew Sam didn't actually touch Baker, couldn't. After all, he's dead. And I doubt Baker touched this file folder. So, I'm just trying to get a better understanding of how her map came about."

"And there's the mystery. Can't fight the spirits, can we. Sam also said you had connections in the Bureau."

"Yes. They will have a plane available soon. One with high frequency penetrating radar."

"That would be one hell of a story if they actually found those bodies. I can smell a Pulitzer Prize from here." And did her eyes just light up? "What about identifications?"

"My FBI contact is collecting data on missing persons from that time period so, yes, this will be a real breakthrough. And closure for those families."

Robinson stood, ending the meeting before she dragged details out of his mouth. Sheila stood and followed him to the door.

His smile dropped as he closed the door. "Whew, that was close," he whispered. His phone rang just as he settled into his linebacker-sized chair.

"Did you hear about the bust last night?" Padre asked.

"Yes. Can't believe that operation has been in business for three years and no one noticed."

"Skizzy may not have found Crane, but he helped the authorities nab thirty identical trucks with identical stock operating in eight other states. At least now we confirmed the dancing fruits and vegetables the nut case had seen that night. It was a big night for the DEA," Padre reported. "Now, how did it go with the platinum witch?"

"She's everything you said she was, very clever in her wording. Seemed a little too interested in how Sam was able to glean info on a folder and papers that Baker never touched. I could only be truthful that I had no idea how and I have never questioned Sam's abilities." Robinson told Padre about the ground penetrating radar that would be used.

"Well, don't be surprised if something comes out soon in the Daily Herald, a little prelude to whet the readers' appetites. That's what Sheila is good at. She'll make it some four-part exclusive."

Robinson laughed at that, although he was sure Padre wasn't joking. "She's probably thinking of which spot to clear on the fireplace mantel for her awards."

"Miss Monroe will have deserved it if everything on the map comes true."

Dillon placed a book on Sara's lap. "See-See, up?" Dillon held his arms out to be picked up.

"Uh, oh. You're in trouble. He'll ask you to read the book five times," Sam said with a laugh. She cleared the last of the cups and plates. Abby had invited Sara and Dagger for coffee, but with Abby it was never just coffee. Jake had taken Dagger to his man cave above the garage to show him his telescope. They had been gone a little too long for comfort. So far the women had not heard any arguing. Sam was just going to warn Sara that Dillon weighed a ton and to be careful lifting him. Her fears were dismissed when Sara appeared to lift Dillon as though he were as light as a feather.

"*The Disappearing Squirrel*. Interesting title. How does the squirrel disappear, Dillon?"

Dillon pointed at the first picture. "There."

"He'll point more than say the words." Sam had been teaching Dillon the names of various birds and animals. Alex also introduced Dillon to animals and plants by the carriage house.

They heard the screen door in the kitchen open and men's voices.

"How was the man cave?" Sara asked.

"Manly," Dagger said. "Has all the conveniences, especially a stocked mini-refrigerator."

"You should come at night when you can see the stars," Sam suggested. "It's been cloudy all week, but it has to clear eventually."

"Is Dillon teaching Sara how to read?" Jake asked. Sara gave a withered smile. He pulled out a chair and sat next to Sam. "You had visitors again last night?"

Sam shrugged. "Just about every night, as you well know."

Dagger hoped by remaining standing Sara would get the hint to leave. No such luck. He pulled out a chair and sat down. "Why don't you sleep in that tipi out back. Maybe those spirits can chase them away."

"You know, that's not a bad idea." Sam was actually serious, although she was still curious to know what the remains meant when they said we weren't done.

"Bird fly." Dillon pointed at the picture.

"Yes and the bird flew because the squirrel was chasing him."

Dillon turned his head and pointed at Sara. "See-See fly."

Oh shit, Sam thought. She caught Sara's shocked face and didn't want to chance looking at Dagger's. "Squirrels can fly, too, Dillon. Uncle Alex showed you a flying squirrel."

"There, not there." Dillon pointed at the next page.

"You're right, Dillon," Sara said, "The bird hid behind the leaf so the squirrel wouldn't see him."

"There, not there," the toddler repeated.

Sara felt the blood rush to her head. "There, not there," she whispered. Sara turned to Dagger. "There, not there. I know what was wrong with that monkey island we saw. The building was there but not there. And the monkeys weren't monkeys."

"What?" Jake looked from Sara to Dagger.

"I don't understand." Sam was also puzzled by Sara's comments.

"The monkeys were holograms and there was a building on the island covered in that camouflage fabric, like what Sophia showed you from the invisible theft case."

Dagger understood exactly what Sara was referring to. "We have to get to the Hideaway office and contact Sophia."

"We'll come, too," Sam said, lifting Dillon from Sara's lap. "Let me get mom. She's in the laundry room."

Within twenty minutes they arrived at the Hideaway. Dagger arrived five minutes before Jake since he had a lead foot. He had pounded on the back door of the bar and waved to Stan before climbing the wrought iron stairs up to his office.

Jake and Sam didn't know what to say as Dagger's desk suddenly lit up with a virtual keyboard. More surprising, though, was the lack of a monitor, yet Sophia's face hovered over the desk with Carl's image directly behind hers.

"So, camouflage material created by Quantum Stealth. Interesting," Carl said.

"How many floors do you think the building had, Sara?"

"Hard to tell. There weren't any windows."

"Of course not. And the monkeys were definitely holograms?"

"Yes. They had a slight shimmer to them, just like the people in the underground lab in Nebraska. Dagger thought they were real until I walked right through one."

Sam and Jake exchanged glances. There were so many questions they each wanted to ask but they remained quiet. This was unchartered territory to them.

"Anything else unusual, or some type of identifying marks or signs?"

"No, Sophia. I didn't see a betta fish emblem." Sara thought about it for a moment. "Wait. There was a sign several yards from the beach. It looked partially eroded but I remember it looked like it said *pet refuge*, although there were washed out letters after *pet* and an *n* with a space before *pet*."

Sophia slowly turned to look at Carl. "It couldn't be, could it?"

"Couldn't be what? Dagger asked.

"*Mon Petit Refuge* which translates in French Canadian to My Little Refuge. The Director on more than one occasion told me if he were ever to retire he would find an island somewhere, *Mon Petit Refuge*."

"So, this might be another lab with lord knows how many floors underground." Dagger gave that some thought. "Or another seed vault below for his own personal use. If he wanted a retirement home and island, do you really think he would have a lab there? That doesn't sound like retiring."

"Did either of you see any guards there? Cameras?" Carl looked directly at Dagger, close enough to believe that he was actually in the room.

"No. What about you, Sara?"

"No, but we didn't see the whole island from the lighthouse." Sara certainly wasn't going to tell them she had circled the island at night, not with Sam and Jake in the room.

"Well, then. We will just have to send a drone there to videotape the area."

"Why a drone, Carl?"

"Because, Jake, if there are guards they might be alerted if we take a boat ride and get too close or if we were to buzz the island in a plane. Keyes may be dead, but it doesn't mean there aren't a few people there conducting more questionable activities."

"Maybe that's why the body parts said they weren't done. Maybe they were supposed to relocate to the island before their research ship was blown up." A chill clawed at her spine. How long were those body parts going to haunt her?

53

Crane looked the part of a tourist as he sported a casual shirt, chinos, sunglasses, and a baseball cap. He sat at the outdoor cafe enjoying a croissant and coffee. The morning paper was folded to the article on the veteran who was recovering in the hospital from an overdose. Crane had wanted to make sure the man had survived. That night he had pushed aside the voices in his head, words that admonished him for not finishing the job. Instead, he had focused on his father and the work he had created to save people, not destroy. Destroy. That word alone made him think of Jonathan Keyes. He ran a finger across the watch he had taken off the dying Director. How that man had managed to live as long as he did was a miracle. The man had been a pariah, a threat to humanity and the entire world. His father had warned him to be careful whenever they spoke about the Director. He had spies everywhere and one negative word about the Director could vanish you by morning. "Keep your head down and do your work," his father had cautioned. At the thought of his father, he touched the ring on his left hand. His father had given it to him before he passed away. Caduceus…a winged staff with two snakes, the medical symbol. Something to remind him to stay focused and to fight the good fight. But there had been more to the ring.

Tomorrow, maybe, he would think about moving on. Yes! More places to visit, more people to kill. How had these evil voices been injected into his mind? It was puzzling...and frightening as hell.

With calls made and the first article almost finished, Sheila only had to wait on the availability of the plane. She swiveled her chair so she could look out on Lake Michigan, the sailboats in the distance, and the Chicago Skyline. On a sunny day, her office was blinding with white carpeting and furniture. The white walls were covered in family paintings and awards. One day this newspaper would be all hers, but she wasn't in a hurry. On a bad day her father was one day away from retiring. On a good day, they would have to drag him feet first out of the building. Sheila thrived on the investigative part of journalism. She wasn't made for babysitting people and sitting in the office all day.

Looking back at her computer, she made a decision. She didn't actually promise, crisscross promise, to keep Sam's name out of the article. After all, what's a name drop or two. And just to sweeten the pot, so to speak, she was also going to include the map.

The four detectives returned to the Hideaway where they encountered Stan talking to Sophia. Sam stopped and turned to Sara. "I thought Sophia was in Heyward Bluff when we just spoke to her?"

"That's a hologram," Sara explained. "Looks real, doesn't it?"

While Dagger and Sara claimed two seats at a table, Sam and Jake remained standing, examining the computerized marvel. Sam wanted to walk around Sophia to check for wires from the ceiling.

"Sophia was just telling me that Hurricane Earl was expected to hit the coast by the end of the week."

Sophia nodded. "Carl and I discussed it, Stan. And for the interest of your other guests, we feel the hurricane will work in our benefit."

"How's that?" Dagger knew only Sophia could turn a potential catastrophe into an advantage.

"Once the drone confirms what we are dealing with, we will have our divers survey what exactly is underneath and surrounding the island," Carl said as he appeared next to Sophia.

"An implosion?" Jake asked.

"That would work best we feel, especially with Hilton Head Island being evacuated, the high winds, rain. It would be a perfect storm, so to speak. There won't be any questions asked when and if debris washes up on the beach. You should have seen the debris after Hurricane Matthew. Many of the boats were ripped from their moorings and washed ashore."

Sam was still examining Sophia's image. It looked so real she could swear Sophia was actually in the room. "Won't you both be in danger, especially since authorities feel the storm is a threat and you aren't evacuating?"

"We have a secret panic room and don't forget the metal hurricane shutters you saw the first time you were here, Sam."

"I know, Carl, but...wait. You have a panic room? How come we haven't seen it?"

"There's a reason it's called a secret panic room, Sam."

The door burst open and in charged Skizzy. "Yo, I didn't know you had company." He gave a wave to Carl and Sophia. "Kinda far from home aren't you?" He gave a nervous laugh. Carl was familiar to him, but he had yet to meet Sophia.

"We need to make plans. Let us know of any updates on your end." Sophia gave a nod and both her and Carl's images vanished.

Skizzy's eyes bulged. "Whoa, what just happened?" He turned to Dagger, then Sara. "I knew it. They were sucked up to the mother ship, weren't they? Holy cow!" He headed to the door, probably wanting to check the sky and confirm his suspicion.

Dagger grabbed ahold of Skizzy by the collar and stopped him. "They were holograms, Skizzy."

The skinny guy was actually shaking. "So you think." He looked at the five sets of eyes studying him. "I'm right, aren't I?"

Stan started laughing. "Mother ship, that's a good one. Damn, he would have been fun on the flight to the coast."

Skizzy wasn't amused. He pulled out a flash drive from his pocket and handed it to Stan. "I have some feed from the camera I set outside the pharmacy. I wanted you to see the dancing fruits and vegetables so you didn't think it was my imagination." Stan inserted the flash drive into his laptop. The large screen TV hanging on the opposite wall came to life.

"The fact that DEA made the bust is all the proof we need, Skizzy." Dagger shook his head. Maybe he did think it had been Skizzy's imagination. After all, it was foggy that night and the squirrelly guy wasn't all that reliable during the best of times.

"There, see?" Skizzy pointed at the screen. "I scurried after that truck when I saw it from our coffee klatch around the fifty-gallon drum. It drove to the end of that block and turned down an alley." The side of the truck could be seen clearly. It was marked as one of the food pantry type trucks which loads up on produce and meat from area grocery stores.

"Back it up," Jake said. Something else had caught his eye. "All the way to the beginning when you move away from your homeless version of a fireplace."

"Well, that's a nice and considerate comment, although not unexpected seeing who you hang around with." Skizzy gave a nod in Dagger's direction.

Jake's comment brought the rest of the group's attention to the screen. "There."

"What, there?" Skizzy said. "You gonna make fun of the way I scurry now?"

"No."

"I see what you mean, Jake." Dagger motioned to the screen. "Someone's following you."

Stan let the video play out until Skizzy and the man were out of sight. "He certainly looks interested in either you or the truck."

"Can't see his face," Sam said. "He never turns around. Not even a side view."

"Same height and build as Crane, though. He's wearing a hat so we can only guess, with it being so dark, that he's partially bald."

"I don't see a priest's collar, though, Stan," Sam commented.

Skizzy gasped. "OMG. I was his next target?"

Sara asked, "What were you talking about to the other homeless people that might have drawn his attention?"

"Well." Skizzy let that word drag out. "I might have put it on a little too thick."

"Like?" Dagger prompted.

"I might have mentioned that I killed two or three wives." Five heads slowly turned in Skizzy's direction. "Also, might have mentioned that it's illegal to rip up native plants in this state so the trick after burying the wives was to plant native plants right on top of their graves."

"Holy hell. Who said this guy wasn't brilliant." Stan barked out a laugh.

<h1 style="text-align:center">54</h1>

Dagger parked down the street from Sam's house. It was after ten o'clock. He had told Sara he had to do something. He swore he would fill her in at breakfast as long she promised not to follow him.

He had no idea why he picked tonight and wasn't even sure if anyone was still awake. Ringing the doorbell wasn't his first option. Instead, he thought he would walk back to the tipi. She might be there.

The wrought iron fence was easy enough to climb over in the dark. Driving up to the gate where the camera would announce his arrival had not even entered his mind. Dagger kept close to the house as he made his way up the drive. A sound drew him closer to the building as he waited and listened. Switching to his nighttime vision, the property looked as bright as daylight. Seeing that there wasn't a light on above the garage nor any more sounds, he switched back to normal vision and rounded the corner.

"Come, Mister Dagger. I have been waiting for you." Abby was sitting in one of the cushioned chairs on the patio, a stone firepit nearby with amber glass beads glowing in the dark. She reached into a cooler and pulled out three glasses. "You might want some bourbon instead of beer tonight." She filled each glass halfway.

Dagger was frozen in place until a dot of amber drew his attention. Several yards away in the shadows, Alex sat smoking a pipe. Did this man ever let Abby out of his sight? Or did he not want her anywhere alone with Dagger? Sam had once said Alex was Abby's protector. Ignoring Alex, Dagger claimed the chair next to Abby, studying the three filled glasses and wondering which one might have some herbal poison. Abby must have read his mind because she said, "Pick whichever one you feel is safest." There was a slight smile on her face as she said it.

"You obviously know why I'm here."

"Of course. I just wasn't sure when you would get up the nerve to come. I felt tonight would be the night."

He wasn't about to ask her how she knew. "You have to realize that I'm very skeptical."

"And yet, here you are." She handed one glass to Alex then let Dagger pick his before she took the remaining glass. "You have a very traumatic background, not unlike Sam's. It takes just one incident to shut down a young mind."

Dagger took a sip of his drink and stared at the glowing stones. He focused on the liquor, waiting to see if some hallucinogenic was going to affect his thinking. Maybe this was a bad idea. If he can't remember anything of his life before the underground facility, how could Abby?

"The spirits only showed me what they felt affected you the most. There is someone else you know who can fill in the blanks. If you want a city or names, I can't help you. All I can say is you are from out east, Philadelphia maybe, or New Jersey comes to mind. You were forced to witness something that was horrendous."

"Forced?"

"There were family members killed."

"Mine?"

"I'm not sure."

"How can you not..."

"Patience," came a firm voice from the shadows.

"If you want to know your heritage, I feel it is Greek or Italian, which is quite evident as I think even you know just by looking in the mirror. There were various powerful mafia types."

He figured his dark eyes and olive complexion didn't scream Scandinavian. Sophia hadn't been wrong when she said she had erased his memory. Which begged the question, how did she know he witnessed something so tragic that his mind couldn't process it?

"So how did I get from Philadelphia to Nebraska?" Everything Abby had disclosed so far did not spark one memory cell.

"There was a woman who pulled you away from the events taking place."

"A woman?" Dagger felt his anger building. Of course, he didn't take a cab to Nebraska or been picked up jaywalking. "So, this woman kidnapped me." He downed the rest of his drink, wanting desperately to smash the glass into the firepit.

Abby reached out and clasped his hand, making sure she had his attention. "No, Dagger. She didn't kidnap you...she rescued you."

"Do you have any idea what time it is?" Sophia was none too happy to be jostled from bed by the continuous beeping from her computer alerting her that someone was impatient and relentless to get her attention. It was past midnight in her time zone.

"Tell me about Philadelphia." Dagger had gone directly to his office above the Hideaway after speaking with Abby. He wasn't going to go back home without getting some answers and, the computer in his office was the only one that linked directly to Sophia.

"Philadelphia?" Sophia's brief look of confusion quickly changed to shock. "I'm not sure..."

"Don't." Dagger's anger immediately increased the pupils of his eyes, all the whites erased. It was all he could do to keep the demon from picking up the desk and flinging it across the room.

"Sam's mother I take it?" Sophia sighed. Carl had told Sophia about both Sam's and Abby's abilities, but she had no idea if Abby could actually sense anything about Dagger since he didn't remember his youth. "How much did she tell you?"

He took a deep breath to calm down. "Only something about my witnessing a murder that traumatized me, something about rival mafia-types. She said you rescued me, so start talking."

She raked her fingers through her hair, then sat back. "I was in Philadelphia for a conference. I'm sure you remembered from your visit how we had planned for me to get Director Keyes' attention. After all, I had a skill that would be useful to him. After the conference, having not been approached by anyone, I went for a walk. I didn't want to roam too far from the hotel since I had heard there were parts of the city that should be avoided. When I turned to head back to the hotel I heard loud voices, angry voices, and screaming. Should have fled, but..." She leaned forward, her face suddenly showing, of all things, motherly concern. "The screams were from someone young. I crept closer and saw two men holding you back. There was a light on in a building, a deli business I believe. Through the picture window I could see a couple and a young girl. It didn't take much for me to realize it was a shakedown, a payment to the mafia family. The man was refusing and without one hesitation he shot the young girl in the head. She couldn't have been more than your age at the time. Just as quickly, they shot the mother. You screamed and tried to turn away."

Still, everything Sophia was saying had yet to spark a memory. "So, it was my sister and mother who were killed."

"That's what I had thought, but one of the men grabbed your head and ordered you to watch. He said, "This will be your job in a few years unless you want to disappoint your father.""

Dagger was stunned. He was the son of the head of some mafia? Could he trust Sophia to tell him the truth after all the years of mistrust and lies? "So how did I get to Nebraska?"

"The father pulled a gun from a drawer and started shooting. The two men holding you ran into the store to help. Then someone pulled out a machete and started chopping at the man. Took his arm clean off, the one holding the gun. You were frozen in place, catatonic from all I could see. I ran up to you and ushered you away. Had to force you to run. It was only a few blocks until a black van stopped, the side door slid open, bags were placed over our heads. I felt a needle in my neck, and I didn't wake up until Nebraska. It was days until I discovered that they had taken you too."

No matter how hard he tried, there wasn't one thing Sophia just said that made sense. She had done a great job erasing his memory. "Did you follow-up at all? Find out who the victims were or the killers?"

"You forget where I ended up. I couldn't research anything. Years later when I was able to get a message out to Carl, he used his contacts to search for information. The local police said it was useless. There wasn't any evidence of a crime in the area I had described to Carl. Not one report of a missing family or of a hit by a mafia clan. No witnesses had come forward so police had nothing to go on."

And nothing to confirm your side of the story, Dagger thought. He had reason to have doubts. After all, he had been lied to all of his life. But then he thought of Abby. She would have no reason to lie, unless Carl had called her and told her what to say.

55

Crane had been nursing a cup of coffee for ten minutes. Having barely slept all night, he found himself the first customer in the hotel's outdoor cafe. His suitcase, open and fully packed, rested on his hotel bed. Something was happening and it wasn't anything good. It had been exhausting fighting back against the urge to roam the streets for victims. What would his father say? That was the only question that kept him centered.

"Would you like a warmup, sir?"

Young eyes looked down on him. Were the pupils dilated? Were there injection marks on her arm? He was again looking for a victim. "A fresh cup if you don't mind, please." He watched her walk away and shuddered. What was happening to him?

He unfolded the newspaper and scanned the words without reading, his mind still on the waitress, his suitcase, the pull of the streets and nighttime. The pages turned without purpose, eyes unfocused until he turned to page two and saw the map. Crane didn't even notice when the waitress brought him a fresh cup of coffee.

The article was written by Sheila Monroe with very few details, no location or explanation of the X's. It was a teaser article mentioning that the map had been in the possession of a local psychic or Native sage by the name of Samantha Casey. Slowly Crane pulled his own map from his pocket and set it next to the picture in the article. It was an identical match.

Dagger motioned Jake to the opposite end of the bar. They were again at the Hideaway, which was the best place to hold meetings. Dagger had filled Sara in earlier on what had happened at Abby's last night and his subsequent call to Sophia.

"I made a trip to your house last night, hoping to find Abby. And no, I didn't call first, nor ring the buzzer at the gate. For some reason she was sitting on the deck waiting for me."

A slight smile tugged at Jake's lips. "She did that to me once. Even had a cold beer waiting in a cooler."

"Is she on the level? I mean, I thought she might have some answers I was seeking but Carl could have called and told her what to say. How can I be sure..."

Jake stopped him there. "I can assure you whatever my mother-in-law told you is on the level. I don't know how she or Sam do what they do. Even Alex. I've seen animals come up to him for medical aid and they seem to understand the language he uses when he talks to them. If Carl were to call her and even start to ask or offer information, she would not let the conversation continue or even be influenced. As far as Carl, he has kept a lot from me over the years, as I'm sure you have learned by now. He has a great deal of respect for Abby. My personal feeling? Whatever Abby told you can be taken to the bank." Dagger let the silence stretch as thoughts collided in his head. "If you're thinking what I suspect, I would say it's a bad idea," Jake said.

"What's that?"

"You are thinking of doing your own investigation. Abby gave you a suggestion as to where to look."

"Abby told you."

"No. Just logic. Sophia told us your background when we were in Heyward Bluff, how she had wiped out your childhood memories permanently. You're trying to fill in the blanks. Then you heard Sam mention that Abby can tell everything about you by holding your hand. So, logically, you would go to Abby."

Dagger was never an open book but working with Jake lately he felt like his wounds had split open for the world to see. "If it were you, wouldn't you want to know about your earlier missing years?"

"It's been a while, though. Twenty or so odd years?" When Jake saw Dagger look toward the table where Sam sat, he shook his head. "Don't even think of asking Sam. I know she'd jump in to help. What do you really hope to accomplish? If your search is a dead end, then what? You can't chase ghosts, trust me."

Sara glanced at the end of the bar. "Is it my imagination or are those two bonding?"

Sam couldn't help but laugh. "That would be something, wouldn't it?"

Stan clapped his hands. "Updates, people. Get your coffee, pastry, tea, juice, and let's get to it." They gathered around the table, only the five of them since Padre and Robinson had other meetings and Skizzy was in his bunker hiding from any errant drug dealers. "I've been watching the weather for the east coast. Seems that Hurricane Ferdinand is building steam. The drones have confirmed that the faux monkey island is definitely what we suspected. Plans are proceeding accordingly."

"Which are?" Dagger prompted.

"Need to know," Stan replied. "Now, regarding Doctor Crane, it's been three days since the last victim was found. What do we know? Has he left town? Are there bodies we haven't discovered yet?"

"We know from camera footage that someone followed Skizzy the night he found the warehouse. Only the back side of the stalker was visible, though."

"That's good enough for me, Dagger. At least we know Crane was in town two nights ago," Stan said.

"Maybe almost killing a war vet with PTSD went against his principles," Sara suggested.

"I think he's confused."

"How's that, Sam?" Stan pulled the tray over and selected a pastry.

"I feel Crane has always been a gentle man. Baker, on the other hand, is possibly getting more dominant and it scares Crane. I wouldn't doubt that the doctor would like to pack up and leave. However, if Baker is growing stronger, he won't let Crane leave a very fertile killing field."

"I would think Baker can kill anywhere. Just about every town has a drug problem." Jake couldn't completely dismiss what Sam said. After all, most of the recent deaths could all be chalked up to an overdose, not murder…except for those sketches.

Sam's phone rang. She answered without looking at the number. The voice was male and no one she recognized. "Yes, this is Sam Casey." She rolled her eyes, then covered the mouthpiece on her phone as she mouthed to the others, "wait til I get my hands on Sheila." Sam had noticed in the morning paper that Sheila had used Sam's name and a picture of the map. "Yes, I'm still here." Her face suddenly turned pale. She put the phone on speaker and set it on the table. "What do you mean you have the same map?"

"I have been drawing the same map. It's identical to the one in the paper."

Sam looked at Stan. She wanted to ask what he thought she should say. Everyone was too puzzled or shocked to offer her advice. She made an executive decision. Protocol be damned. "Doctor Crane?"

"How do you...am I on speaker?"

"Yes and I want to meet. I'm sure you are curious why you and I both drew the same map. I have the answers, Doctor Crane."

The silence dragged on so long Sam was certain he must have hung up. "First prove how you know who I am."

Sam looked at Dagger and he nodded. "Okay, BettaTec and Jonathan Keyes."

Silence again stretched. A faint gasp and measured breathing could be heard. "If you know of what I've done than you are familiar with the location of where the first victim was located."

"I know it."

"Eleven o'clock and come alone."

"Eleven o'clock and I won't be alone. That's not up for negotiation." Sam hung up and breathed a sigh of relief. "Well, that was interesting."

56

It was decided that only Dagger and Sam would meet with Crane. They didn't want to overwhelm him. Jake and Sara were waiting nearby in Jake's vehicle. He used binoculars and watched from the gate by the salvage yard for Crane to arrive. Dagger paced while Sam sat on a concrete barrier.

"You seem a bit nervous. It isn't like you, I would think."

Dagger just glared at Sam before looking away quickly. "I saw Abby last night."

"I figured someone showed up. Abby had packed a bottle and three glasses into a cooler with ice so I knew she was expecting someone. I also saw Alex making a sage bundle several days ago which Alex and Abby usually do before a ritual to contact the spirits."

He stopped pacing and took a seat next to her. "It's hard not to want to check into my past, to find the memories missing."

"Did what Abby tell you suddenly defrost your memory cells?"

"No. Even Sophia could only tell me what she saw when she dragged me away from a murder. Then both of us were kidnapped by BettaTec."

"Then how do you expect going back to wherever this happened to help in any way after all these years?"

What Sam said made sense. It was the same thing Jake had told him. "I read about the one case you stumbled onto, the twenty-year-old button you unearthed at a construction site. You were able to solve that crime."

"True, but I was able to question the accused in prison, to get more details as to what had taken place, how he had met the victim, the other people the victim had associated with, even her parents. You don't have any of that, not even any clothes or possessions from when you were kidnapped. I bet the spirits weren't able to even tell mom your real name."

"No. BettaTec used numbers to identify their operatives."

"Six-one-seven?"

"Right. I came up with Chase Dagger. When I arrived in Cedar Point I saw a magazine article on Chasing the Elusive Dagger. Thought it had a certain ring to it."

"I like it. Could be worse. You could find out your real name is Bruno Buttkiss."

Sam's cell phone vibrated. A signal from Jake that a car was nearby

Levitt Crane was not what they had expected. Even without the priest's collar Crane looked like a man of the cloth, a friendly neighbor, a gentle family doctor. His nervousness did show, though. Crane checked his surroundings, possibly afraid police were waiting in the brush.

Dagger stood as Crane approached. The doctor's eyes roamed, glancing at nearby brush and at the far end where he had killed his first victim. His face and body may be identical to Crane, but there was something threatening in his eyes.

"We're alone." Dagger motioned to Sam. "I'm Chase Dagger. This is Sam Casey." He took several seconds to scan Crane's background, surprised that it was blank. It didn't even reveal anything about Baker.

Sam reached out a hand to Crane. "I'm really curious to see your map."

Crane only nodded, then looked suspiciously at Dagger. "You look like you might have been one of the director's operatives."

"I was. Not anymore. I was one of the lucky ones to escape."

"Ahhh, of course." He turned back to Sam. "You brought your map?"

Sam pulled it out of her pocket and opened it. Crane did the same. The three of them studied the maps, noting the placement of the various lines and X's. "Damn. You were right. They are exactly the same." Dagger had thought there might be some telltale difference but there wasn't.

"So tell me. What does it mean?"

"The real Doctor Levitt Crane is dead. Before he died he had bio-printed his body so his work could continue. You have his exact features and memories except for one difference. He needed to stay alive while he did the creation. Unfortunately," Sam said, "and unknowingly, he combined a few of his with the brain cells of a dead serial killer by the name of John Wallace Baker."

Crane's hand started to shake, and he stumbled over to sit next to Dagger. "Serial killer?"

Sam filled him in on Baker's killing spree and how he had died before revealing the location of his last eight victims. "We believe these X's mark the location."

"Dear god." Crane lifted his glasses and wiped tears from his eyes. "That explains this compulsion I have which is entirely out of character." He studied Sam's face for several seconds. "But how could you draw the map? You didn't know me or this guy Baker?"

"All I had to do was touch the black marker you discarded in the abandoned real estate office." Sam gave a slight shrug. "It's what I do... touch a victim or something the killer touched. I obviously picked up Baker's vibes. After that I found myself sketching this, adding more details each day."

Crane pulled a bottle of water from his pocket, unscrewed the cap, and took a sip. "This experiment wasn't exactly the breakthrough I, I mean the real Crane, had thought it would be. Does this reporter know about me?"

"No. I only told her about Baker. Now she's on a quest to find the bodies and make a name for herself. Your name will never come up." And Sam hoped it was kept that way.

Dagger nodded toward the doctor's wrist. "I see you have the Director's watch." He had always considered the Jaeger-LeCoultre or any extravagant purchase like that to be nothing more than a vanity gift.

"What's so great about a Jaeger-LeCoultre watch?" Sam thought it was a bit gaudy with all of the bling on it.

"Looks like he upgraded," Dagger said. "This one is a Gyrotourbillion, rhodium plated with sapphire crystals and a crocodile band. Costs over four hundred thousand."

Crane removed the watch and handed it to Dagger. "Take it. It's a fake anyway. The seconds hand on an authentic Jaeger-LeCoultre sweeps. This seconds hand jumps so you can tell it's a fake. Besides, I won't be needing it anymore."

"I heard about your inroads with bio-printing organs. That's truly a life-saver," Sam said as Crane took another long swallow from the water bottle. "It's a pity that scientists today haven't progressed as far as you and your dad."

Crane studied first Sam, then Dagger as Dagger's brain scanned the doctor for wires or an ID chip. He didn't detect anything that might be transmitting their images or audio. "Who are you people?" Crane asked.

"AlphaTec. Mother is still alive."

The doctor burst out laughing. "My father and I always knew Mother was the smarter of the two." He took another long swallow as a shuffling behind him drew his attention to two men clad in black at the entrance. Crane pulled a ring from his finger and handed it to Dagger. "This was my father's. I'm sure Mother will know what to do with it."

Dagger studied the water bottle as Crane lifted it to his mouth. He stopped Crane before he could take another sip. "Would you do something for me first?"

57

"I can't believe you!" Sam swiped Dagger's arm several times.

"Hey, can you call her off? She gave me the silent treatment all the way here and then she unleashes."

"Why didn't you stop him if you knew what he was doing?" Sam slapped his arm again.

"Really, Dagger." Sara shook her head as she studied the drawing of a demon on his wrist.

"Right. The only time Dagger stopped him from drinking all of the laced water was when he wanted him to do the sketch for him. You know you could have given him Narcan and prevented him from dying."

"Sit," Stan ordered everyone. "Sam, Crane knew he couldn't go on, not with Baker controlling him. Killing was not in Crane's DNA and he hated what Baker was making him do. There was no other alternative."

Jake studied Dagger's wrist. "Why did you have him draw it facing you rather than away, like all of Baker's victims?"

"Because I wanted to see it." Dagger knew it would eventually wash away, but for now it was a reminder of his own demon. "He didn't want saving, Sam," he said as he took a seat across from her. "Baker would have always been with him."

"At least you got the watch."

"What watch?" Stan looked from Sam to Dagger.

Dagger pulled the watch from his pocket. "Looks nice, but gaudy, and it's fake according to Crane. He said the seconds hand jumps rather than sweeps which is an indication that it's..."

"Oh no, no, no." Stan pounded away on his laptop. Seconds later Sophia and Carl's images appeared on the wide screen hanging on the wall. "Sophia, the watch Crane took from the Director is fake."

"I knew it!"

"What does that mean, Carl?" Jake asked.

"The man Crane killed was a double."

"You mean like a clone?"

"No, Sara," Sophia replied. "The Director had at least three doubles that we knew of, so he didn't have to appear in public often. Plastic surgery, voice alterations, you name it. Even fingerprints. They literally could pass for the man. Dammit!"

Dagger could feel the anger build. "So the real one is still out there."

"On Sara's monkey island."

"Are you certain, Sophia?"

"About ninety-nine percent," Carl replied as he looked at his cousin. "Ever since we saw the video of Crane killing Keyes Sophia felt something wasn't right. And I've always learned to trust her instincts. She has a good feeling about that island. And with that category one hurricane headed our way tomorrow night, we can hopefully bury that island in the Atlantic."

Stan gave a thumbs up. "I've always trusted your instincts, too, Mother."

Dagger pulled the other item from his pocket. "Crane said to give you his father's ring. Don't know why." He placed it on the table.

"You told him Sophia was still alive?" Carl's bark was showing.

"I scanned him. He didn't have a chip or recording device that might be transmitting somewhere."

Jake picked up the ring from the table. "Has a medical insignia on it. Think it's called a Caduceus. Why would he think you would want it?" When Jake pressed a finger against the opposite side of the ring, something jutted from the side of the insignia. "Hell, it's a flash drive."

Stan held out his hand. "Let's see what this puppy is hiding." He inserted the flash drive into his computer. The screen filled with a variety of folders, all with organ names.

"I think he's giving you all of his bio-printing notes, Sophia." Stan opened a folder labeled Crane. "Here's a folder of his research notes when he had bio-printed his own body."

"Send me the entire contents but delete the Crane folder first. I don't want anyone setting eyes on that. The world isn't ready for bio-printing people. Once I confirm that all the folders were received on my end, destroy the flash drive."

Dagger's bullshit meter started banging. "You don't want to sell it to the highest bidder, Sophia?"

"Bastard," Carl said under his breath.

Sophia displayed a rare emotion of hurt and disappointment. "No. I'm going to create a foundation called the Russell and Levitt Crane Bio-print Institute and employ the best scientific minds in bio-printing to work on his research. I think the medical world has been dragging its feet far too long when it comes to providing organ transplants."

"We have plans to make for tomorrow," Carl said. "Make sure you verify that we received all of those files before you destroy the flash drive, Stan."

"Well, aren't you a ray of sunshine, Dagger." Stan started uploading the files from the flash drive.

"Why couldn't you get the plane?" Sheila whined. She knew it wasn't ladylike and her mother would definitely disapprove. She was sitting in an unmarked black van with her former college sweetheart, Carson Hartford the third. Any guy with a junior, the second, or the third after his name spelled wealth and family heritage. Not to mention his chiseled body, striking blue eyes and hair so blonde it looked white.

"I had to bend over backwards to get the drone. The boss didn't feel there was enough valid proof to warrant the plane. And I had to admit this is really farfetched. You didn't give me convincing enough proof that you aren't putting me on a wild goose chase."

"But one day, that's it? You could only get the drone for one day?" Sheila crossed her legs, revealing flesh above her thigh high boots, which didn't go unnoticed by Carson.

"Flirting is still in your DNA, I see," he said with a smile, his eyes moving from Sheila's legs to the monitor which had yet to light up anything that might resemble human remains.

"Can't help it, but if I wanted to flirt with you I wouldn't have worn the boots or a sweater that zips up to my neck. How is Lacey by the way?" How like a guy with the third after his name to marry a girl with Lacey for a first name?

"Doing great. We just had our third baby, a girl this time. Two boys and a girl. What about you?"

Sheila waved the bling on her hands. "Two engagements. One broken, one deceased."

"Sorry to hear it. You'd make a great wife, but I'm not sure about the motherhood part."

"I'm sure you've heard of nannies and boarding schools."

The van was parked near the Wildlife Sanctuary, which was the closest location to the Illinois border where the first X was marked on the map. Sheila could see the drone overhead, an orange box hanging from its underside. "Why does it fly so low?"

"The radar can track to a depth of around twelve feet, depending on the composition of the dirt. The harder the dirt, the less depth it can penetrate."

"Why is it stopping?" Sheila's question was cut off by a knock on the side window. The drone was now hovering.

They both emerged from the van and made their way around to the back where a man in jeans and a flannel shirt was manipulating dials and buttons on a computer. With the Russian hat and ear flaps, he would look more at home in a hunting cabin. "

"Found something." Lou Jeffers was the man the FBI often called on when they needed a GPR forensics drone expert.

"What are we looking at?" Carson asked.

The monitor showed a variety of colored lines. "There's something here. You can tell by the lines that are domed. The stats estimate it's no farther than four feet down. I'll send the coordinates to your laptop." After sending the coordinates, Lou pressed a button and the drone took off again, reviewing the copy of the map Sheila had given him which showed another X just north and a little east of the X the drone had just located.

Sheila could feel her heart racing. This could be big. She shouldn't get ahead of herself, though. If it's a grave, it could be a deer or someone's dog. The X's were not that far apart, running from the Sanctuary to just north and west of LaPorte, Indiana.

Carson clapped Lou on the back. "How far can your baby go?"

"Get comfortable, eat lunch, whatever. How far is the very last X, little lady?"

Sheila hated that term but easily forgave him. After all, it was his drone. "By my estimates, about ten miles away."

"Then we're good to go."

58

"I don't blame you for being furious with Dagger. That guy takes distrust to a whole new level."

"I'm not mad, Carl. I'm just disappointed, but I understand where he's coming from." Sophia watched as Carl pointed the remote at the outside hurricane shutters. The sky was grey as the wind whipped the palm trees near the house. The category one hurricane was expected to hit landfall around ten o'clock in the evening. Traffic on the bridge was sparse as most residents who planned to evacuate had left a couple days ago.

"The Director made me suspicious of everyone around me. He had spies, people who tried to befriend others, and it was difficult to know whom to trust. Rooms were bugged and videotaped. It was a terrible place to work and live, so I just kept my head down and did my job." Sophia followed Carl to the deck where the push of a button brought tarp-like shields down to the decking. Sophia pulled the tarp tight and fitted the eyelet over the hook, then clamped it down.

"Are the cameras working?"

Divers had placed underwater cameras to hopefully catch the explosion and provide live feed back to Sophia's monitor. Calculations had already been made based on the storm's direction as to where debris might wash up. If they could find just one body part, no matter how gruesome, that could confirm if Director Keyes had been on the island.

"Even if we lose power the monitor should still work with the backup generator." Sophia's phone rang. She checked the screen. "It's Dagger."

"Should I pour you a drink?"

"A stiff one, please."

* * * *

Jake turned the steaks over on the grill as Alex kept an eye on the shrimp and salmon. "What are the odds that Dagger and Sam would be on their phones at the same time?"

"Maybe they are talking to each other," Alex said. "Keeping secrets."

Jake laughed at that. "Guess Dagger isn't the only one who has trust problems. He isn't as bad as you think. Sara has softened his edges quite a bit, I would guess. And Sam and I have been a great influence on him."

"Oh, really?" Alex huffed.

"He might not agree, but Sara seems to think so."

"Agree about what?" Dagger closed the patio door behind him and stepped out into the crisp fall air.

"Jake seems to think that he and Sam have been a positive influence on you."

Dagger slid a dark gaze Jake's way as he grabbed a beer from the cooler. "Really?"

"Same thing I said." Alex slid the fish onto a side plate and covered it with aluminum foil.

"Are the steaks ready?"

"Just about."

They carried the food into the house where the dining room table was set with Abby's best stoneware. Two lit candles were on the table while overhead lighting was dimmed. One would have thought Abby was celebrating Thanksgiving early.

Sam and Sara brought in the side dishes of baked potatoes, beans from Alex's garden, and condiments. Dillon was already fed and in his crib upstairs.

"This looks like a prisoner's last meal. Should I be worried?" Dagger pulled out Sara's chair for her, then took a seat.

"It's more a celebratory meal," Abby said. She again sat at the head of the table and started passing the plate of steaks around while Sam started with the dish of vegetables. "You have worked well together and solved the case."

"Actually, I think we've solved two cases. I just spoke to Sheila. They have found all eight bodies using the ground penetrating radar from the university. Or I should say they found eight graves. They will start digging tomorrow. I let her call Captain Robinson with the information."

"She's probably at a spa sprucing up for her television interviews."

"How cynical, Dagger. Now what was your phone call about?" Jake asked.

"I called Sophia. Everything seems to be ready for when the hurricane hits." He checked his watch. "And it should be hitting in about three hour."

Sara grabbed the plate of fish from Jake and slid a piece of salmon and some shrimp onto her plate. "And I'm sure you apologized for the accusation you made."

All eyes slid in Dagger's direction. "I didn't have to."

"Humff," Alex grunted. "Never claim fault appears to be your motto."

"I didn't have to because she answered the phone with 'you are forgiven.'" Dagger passed the salad bowl, opting to stick to steak and potatoes. "I don't think Sophia and I are the only two people who find a lot in life to distrust." He stabbed a glare in Alex's direction.

Another grunt from Alex. "Point taken," Abby said while she, too, glanced at Alex.

Jake raised his glass of beer. "To a successful case."

Sara raised her glass of wine. "To a successful working relationship."

"Once Sophia's suspicions are confirmed regarding Director Keyes, I'd say there won't be any more cases to solve, so don't start changing the names on your business cards, Sam." Dagger raised his glass of beer.

"I could probably confirm it before she does," Sam said. "I'll let you know when I'm no longer seeing crawling body parts at night."

Epilogue

The morning after Hurricane Ferdinand's one hundred mile an hour winds whipped the coast of South Carolina, Sam realized for the first time that she had not been visited by the body parts. She had quickly informed Dagger and Stan.

For the first month after the hurricane, as County crews and volunteers continued to clean up the debris, unidentified men attired in black work boots, black jeans and shirts, made their way farther north. They moved past sailboats lying on their sides like beached whales and houseboats broken into pieces. The results of hurricane force winds had ripped dinghies from their moorings, business signs from storefronts as well as yard ornaments from estates that residents had neglected to bring indoors before evacuating.

The AlphaTec crew had studied the map Carl provided which gave the best guesstimate as to where debris from the Director's island might wash up. Sophia had doubts after learning there had been a strong undertow following the hurricane.

With the passing of Mother Nature's wrath, the sun's rays had been intense, as if she were apologizing for bringing such destruction. On the forty-fifth day on a small sandbar about two blocks from shore, several pieces of what looked like computer parts, wooden shutters and tree branches had gathered. A partial weathered sign was entangled in one of the branches. Only the letters *pet* were decipherable and, so far, the only item that could possibly be from Keyes' island...*Mon Petit Refuge*. It wasn't until another section of the sign was discovered wedged into a lower part of a sand dune on shore that they found a partial arm with an intact hand. On the wrist was a Jaeger-LeCoultre watch with a sweeping seconds hand.